ROCK My Body
(Black Falcon, #4)

By Michelle A. Valentine

Dedications

To the readers: Thank you for
always being amazing.

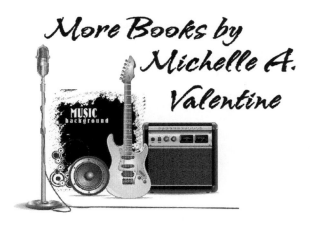

More Books by Michelle A. Valentine

Black Falcon Series Reading Order
Rock the Beginning (Black Falcon, #0.5)
Can be found in Stories for Amanda
or in the back of Rock the Beat
Rock the Heart (Black Falcon, #1)
Rock the Band (Black Falcon, #1.5)
Rock My Bed (Black Falcon, #2)
Rock My World (Black Falcon, #2.5)
Rock the Beat (Black Falcon, #3)
Rock My Body (Black Falcon, #4)

Hard Knocks Series
Phenomenal X (Hard Knocks, #1)

The Collectors Series
Demon at My Door

Coming Soon
Xavier Cold (Hard Knocks, #2)
Elite Invitation
Demon in My Bed
Wicked White

"Rage, rage against the dying of the light"
– Dylan Thomas

Prologue

"Coming Down" – Five Finger Death Punch

One Year Ago...

Tyke

I nod my head to the beat, glad that, for once, we are in our element in playing to a sold-out crowd.

I'm not exactly sure where everything started falling apart. Wait...that's a lie. I know *exactly* when my blissful happiness began to deteriorate. It was the day Riff brought a woman on our bus for a long-term stay. A woman who fucked everything up and started Black Falcon on our downward spiral.

One day things were great—every guy in the band practically floating on cloud nine and all that shit—but somehow in the midst of our happiness and living out our life-long dream, things turned to shit. Sophie, Riff's temporary fuck-of-the-month, single handedly drove a wedge into our foundation and rocked our ship by claiming she one-nighted Noel and was knocked up by him. For a while, I wasn't even sure if the band would make it, but we did, ironically, with the help of two women, Lanie Vance and Aubrey Jenson. They were all right chicks at first, but eventually became thorns in my side too. Noel and Riff are so lovesick; they can't see that their constant need to "*take a break*" for "*family time*" is destroying us.

My twin brother, Trip, used to look at the situation like I do. He wasn't happy about the disappearing acts that both Noel and Riff insisted on pulling all the damn time. That was until my baby brother took it upon himself to seek out other interests besides the band. He not only found a dirt bike track to invest his money into, he also found a chick to invest his time into. He had to go and fall for the fucking track owner's daughter, Holly. After that, he had a change of heart, and started empathizing with my other bandmates.

Fucking pussies.

All of them.

Black Falcon might as well be a label-made band like those Embrace the Darkness douchebags who are always trying to upstage us and ride our coattails. Like them, we don't really give a fuck about each other anymore. Seems like this band is nothing more than a paycheck, which is sad. When we all vibe well together, magic truly happens.

Trip pounds out the last few beats of the song and the crowd explodes, instantly begging for more.

This is what I love. There isn't any other feeling like it in the world. Nothing can ever top this rush, but because our performances are so few and far between,

I've been forced to find other things that really get my blood pumping.

When my eyes lock with my twin's green ones, we both have the biggest grins on our face, I know he loves this, too—the euphoric energy from the crowd.

How can he not miss this?

How can he put anything above this? How can any of them?

Our band's front man, Noel Falcon, chuckles into the mic as he stares out into the crowd. "Damn. You fuckers are insane. We've got one more song left for you." He pauses, running his hand through his dark hair, giving the twenty thousand bodies here to see us perform time to respond, their screaming getting louder and louder. "I feel the love." He readjusts his mic stand. "Since we're all friends here, I'm gonna tell you all a little story about a girl who shredded my heart back in high school without any hesitation. It's called 'Ball Busting Bitch'. If you've ever had your heart fucked over by a woman, sing along."

Noel smirks and the laughter in his eyes is evident. Ever since he married Lanie Vance, it's pretty funny to see him keep up appearances with this song—even though he's madly in love with that ball buster.

Trip kicks up the beat, and I thump away on the strings of my bass, creating our signature dark and dirty beat while we wait on Riff to join us, who makes the lead guitar scream like a woman in heat.

I close my eyes as the rhythm of our biggest hit pulses through my body. Music is the one thing I can completely lose myself in. When I'm in the moment, feeling the beat, I'm untouchable; nothing else matters but the way each note engulfs my soul, scorching itself onto me permanently, reminding me that music is what I live for. It's what I was born to do.

I slide my fingers down the thick strings, finding the sweet spot, and slap them hard with the thumb on the opposite hand. My head rocks back and forth as I play the hell out of the song. I can't remember a time that we've ever sounded better.

Surely, they'll want to celebrate like old times after this show—the four of us together, cracking open a few cold ones and just being *together*.

That's what I miss the most.

The final notes in the song play out, ending our forty-five minute set, and Noel shouts, "You've all been a fucking beautiful crowd. Thank you!"

As soon as my eyes snap open, they land on my brother, tossing his drumsticks into the crowd while Noel and Riff exit the stage. And just like that, the song disappears, taking my euphoria along with it, and the warmth I was just feeling is completely gone from my heart, replaced by an arctic chill.

What's their big fucking hurry?

I set my bass down on the stand and follow Trip off the stage. The remnants of the crowd's energy still linger in my veins, and I'm ready to burn it off and party with my buddies.

I throw my arm around my twin's neck as we make our way backstage. "Where are we partying tonight, baby brother?"

Trip shakes his head and smiles as his eyes drift off like he's thinking of something else. "Can't, man. Holly just flew in, and she's waiting for me at the hotel."

I sigh and pull my arm away. "You suck. Can't you see her after we go out for a while? I need my wingman."

"Wish I could, but I can't let my girl down. Besides, it's been two weeks since I've seen her." He gives me a quick jab to the ribs. "Stop frowning, Sunshine. We'll do something soon. Promise."

I roll my eyes. "That's what you always say, but it never fucking happens. Just go the fuck back to your girl and forget about me."

Trip's brow furrows. "What the fuck's with the attitude? Are you pissed that I'm happy."

My lip rises as my face contorts with disgust. "No, I'm not *pissed* that you're happy."

"Then what the fuck is the problem? You've been nothing but a drunken asshole most of the time I'm around lately, so why in the hell do you even care that I want to spend some time with my girl? It's obvious that you're perfectly capable of partying on your own. You don't need me for that."

I blow out a rush of air through my nose. Starting a fight with him wasn't my intention. But doesn't he see what spending all his time with his woman is doing to the band?

Do any of them see?

Jesus, it's like we have three fucking Yoko Onos, yet no one sees the problem here except me. These women are dictating the future of this band. It's all going to fall apart, but it's like all of them are too fucking pussy-whipped to see it happening right before their own eyes.

Noel and Riff walk over toward us, both wearing perplexed expressions.

"What are you two dipshits fighting over now?" Riff mocks. "Can't you assholes just kiss and make up. The tension between you two lately has been fucking ridiculous. What's up?"

5

Trip shakes his head. "Nothing's wrong. My brother is just acting like a chick here, crying about how I never spend time with him anymore."

I scrub my hand down my face, not wanting to waste any more of my time. "Fuck it. I'm out of here."

I can't get into this with them. None of them will ever see things like I do, so there's no point in even trying to reason with them.

I turn toward the exit, and I hear the guys calling my name but don't bother to turn around. If none of them care what happens to Black Falcon then why should I?

I'm done being the goddamn babysitter of the group: keeping everyone on task and writing eighty percent of the music. It's time I start living *my* life and forget I give a fuck, too.

The pounding in my skull is relentless. Holy fuck. What in the hell did I get myself into last night? The last thing I remember is being at the club that Lou, one of the roadies, dragged me to. Everything else is fuzzy as shit.

I rub my eyes as I try to remember, but a loud buzz echoes around the room and keeps me from focusing on anything but the God-awful sound.

What the fuck?

I peel my eyes open and blink hard as my gaze lands first, on a brick wall, then, a small window with bars on it. I push myself up slowly, studying the unusual window as I try to get my bearings. After my eyes slide around every inch of the room and find nothing but bars surrounding me, blocking my freedom, my heart rate kicks up a notch, and the panic sets in.

How in the hell did I wind up in *jail?*

I push myself to my feet and wobble a split second before I regain my balance. Whatever I drank last night is still obviously in my system. My feet shuffle toward the bars, and I wrap my fingers around the cold steel. I strain my neck to look down the long hall, but all I hear is the sound of other prisoners talking. I need some answers.

I press my head against the bars. "Guards? Hey? Guards!"

Heavy footsteps fall down the concrete hallway, each step coming closer to the small cell I'm stuck in.

A gray-haired guard dressed in a dark blue uniform that's a size too small wears a scowl on his plump face as he sets his stern eyes on me. "You need something?"

My shoulders stiffen, and I'm instantly riled by his tone, especially considering I don't have the foggiest idea why I'm here. "Yeah. What in the hell am I in here for?"

The guard sighs heavily. "DUI. We picked you up last night on I-95 swerving all over the lanes."

My shoulders slack and I push back from the bars but still hang on and drop my head. "Fuck. Does my brother know to come and get me?"

"Doubtful. You were too toasted to make your phone call last night. You kept fighting us off you, so we tossed you in here to sleep it off. You're welcome to that call any time. Call anyone you'd like."

I take a deep breath. When Trip finds out about this, he's going to flip his shit. Usually, I'm the one thinking about how things like this will affect the band, not him—hell, not any of the others. Riff is known for giving out golden tickets to chicks who hang out backstage to sleep with him. Trip never gives two shits about anything, and Noel...well, he's no angel either. Back in the day, me getting this DUI would've just been something we laughed off, but now that they're all on the straight and narrow, I imagine they'll give me the third degree over this.

But what choice do I have? Who else can I call?

After a long moment, I push away from the bars and look the guard in the eye. "I think I'll make that call now."

A few hours later, I'm finally at the front desk, gathering all the personal items I had on me when I was booked.

"One wallet, a set of keys, two hundred and fifteen dollars in cash, four guitar picks, a sheet of folded up paper, and one cell phone," the middle-aged brunette clerk says as she hands me all the items. "Sign here and here, and you'll be on your way."

I scribble my name in the sections she's marked and gather my things. Before I can even turn around, I feel Trip's eyes, judging me.

I head toward the door, Trip close on my heels. Once we're outside, my brother clears his throat. "I called the rental car company to come pick up their car from the impound lot. Kyle is waiting around the side with the Escalade to take us to the airport."

I raise my eyebrows. "That's it? No big lecture?"

Trip sighs. "What do you want me to say, Tyke? Do you really need me to tell you how much you fucked up? How bad this is going to look for the band? You know better than anyone this isn't good fucking PR, so why voice it? As long as I can remember, you've been the stable one. I'm sure this isn't going to happen again. You always do what's best for the band. It was a one-time mistake. We all make them."

"Glad to hear you actually still care about the band."

Trip flinches. "What the fuck is that supposed to mean? When have I ever *not* cared?"

I shake my head. "Come on, brother. Don't act like you don't know what I'm talking about. No one has cared for a while now, including you. You guys spend all of your time with your women and leave all the work to me. I'm the one writing all the songs while Noel and Riff are off being husbands and fathers and you're out there playing house. Do you think that's fair? You guys get to fuck around and not give a shit about the future of this band?"

He licks the corner of his mouth as he huffs. "Fuck you, Tyke. Just because we settled down and found other interests, don't think for one goddamn minute that we don't care about the band anymore. Nothing with the band has changed. *You're* the one who's changed."

Anger boils inside me. Is he really that blind? Can he not see how so much has changed in the year since Noel and Riff got married, and he got with Holly? I love my brother. I don't want to lose him, but I'm not going to stand here attempting to make him see my side when I know it's a lost cause. I'd be better off beating my head against a brick wall.

"You're right, Trip. Things are most definitely different and are going to change even fucking more."

Without another word, I turn on my heel and walk away from my baby brother. It's not the best option, but it's the only one I've got. Whatever it takes, I'm going show the rest of these guys that they're letting this band die. And despite what they think, I'm the only one fighting to keep us together.

Chapter One

"Evil Twin" – Arctic Monkeys

Present Day

Tyke

Fuck.

I've done it again.

I turn my head and survey my surroundings. Four white hotel walls and a horrible painting of a man fishing in a pond are the first things that come into my hazy line of sight. The second thing is the blonde knocked out cold next to me, her tits hanging half out her shirt.

Damn. What in the hell did I do last night?

I squeeze my eyes shut while the pounding in my skull beats continuously. Raising my hand, desperate to pinch the bridge of my nose to ease the pain, my arm stops far short of my face. My gaze snaps down to my wrists, bound at my sides with a thin rope, and I yank my arm, attempting to move my feet as well without much luck.

What in the hell?

My heart thunders in my chest as my foggy brain quickly pulls together that someone has no intentions of allowing me to leave this bed. Panic rolls over me when I can't recall whom I came here with, or even how I got here. As much as I hate to admit it, Trip was right—some chick has finally gone all *Misery* on my ass.

I survey the knot tied in the rope. It doesn't look like it'll be that difficult to loosen, if I can just figure out a way to get my hands on it. Twisting my wrist side to side, I attempt to wiggle out, but it's no use. It's tied too tight.

I shift beneath the sheet that's draped over me, and realize I'm completely fucking naked.

Shit. Being naked and tied to a bed is never a good thing. This isn't going to end well.

The bathroom door opens and I freeze, unsure of what the hell might be walking toward me. A slender brunette in a black mask with a great set of tits struts into the room wearing a tight leather outfit that wraps her body like a glove. As if the outfit wasn't over-the-top enough, she's also toting a black whip in her left hand, alongside an expression that screams she's ready to inflict some major pain. I tense at the sight of her.

What in the holy fuck have I gotten myself into?

I yank my wrists, attempting to free myself, and the woman cusses at me in Spanish, clearly unhappy with my change of heart. "Hijo de puta!"

It only takes a split second for me to recognize the voice before I burst out laughing, instantly relaxing against the stark-white sheets. "Gabby, what the fuck?"

Her lip pokes out in a distinct pout as she pulls the mask off, revealing her smooth, tan complexion. Her big brown eyes complement her perfectly round face and button nose, reminding me of just how attractive she is. "Aww, come on, Tyke. I'm not done playing yet. Don't you want to have some more fun with her? She was a good sport."

The woman next to me continues to breathe softly, and while I'm positive that this woman provided great entertainment for Gabby and I last night, I can't remember a damn thing about it.

There's no time to try to remember it though, because the moment I sit up a little straighter, the sun's harsh rays poke through the thick drapes, letting me know I'm already late. "Can't. I have a band meeting at one."

Gabby's harsh laugh cuts across the room as her lithe fingers work at the knots in the rope. "Hate to break it to you, slick, but that ship has sailed. It's nearly three."

I sit up once I'm free and rub my wrists. "Fuck. The guys are going to be pissed. I've blown off the last three or four band meetings. Doing it again isn't going to sit well with them."

Gabby sits at the small desk in the room and fixes a line on the mirror for herself before snorting it up her nose. "Fuck 'em. Those douchebags need to learn to fend for themselves."

"Don't, Gabby," I warn, not liking her putting the guys down. It's one thing for me to do it, but someone else baggin' on them pisses me off. They're my brothers.

I roll out of bed and grab my jeans off the floor, quickly yanking them up on my hips. There's no sign of my underwear, but whatever; I'm not about to waste my time looking for them. I have to get the fuck out.

The blonde rolls over onto her back, and I freeze just as I pull my black T-shirt over my head. When she doesn't wake, I turn to Gabby. "You taking care of this one?"

She nods and wipes her nose, but a small dusting of white powder still remains. "Yeah. I'll check her phone for any pictures and videos and then call her a cab."

I fasten my belt and then slip my feet into my boots. "Good. No more groupies with sex tapes of us. That shit didn't go well last time."

She laughs. "Speak for yourself. That fucking tape got my band noticed and put on tour with Black Falcon."

I roll my eyes. "Just check her shit before she leaves. Trip and Noel will blow their fucking tops if I keep bringing the band down with negative publicity."

This time she rolls her eyes at me. "Whatever. I forgot what a Debbie fucking Downer you are when you sober up. You want a bump before you go?"

My nose twitches in anticipation, and while I know I should say no, I can't help myself. Gabby puts a small amount of coke between her index finger and thumb and raises her hand to me. "You know you want to."

I pull her hand up to my face and quickly snort every last bit of nose candy; the white powder stinging as it coats the warm, moist skin inside my nasal passages, sending me on a near-instant high in the process.

I close my eyes as every nerve in me comes alive, making me forget why the fuck I felt so anxious a few moments ago. I lean against the desk next to Gabby and she looks up at me and smiles, nodding over to the chick still sleeping in the king-size bed. "You wanna play?"

Gabby runs her hand down my torso, my toned abs flexing beneath my shirt in response to her touch. She pauses at my belt and yanks it open before allowing the tips of her fingers to rub against the growing erection inside my jeans.

A wicked grin crosses her face as she licks her lips. "I'll take that as a yes."

Unable to resist her, I give in and grab the nape of her neck, pulling her a little more roughly than I mean to out of the chair. I yank her slender body flush with mine. "Why the fuck do I let you do this? You're no good for me."

She bats her long lashes at me, attempting to look innocent. "Because you like getting crazy. Because you were bored out of your fucking skull until I came around. Because, deep down inside, you're tired of being the scapegoat for the other guys in Black Falcon, and you're done being their bitch."

I flinch at her cold words. "Fuck you, Gabby. I'm no one's bitch."

"Except mine," she purrs.

I shove her away. "Especially not yours."

I refasten my belt as I turn and head for the door.

"Tyke..."

I don't bother turning around. Good time or not, there's no way in hell I'm going to be talked down to by a chick I've known for three months.

Who the fuck does she think she is?

If it weren't for a groupie catching me drunk fucking Gabby after a show and blasting it all over the web, she and her band, Sex Arsenal, would still be playing small

15

dive bar gigs with a weak-ass following. Now that bitch has the nerve to insinuate I'm a pussy? Fuck her.

I don't need her. There are plenty of other people to party with. Her pussy isn't made out of gold, and I damn sure never made a fucking commitment to her.

She's a chick I like to get high with and fuck—that's it. Nothing more. She better not have it in her head that we are more than that.

Jesus.

When the elevator opens up to the lobby, the full effect of the afternoon sun begins to assault my eyes and I flinch, fishing my sunglasses from my pocket and slipping them on my face. The moment I'm outside I pat my pockets, hoping to find some car keys, but I have no such luck. I obviously didn't drive myself over here last night. Actually, I have no fucking clue where in the hell I am. Reaching into my back pocket, I whip out my phone and use the GPS feature on it.

Orlando.

Thank God I'm still in the right city. We play the Amway Center tonight to a sold out crowd. At least I know I can still make it there on time.

The young valet approaches me with a pen and paper in hand. The small cluster of pimples on his forehead does nothing to conceal his youth, and the eager smile on his face tells me one thing: he's a fan.

"Excuse me? I hate to bother you, but you're in Black Falcon, aren't you?" he asks in a voice that's just above a timid whisper.

I shove my glasses a little further up my nose. "Yep. Sure am."

He stretches his arms toward me. "Can I have your autograph?"

I take the pen and small notepad from him. "Sure, kid. Can you get me a cab?"

He nods vigorously as he takes back the signed paper. "No problem!"

While he scurries off, I check the messages on my phone.

Trip: Where the fuck are you?

Trip: Goddamn it. This shit is getting old. It's not cool to take off and not tell anyone where you are. I need to talk to you.

Trip: ?????

The final text catches my attention.

Trip: I hope you at least show up tonight.

My brow furrows at that comment. I've only ever missed a couple shows, and I felt like a total piece of shit for doing it. I hadn't realized we had a few early shows and may have been sleeping off the previous night's activities. It wasn't like I missed them on purpose, and yet that's all Trip ever seems to remember lately. He's conveniently forgotten all the times I've saved their asses. I fuck up and I never get to live it down.

I fire back a text telling him I'll be there and slip my phone back in my pocket, just in time to hop in the cab that's pulled up.

The ride over to the arena is pretty quick, which sucks. It used to excite me to spend time with my boys, but now I fucking dread it. None of us are on the same page anymore. Everyone is going in different directions, and our communication is shit.

Pulling up to the arena, I text Kyle to meet me out back and get me in through the crowd that's already building. I don't have a scrap of proof that I'm with the band and security can be real dicks if you don't have a pass.

"How much longer?" the cabbie asks after five minutes of me refusing to get out until I see Kyle.

"Chill, dude. I'm good for it. Trust me." He glances at me through the rearview mirror, and I can tell he's having some serious doubts about whether I can pay the fare.

I glance down at my wrinkled clothes and the tats that cover most of my arms. Granted, I don't exactly give off the best first impression right now, but damn, I hate it when people are judgmental.

Shrill screams from a group of fans surrounding the back gate catch my attention in time to see Kyle pass through the crowd alone. I dig my wallet out from my back pocket and pay the fare, along with a generous tip, before letting myself out of the cab.

Fans swarm around me, practically shoving pens and pieces of paper in front of my face begging for autographs, while dozens of flashes go off simultaneously. Kyle does his best to part the way for me as we push through to the gate.

Once inside, locked away from the fans, Kyle turns to me and hands me a backstage pass. "Where the hell were you? The guys are pissed."

I pull the lanyard over my head, adjust my sunglasses on my nose, and shrug. "What's new? They're always pissed at me for one reason or another lately. They'll get over me missing the stupid meeting. They never talk about anything other than scheduling more time off. It's not like my vote ever gets taken into consideration anyhow."

Kyle opens the door to the arena and motions me in. "I think they notice you being absent from more things than you realize."

"Doubtful."

I follow him through the maze of roadies, instruments, and stage props until my brother and the other guys come into view. The three of them stand there, talking quietly amongst themselves, until Riff glances up and notices me walking in their direction. He throws a swift elbow at Noel and nods toward me.

A strange vibe washes over me, and I can tell by the expressions on their faces that none of them are too happy with me right now.

Trip turns to look at me, contempt written all over his face. "Nice of you to grace us with your presence, asshole. Where were you?"

The sunglasses still covering my face shield the dramatic eye roll I'm giving him. "I was with Gabby."

He narrows his eyes at me. "I thought you said you were done with that shit?"

"Not that it's any of your fucking business, but I'm not using again."

I hope Trip doesn't see through the lie and figure out I've been dabbling a little on the white horse. I don't need the headache that comes from dealing with him. Besides, I don't have to report what I'm doing to him.

A harsh laugh rolls out of Trip's mouth. "I suppose you just enjoy her fucking company. Come on, man, this is me you're talking to. Your identical twin. Girls like Gabby Rodriguez are fast and easy; not exactly dating material. So don't try and bullshit this bullshitter—I know the kind of shit you do when you're with her."

The condescending tone in his voice makes my blood boil. I don't see where he gets off. He's not our fucking father. I can do what I want, when I want. "Since when does what I do and with who affect you?" I swing my gaze to Noel and Riff, who are both watching our exchange intently. It's time I let them all know how I feel. "Since when does my business affect any of you? All of you have your own fucking things going on. What does it matter if I'm out having a good time?"

Riff narrows his eyes. "It fucking matters when you miss important shit because you're too high to remember your goddamn priorities. That's the sixth band meeting you've blown off. Do you even know what the fuck is going on with the new album?"

I stare at him, the expression on my face blank. "What the fuck are you talking about? There's absolutely nothing going on with the new album because I haven't finished any of the fucking songs for it yet."

"Jesus, fuck, he's out of it now," Riff says as he shakes his head. "Do you even know what day of the week it is?"

I hesitate and swallow hard. I start to reach for my phone to check the date because, honestly, I don't have a fucking clue, but I stop short because doing that would just prove Riff right.

Riff shakes his head and turns to Noel with raised eyebrows. "I told you he didn't have a fucking clue. He's bad for business."

I flinch. "When have I ever been bad for business? I'm the glue that holds this piece of shit band together."

"Not anymore," Riff replies coolly.

ROCK MY BODY

I shake my head, not missing the disgust in Riff's eyes. It's a look I remember all too well. It's the same one he had a couple of years ago when Noel struggled with his addiction. The same look he had when he wanted us to boot Noel from the band.

I narrow my eyes at my childhood friend. "You got something to say to me, Riff, just go ahead and fucking say it."

Riff looks from Noel to Trip and his Adam's apple bobs as he swallows hard and then lifts his chin. "You're out, Tyke."

My eyes widen as every muscle inside me tenses. "What?!"

"You. Are. Out. You've become a liability. Noel knows it, and so does your brother. You need help. We won't stand by and watch you destroy yourself and drag this band down with you."

Rage rolls through every inch of me. "You're kicking *me* out? I fucking started this band. You can't kick me out."

Trip lays his hand on my shoulder. "Tyke—"

I shrug away from his touch. "Fuck you, Trip. Don't fucking touch me!" I level my heated gaze on the other two guys. "Fuck all of you!"

I take a couple steps back while my mouth hangs agape. I can't fucking believe this. They're giving me the boot, just like that? No chance to explain myself? Just out—like I'm a piece of fucking trash they can't wait to get rid of.

Fine.

Fucking Fine.

They'll see.

They need me.

They'll get over it.

I storm out of the arena, needing time to clear my head and figure this shit out, but before I get through the door, Kyle stops me. "Where you off to?"

"Hotel," is all I can manage to say.

The thick cords of muscle work beneath Kyle's skin as he pulls a set of keys out of his pocket. "Come on, I'll drive you over."

I follow our bodyguard to the Escalade. Kyle uses the key fob to unlock the SUV, and we both hop inside.

As I pull the heavy door closed behind me, I reconsider leaving. I should go back in there and hammer things out with the guys now. After all, I don't want tonight's show to be tense. But my head's still a little foggy from the coke I snorted, and I know I won't be able to speak to them rationally about this until I've had time to calm down.

I scrub my hand over my face. Tension in the band always fucking sucks—it's even worse to be the cause of it. They blame me for it, I know, but they don't see that all this shit started with them not caring enough. Not being committed enough. Not living for the band like they used to.

"Wanna talk about it?" Kyle asks, killing the silence that has allowed me to go deeper into my own thoughts.

I sigh. "What's there to talk about? The guys just kicked me out. They're pissed, I get it, but it won't last. We never stay mad at each other. We're brothers."

Kyle adjusts in his seat as he stares out at the road ahead. "That would be great. Things were going so good for a while, and I hate that there's this underlying tension between you guys. It makes things uncomfortable for us all when you guys aren't getting along."

"Come on, Kyle. Things haven't been that bad. We've been through far worse."

He sighs. "If you say so. I would just hate to see this great thing you all have going fall apart."

"We're not going to fall apart," I say with a slight huff.

We're quiet for the rest of the ride. I don't really feel like rehashing band issues with Kyle when I'm not even sure what in the hell is going on myself. After I spend a few hours sleeping and getting my head clear in my hotel room, I take a long hard look at myself in the bathroom mirror. My shaggy sandy-blond hair is a bit shaggy, a far cry from the short buzz cut I used to sport. Lately, I haven't really felt the need to be so clean-cut. The green of my eyes looks a little dingy, a little lifeless, but that's not completely my fault. Anyone in my shoes who's losing everything they've ever worked for would look the same way.

I rake my hair back with both hands and sigh. We just have to get back on track. I'll go to the guys and promise to stay sober, as long as they agree to start taking this band more serious. What we need is a heart-to-heart, as brothers. We need to squash this beef between us so that we can get back to doing what we do best—making great music.

I grab my backstage pass and slide it around my neck and slip out the door. I call a cab to take me back to the arena. It's time to get this shit back on track.

With a clear head, I set out to have a discussion with the guys about us all changing our ways, mending what the last few years have broken.

The cabbie drops me off near the back gate of the arena and with the help of my pass, I have no problem slipping into the backstage area on my own.

I pull my phone out of my pocket and check the time. It's nearly nine, the time we are scheduled to take the stage after Gabby's band, Sex Arsenal, opens for us. A few of the roadies nod at me as I pass by them on the way to the stage.

One roadie I've been partying with quite a bit lately, Lou, stops in front of me the moment he recognizes me. "Tyke? What are you doing here, man?"

My brow furrows instantly. "Why wouldn't I be here?"

Lou's mouth opens like he wants to say something, but he quickly closes it and shakes his head. "You're right. Forget I said anything."

I clap him on the back as I pass by. "All right. Catch you later."

I shove my hands deep into my pockets as I keep pushing forward, thinking about how odd Lou's reaction to seeing me was. I mean, why wouldn't I be here? We have a fucking show to do. He's obviously been smokin' something.

The rumble of Gabby's voice blasts through the arena. "You guys have been an awesome fucking crowd! Thanks for coming out early to hear our set. I need beer money, so make sure you pick up our newest record and buy a goddamn T-shirt out front." There's a roar of support from the fans. "Give it up for Black Falcon! They're about to come out and rock your faces off. You assholes will love that shit! We are Sex Arsenal! Goodnight!"

After a couple thumps on the bass drum, the only noise left is the hum of the buzzing crowd. It won't be long until we take the stage, so this little talk with the boys will have to wait until our set is over.

I begin tapping out the beat to "Ball Busting Bitch" with my thumbs which are still wedged in my pockets. Even though that's one song I didn't write, I still love it. It's the song that put us over the top, and I'll be forever grateful to it for our success.

I nod my head to the melody repeating in my brain, but the moment I round the corner and my gaze falls on the guys with Sergio Alvarez from Embrace the Darkness, the song drops out of my mind.

What the ever-lovin' fuck? We hate those douchebags. Since when did we decide to get fucking chummy with their bass player? I don't know the guy personally, but if he's in Embrace the Darkness, then he's got to be just as big of an asshole as Donovan and Striker.

I lift my chin and head straight for them, determined to get to the bottom of this.

Noel elbows Riff, who is busy explaining chords of some sort to Sergio while Trip looks on with a frown on his face. After Noel spots me, he nods to Trip who finally notices me, too. I hate this tension between us. I'll be glad when we squash all this later tonight and shit *finally* gets back to normal.

"What's up, guys?" I meet each one of their stares a little longer than necessary, but I'm trying to get a read on the situation.

"Sergio." Even I can hear the tension in my voice as I greet him with uncertainty, trying to figure out why he's here, since his band isn't on this tour with us.

Sergio's mouth twists as his eyebrows shoot up like he's surprised to see me. He looks to Riff, who only shrugs at him, before he says, "I'll give you guys a minute."

Sergio rotates the strap on his shoulder, sliding his bass onto his back before walking away. I turn back to the guys and Noel runs his hand through his hair while Riff pinches the bridge of his nose, drawing my attention to his crazy Mohawk. I know these moves; both of them revert to their nervous tics when they are frustrated and don't know how to handle it. I swing my gaze over to my brother, who grabs the bill of his baseball cap and adjusts it so it's covering most of his jet-black hair.

I fold my arms over my chest. "All right, fucking out with it. What aren't you telling me?"

Trip puffs his cheeks and blows a rush of air out through pursed lips. "We just didn't expect you to show up, that's all."

I scrunch my brow. "Where else would I be? We have a show—of course I'm going to be here."

My twin licks his lips carefully and then swallows. "The thing is, Tyke, we thought we were pretty clear earlier—"

I don't even give him a chance to finish. "You mean about throwing me out of the band?" I wave him off dismissively. "You guys were pissed, and I get why you said it, but we can sort all that out after the show. I've already forgiven you guys."

They exchange expressions bordering on surprise and sadness.

"Look, Tyke, we—"

My brother throws a hand out to stop Riff from saying anything else.

"Let me," Trip says, turning to me. "Tyke, we love you, man, but you need help. I know you believe you have a handle on all this partying you're doing, that you're in complete control, but the truth is you don't, and you aren't. I'm not sure what's going on with you because you won't talk to me—or any of us—but whatever it is, you need to figure it out."

I don't know whether to be excited that we've finally come to a point where a discussion about this band and my issues with what's happened to it is finally going to happen, or to get pissed that my own brother can't tell that I don't have addiction issues. I'm in complete fucking control.

"I'm so glad that you've finally seen there's a huge problem with the dynamics of the band and are ready to fix them. After we play tonight, I'd love to sit down and talk about adding more dates to the tour."

"No, Tyke." Trip shakes his head. "We've tried talking with you before, and no matter what we say to you, I know you aren't going to stop partying."

I roll my eyes. "I can stop any time I want. I just choose not to. I don't see what that has to do with the band."

"We can't have you with us while you're using," Noel chimes in. "I know more than anyone how easy it is to get out of control. If it weren't for you guys being by my side while I went to rehab—"

"Jesus Christ, are you fucking serious? *Rehab*? I don't need fucking rehab." Just where in the fuck do they get off? I've never been as bad as Noel was. Okay,

27

so maybe I missed a few shows where he never did when he was using, but it was only a few times.

I scrub my hands down my face. This is so fucking stupid, but I know they won't let me get out of rehab if they've made up their minds that I need treatment, so I might as well give in and get this over with.

"Fine. You want me to go to rehab? I'll go as soon as we wrap up the tour."

Trip takes a step toward me and starts to put his hand on my shoulder but hesitates, then shoves it back into his pocket. "You can't wait until after the tour, Tyke."

"Of course I can."

He shakes his head. "No, you can't. You can't resist Gabby, and she's on the rest of the tour with us. We think it's best if you went now."

"Now?" I question. "But, who will—" I stop myself because I don't even need to ask the question. I've already figured out the answer. "You assholes already replaced me? Before I get a fucking say? *Sergio Alvarez*? You've got to kidding me. He couldn't hold a fucking candle to me on his best day."

"Come on, man. Don't be a dick," Riff says. "Sergio's a good dude."

I lick the corner of my mouth. "A good dude, huh?"

Just because someone's a nice person, it doesn't mean they'll work in the band. These assholes will find out soon enough that I'm not replaceable. Hell, I'm going to teach them a lesson. Leave them high and dry, not giving them the satisfaction of kicking me out.

"You know what? You don't have to worry about me anymore because I fucking quit. Have fun keeping this piece of shit band together without me because none of you will put in the work like I do."

I turn and head away from them, listening for them to call my name and beg me to stay and work things out, but it never comes. I sigh and shake my head. Before long, they'll be begging for me to come back. It's only a matter of time.

The rest of the night is a hazy blur...

Going to a bar downtown with Lou...

Music...

Women...

Lots of women...

An assortment of pills...

A bottle of Jim Beam...

Getting behind the wheel of the Escalade I borrowed from Kyle. Driving down the road, drinking straight from the bottle, wondering how my life got so fucked up. Feeling lost. Unwanted, and unloved.

Seeing a concrete wall blocking a housing development and thinking it would be better if I weren't around anymore. After all, who would fucking miss me?

The last thing I remember is mashing the gas pedal to the floor.

Unlatching my seatbelt...

Then...nothing.

Chapter Two

"Mad World" – Gary Jules

Frannie

People say there can be no light without darkness. It's a nice quote and all, but I'm convinced it's just a load of shit people love to hang onto so they feel better. There's been more darkness in my life than I care to admit, but light? There's been no trace of that in a long time.

I watch silently as fat raindrops pound against the window of the train. This—starting over—is a good thing, and has been my main goal since I started my journey to straighten myself up. I've already completed the first two phases of my plan: admitting I had a problem, and taking a stand to overcome it while getting my degree in psychology. Now I'm moving on to the third stage: helping others conquer their personal struggles, too.

It's my new mission.

"Excuse me?"

My eyes drift away from the window to the man standing in the aisle next to me, wearing what I assume to be a very expensive tailored suit. He's clean-shaven; his dark hair is neatly styled. Stunning blue eyes and a perfectly white smile complete this alluring package before me.

If I were still the old me, I would give him my best flirty smile and, despite the gold band on his left hand, I would've invited him to sit down. But I'm trying hard to forget that woman. Absurdly handsome men who never really gave a damn about me are my biggest weakness— a weakness I'm desperate to break away from. Messing around with unavailable men with no hint of remorse was how I knew I had problems: hurting people in order to get my fix is something I did for years. The thought alone is shaming. It got to the point where sex was no longer just a physical escape, but an addiction, too. Like I would die if I didn't have it.

I blink a couple of times, bringing myself out of my thoughts while I do my best to repress my inner flirt. I notice the man's still standing there wearing a mischievous grin. "Yes?"

The stranger's grin widens. "Is this seat taken?"

I lick my lips and swallow hard as the temptation to invite him to snuggle now and fuck later in the bathroom crosses my mind. But as I've learned through my own psychological studies on resisting temptation, no matter how hard it may seem at the time, it's far better than dealing with the fallout of giving in.

I set my purse in the seat. "It is."

The man frowns and takes one last look at my long legs and voluptuous chest before he nods and continues down the aisle to find a seat.

As soon as he's out of sight, I breathe a sigh of relief and allow my head to fall back against the seat. Annie would've been proud, although she wouldn't have approved of how I was living my life to begin with. If she would've been there, things might not have gotten so out of control in the first place.

The train begins pulling away from the station, and I pull out my phone, flipping through my pictures until I find one of her. My fingers press against the screen as I trace the features of her beautiful face. As identical twins, people always said we looked alike, but other than that, there weren't many similarities between us.

Annie was so vibrant; her blue eyes were always so alive with wonder and hope, while mine were dull, filled with dread and despair. She was so optimistic about life, while I was the queen of pessimism. Physically, our bodies were identical—long legs with hour-glass figures like our mother, blue eyes like our father—but our spirits were polar opposites, so I never got why people lumped us together as the same person.

"I miss you," I whisper only loud enough for me to hear, before I kiss my two fingers and press it to her smile.

I quickly lock the screen and stuff my phone back into my purse, picking up the pamphlet for the posh facility I'll be working at. Serenity Hills: Recovery for the Mind, Body, and Soul. When I interviewed last month, the director of the place, Dr. Wayne Shepherd, had gotten me excited to be involved with their program and their mission of helping individuals become the absolute best person they can be.

After nearly eight hours, the train slows as it approaches Cincinnati, the nearest town to Serenity Hills, I begin gathering my belongings and stuffing the books and pamphlets I'd been reading into my handbag. The man who approached me earlier on the train stands and turns toward me, offering a final wink in my direction before heading out of the car. He's leaving the door open if I wanted to follow him, I guess.

I take a deep breath and stand, straightening my shoulders and tilting my chin up as I walk in the opposite direction of the handsome man. Every day that I fight against giving into my addiction, it becomes a little easier to walk away from temptation.

Once off the train, I search around in the crowd for my ride. It doesn't take me long to spot the doctor who interviewed me. He's just as I remembered him; tall, broad-shouldered, with neatly trimmed graying-hair and an athletic build—probably from running. Dr. Shepherd has that whole "distinguished" thing happening, and it totally works for him.

Dr. Shepherd smiles as his gaze locks on mine. He extends his hand in greeting as I approach him, and I set my bag down to shake his hand. "It's good to see you again, Dr. Shepherd."

"Wayne, please, Ms. Mead." His smile is sincere.

"In that case, you can call me Frannie." I want to roll my eyes at myself for sounding so much like a lame-o.

Wayne picks up my bag and ushers me toward the parking lot. "Did you have a good trip? I must say picking someone up from the train station is a first for me. Most people travel by plane or car these days."

I shrug, not wanting to reveal my issue with flying just yet, so I give the best excuse I can come up with. "I prefer it. It's relaxing and flying isn't that much shorter in the long run."

Wayne nods as he leads me to a black Mercedes. "I can appreciate a woman who knows what she likes and doesn't. Flying *is* overrated, I suppose, with its cramped seats and germ-filled cabins." The amused tone in his voice doesn't go unnoticed, and I smile, glad that he's accepted my rationale so easily.

Once Wayne places my bag in the trunk, he escorts me to the passenger side where he proceeds to open my door and help me inside. As I watch him walk around the car, I notice how attractive he is, even though I know he's quite a bit older than my twenty-eight years. I can already tell working alongside him and keeping things completely platonic might prove difficult if he decides to make a move on me, but I'm determined not to sleep with anyone I work with. I'm confident I can keep things strictly business. I have to. My professionalism means the world to me, and I can't allow my demons to influence me and cause problems with this new career that I so desperately want. It will be a challenge, but at least Wayne is a far cry from my normal type— irresistible tattooed, bad-boy man-candy. I just need to keep my distance from him, and any other man who may pose a threat to my newfound vow of celibacy.

It's about an hour drive through the hills of Kentucky before we come to the entrance of Serenity Hills, tucked among a thick line of trees that hide the rest of the property from sight. We turn down the paved drive and wind our way up the gentle slope and through the woods.

The large white Victorian-style home with a wraparound porch that's featured on the cover of the brochure comes into view. Wayne told me how beautiful this place was when he interviewed me in my hometown of Chicago, but I never expected this. It's peaceful and serene—the perfect place for people to relax and recover from whatever demons they're struggling with away from the harsh realities of the real world.

"It's breathtaking, isn't it?" Wayne takes the words right out of my mouth.

"It is," I agree. "I can't believe I'll be staying here."

"Actually..." Wayne pulls around the circular driveway and then continues to drive around to the back of the house, where a series of tiny white cottages sit spread out about fifty yards from the main house. "You and the rest of the staff get your own cottages. They're fully equipped—sort of like an efficiency apartment. They're quite nice."

I like the idea of having my own space to be alone with my thoughts and just read. I do have one lingering question, though. "What about our clients? Where will they be staying?"

He parks the car and cuts the ignition. "The clients stay in the main house, where myself and our head nurse, Timothy, will be as well. We like to keep our eyes on them, and Timothy is quite strong, which comes in handy if a client gets out of hand."

"It's good that you have him."

"It is, but I want to assure you we take staff and client safety very seriously here at Serenity, and have never had an issue with any of our clients behaving in a violent manner. Most are affluent members of society— some are even celebrities."

I raise my eyebrows. Celebrities? I thought the secluded surroundings were just to provide a tranquil atmosphere, but now it makes sense. The lush greenery also helps keep the prying eyes of the paparazzi out. I wasn't even allowed to know the location of the treatment center until I formally accepted the position. The physical address was never listed on any of the informational paperwork I received. "Do many celebrities come here?"

Wayne pauses for a moment and then nods his head. "From time to time."

"Do they receive any special privileges?"

"No. They are treated just like everyone else. We hold group sessions as well as some private ones to maintain a level of privacy for all our clients. Some of the issues they may need our help working through are very private, so we don't begrudge them, or anyone else, of that confidentiality. We don't want to hinder their recovery process."

I nod. "That's understandable."

Wayne smiles, his perfectly white teeth on full display. "I think you'll fit in nicely here, Ms. Mead."

"Frannie, please, I insist, and thank you for that vote of confidence. I'm really excited to be a part of the team here. I'm ready to help make an impact on people's lives."

"I'm glad to hear that, Frannie."

After Wayne helps me from the car and collects my bag from the trunk, I follow him down the cobblestone path toward one of the cottages. Fresh spring flowers line the walkway, and I inhale deeply taking in their floral scent along with the crisp air. I've never been one to covet country living, but I can see how living among beauty like this would be appealing to some.

The closer we get to the cottage, I notice how close it is to a beautiful, lush garden. A huge fountain sits in the middle, water spilling from a female statue's bucket. Four benches surround it, each spaced equally apart. It's breathtaking—like something that belongs in some grand park somewhere for the masses to enjoy, instead of just a few select individuals.

Wayne steps up onto the small concrete stoop of the cottage and watches as I study the garden intently. "I thought you'd enjoy that. I chose this cottage for you since it was right next door to it."

"It's wonderful," I gush.

Wayne smiles, clearly pleased that I'm so ecstatic about his choice. "If you like that, wait until you have a look inside."

Curious as to what could be any better than this, I follow him inside, and my breath immediately catches. This small little house must have been a decorator's wet dream to design. Everything in the places exudes softness and serenity, down to its overstuffed cream colored couch and bedding, both with soft teal accents. It's very fitting considering the name of this facility.

I resist the urge to jump on the bed and test its softness in front of Wayne, choosing instead to walk around the room. A small kitchen area sits along the back wall, and a couch with an entertainment area separates the living room from the bedroom. I push open one of the doors next to the bed to reveal a decent size walk-in closet, and the second door hides the full bathroom complete with claw-foot tub.

I think I've died and gone to my own personal heaven.

Wayne clears his throat behind me, and I turn to find him holding out a key. "Dinner is served promptly at seven in the main house, and I would be delighted to show you around the grounds afterwards—while we still have plenty of light."

I pinch the small piece of metal between my fingers, delighted. "That would be great. Thank you."

A huge smile overtakes Wayne's face, even reaching his dark brown eyes. "I'll leave you to unpack. See you at seven."

The moment the door shuts behind him, I do the thing I've been itching to do since I walked in—I run and jump on the bed, immediately sinking into the thick down comforter.

I shove my loose strands of brown hair out of my face and sigh. "What a start to a new life."

Two years ago, I would never have seen myself here, in this moment. Especially with both a degree *and* a job that I'm excited about. Annie would be proud; I know it.

After unpacking all my things, I glance up at the clock that's hanging on the wall. It's only a little after six, so I still have some time to poke around the place before dinner. I move to grab my purse but decide to tuck it into the closet for safe keeping instead. Since there's not a pocket to be found anywhere on the sundress I'm wearing, I slip the key into my bra for safekeeping.

I step out on the small stoop and take care to lock my door carefully behind me before continuing up the stone path toward the main house. The silence of the natural surroundings is only disturbed when birds chirp in a gleeful chorus. I can't remember the last time I was, or even if I ever have been, in a place so away from civilization that there's absolutely no intrusion on the sounds of nature, but it's delightful.

When I finally make it to the house, I step up onto the back porch. Its grand two-story pillars really give a regal appeal to the place. As I turn to walk to the front of the house, a door behind me opens.

A petite blonde, wearing a white skirt and pale yellow polo shirt, comes bouncing out the door with earbuds in her ears, humming along to a song on the radio.

The moment she spots me, she yanks the cord on her earbuds, popping them out, and grins. "You must be Dr. Mead. I'm Kimmy, the housekeeper. It's so nice to finally have another woman on the staff around here."

I extend a hand out to her. "Please, call me Frannie."

"Oh my gracious, that's an adorable name," she says, and her heavy country accent makes me smile. "Well, Frannie, I hope you like your cottage. Dr. Shepherd allowed me to decorate it for you."

"Wow, I'm impressed. I love the design of the place. Did you put the entire color scheme together?"

Kimmy nods enthusiastically. "I did. It's my dream to be an interior decorator one day. I've been taking some online classes because there are no schools close by that specialize in that. I can't afford to make the drive every day to one of the bigger cities, and I for damn sure can't afford to live there, so online will have to do until I can save enough money to move."

I study the young woman. She can't be more than twenty, and yet, she clearly knows what she wants to do with her life and is already on a serious path to getting it. I'm envious of her, wishing I'd had her drive at that age.

"That sounds like a terrific plan." I strain my neck to peek around the side of the house. "Which is the best way to get into the house? The back?"

Kimmy stuffs her phone and earbuds into the pocket of her skirt. "Come on, I'll show you around. I bet you're pretty anxious to meet everyone and get settled."

"That would be lovely." I follow her back through the door she just came out of, and we enter into a large library.

The grand ambiance that encircles the outside of the place doesn't shy away from the inside one bit. Large wooden bookcases stretch along the back wall from floor to ceiling; every spare inch of the shelves filled with books. I take a deep breath and give myself another pep talk about maintaining my professionalism and not going absolutely gah-gah in front of this young woman. She might not understand my obsession with the written word.

Kimmy catches me staring and laughs. "It's a lot of books, right? I'd never seen so many in all my life—not even in the libraries I've been in. Our towns around here can't afford anything so extreme. We're lucky to have three bookcases for the whole place—for every kind of book."

"That's a shame," I tsk. "There's nothing like getting lost in a fantastic story. No one on earth should be deprived of that."

"I agree." Wayne's smooth voice coats the room, jerking my attention to him. "Sorry, ladies, I didn't mean to intrude, but I was passing by and overheard your last statement, and I couldn't help but get excited right along with you. It's a shame that small towns like this get deprived of a decent library." Wayne turns to direct his attention to Kimmy. "Since I've caught you, do you mind preparing a room in the men's wing? I've just received an urgent request for program enrollment, and our new client will be arriving tomorrow."

She folds her hands in front of her and nods, almost giving off the impression of a slight curtsy, saying, "Right away, Dr. Shepherd," before she hustles out of the room.

I stare after her, and Wayne catches my attention when he speaks. "Bright girl."

"She is," I quickly agree.

"You don't find many employees like her nowadays; smart, kind, and obedient. She follows every rule I set here to a 'T.'"

My mind drifts back to all the previous jobs I've held and how many times I'd screwed off—cutting corners and sneaking time off when I could. I was definitely not the model employee that Kimmy appears to be. Wayne's probably right. Finding someone like her is very much like finding a diamond in the rough.

"I trust you found your living quarters agreeable?" Wayne walks over to the bookcase and rearranges a couple of books on the shelf, like he couldn't stand them being out of order. "If you have any additional requirements, please let Kimmy know. She can arrange to get anything you may need."

"Really, Wayne, everything is perfect," I reassure him.

He turns to me and extends his elbow to me, reminding me of an old movie, where the classic hero, dressed in a perfectly tailored suit, escorts the heroine around. I've always been infatuated with the idea of finding a classy man like that.

I hook my arm in his and allow him to lead me through the door of the library into the main hall of the house. Deep mahogany wood covers the floor, while the crisp white walls lighten the entire space. Black and white portraits of different people are spaced evenly apart and one photo of a young woman with long dark hair catches my attention. Although I can't see her face, the sag in her shoulders and the slight tilt of her head as she stares at a vacant field tells me she's unbelievably sad.

"That's one of my favorites. There's just something about her body language that draws me in and makes me wonder what she's thinking."

I nod in agreement. "Yes."

"I believe hanging photos that represent the possible feelings of our clients shows them that they aren't alone—that everyone feels sad from time to time. You'll find that we have them all over the main house."

From there, Wayne continues the tour through the front parlor and then on to the kitchen, where a heavy-set woman with a deep tan and dark hair pulled up under a hairnet is buzzing around. Her tiny button nose compliments her dark brown eyes which are currently fixed on the cake she's decorating. With a few swift motions of her hand, she creates a tiny red rose and then attaches it to the cake.

"That's amazing. I've always wanted to do that," I say.

The woman glances up and smiles. "Thank you. My mother taught me."

"Dr. Mead, this is Sue, our head chef here at Serenity, and the best baker I've ever had the pleasure of meeting," Wayne introduces us.

I release my arm from Wayne's and begin to extend it toward her, but remember that she's cooking and think better of it. "It's nice to meet you, Sue."

"You, too, Dr. Mead."

"What's on the menu tonight, Sue?" Wayne asks.

"Steak with mashed potatoes and green beans, and of course, chocolate cake for dessert," Sue answers.

"Sounds fantastic. I'm looking forward to it." Wayne turns to me and extends his elbow again. "Shall we?"

Wayne sweeps his arm toward the door on the other side of the kitchen. Before I follow his direction.

"Aloha, Dr. Mead," Sue replies, alerting me to the fact that she's of Hawaiian descent.

We move into an elegant dining room with a table that appears big enough to seat twenty. A grand fireplace sits off to the left side of the table, and it's tall enough for me to walk into, if I wanted. The place settings have been arranged like something from a fine restaurant.

"This is impressive," I tell Wayne. "I would never have pictured all this for..."

I don't finish my thought because I don't want say the wrong thing and offend Wayne.

"A rehab facility?" He lifts an eyebrow and grins.

I shrug. "Yes. I mean, this setup could rival some of the best restaurants in the world."

"Thank you. We pride ourselves on making sure our clients are well taken care of. When they come here to detox, it's not the most pleasant thing to go through, but we try to comfort them by making things nice, allowing them only positive things to focus on while they are here."

Wayne pulls out a chair to the right of the head of the table. "Please, sit. The clients will all be here shortly, and we can get started with introductions."

A few moments later, the sound of laughter comes rolling in from outside the room. It's not exactly the mood I expected from a group of people struggling from an array of addiction issues. The first person through the door is a tall, statuesque blonde, with a model face and legs to die for. Everything about her, from her boobs to her eyebrows, couldn't be more perfect if they were drawn on. Second to arrive is a very handsome man with a broad frame and blond spiky hair. The two of them are smiling, and it makes me think they are the ones I heard laughing just moments ago. Behind them follows a short, balding man with a beer belly who doesn't appear quite as jovial as the two who preceded him. A few more women and men follow in after that, and each and every one of their curious eyes land on me; wondering who I am and what I'm doing here, I'm sure.

Wayne stands as the new group joins us at the table, each taking a seat. "By the sounds of it, it appears you all enjoyed your day out."

"Oh, we did," the blonde says, and then directs her attention to the spiky haired man who came in with her. "Randall ensured we all had a great time."

Randall stiffens his back and directs his gaze at Wayne. "Everyone had fun at the fair and was on their best behavior. It was a nice change of pace to get out of here for a while."

"Good, good," Wayne praises before turning to me. "This is Randall, our activities director."

I return the smile that Randall shoots me with one of my own, as I'm ecstatic to meet another one of my new co-workers.

Wayne clears his throat and addresses everyone who is now seated at the table. "I'm sure you're all curious as to the new face in the room. This is Dr. Francine Mead. She's the new addiction therapist here at Serenity and will be meeting with some of you individually and hopefully develop a relationship whereby she can assist you with your recovery process. I'll ask that each one of you show her the same respect that you show me."

Everyone around the table listens to Wayne intently and they nod in all the appropriate places.

The blonde is the first to speak. I can already tell she is the type of woman who is used to having all the attention in the room. "It's nice to meet you, Dr. Mead. I'm Josie Sullivan. You might've heard of me? I had a hit single called 'Working on a Star' a couple of years ago."

My lips pull into a tight line as I root through the limited pop music catalog I have listed in my head. I haven't had time for much more than studying and spending my time with men. Keeping up on the latest top forty hits hasn't been exactly high on my priority list. I primarily only listen to alternative music.

I grimace. "I'm not much of a music lover, but I'm sure it's a lovely song."

Her expression borders on shock and confusion and then she turns to Randall. "Where did Dr. Shepherd find this one? Under a rock?"

"Josie," Wayne warns. "Please refrain from insulting the staff. You, better than anyone else, know the rules at Serenity."

Josie nods quickly, and I get the feeling this isn't her first visit to Serenity. "I'm sorry, Dr. Shepherd. It won't happen again."

"Good." Wayne unfolds the pressed cloth napkin at his place setting and uses it to cover his lap just as Sue comes into the dining room, pushing a small metal cart with a huge bowl on it. "What kind of soup do we have today?"

"It's a chilled strawberry. I think you'll like it," Sue replies as she begins to ladle a portion into each person's bowl.

The moment the spoon touches my lips and I sip its contents, I fight back the urge to moan. "This is spectacular, Sue."

She smiles at me. "Thank you, Dr. Mead."

The rest of the dinner goes on with small talk taking place between the clients while Wayne interjects every now and then. I learn that most of them have been here for quite some time and were very comfortable stating what they are addicted to, talking very candidly about it.

After it's all over, Wayne escorts me back to my cottage, and I'm still reeling at how open the clients are. "They all seemed to have made wonderful progress. I'm simply amazed at how open they are about their addictions. That's always the first step, admitting they have a problem, but then to be able to talk about it so freely and share their struggles is above and beyond."

Wayne nods. "They don't come here that way, let me assure you. Most come here headstrong and reluctant, adamant they don't have a problem, and that everyone else is just too uptight or meddling in their business, so it takes time for them to come around. We hold a lot of group sessions, encouraging that openness. Eventually, they become more comfortable sharing with us and others around them. Unfortunately, most of their support systems at home hinder more than help their recovery, and more often than not, we end up seeing them back here."

"That's a shame—to see all that progress wasted."

He sighs. "It is. I always have to remind myself that we can only do so much here. Ultimately, it's up to them to remain clean and sober with a positive outlook, and remain open about their feelings and their struggles to those around them."

We arrive at my stoop and I pull the key from my bra. Wayne raises his eyebrows and I merely shrug. "No pockets."

He laughs. "I see."

Once I unlock the door, I turn to him and say, "Thank you for walking me. What time do you want me to start work tomorrow?"

"Eight sharp. We have a new client coming in the morning, and I would like to go over his case file with you before he arrives. Everything we have on the clients is electronic. I'll email your password to access the system so you can look over it at your leisure. I would like for you to take the lead with this one, but I'll be here to help you in any way I can."

I lift my chin, proud that he trusts that I'm ready to jump right into the fire and counsel the new client. "Sounds great. I'll wait for your email."

"I'll send it over as soon as I get back to my office. Goodnight, Frannie."

The rest of the evening, I wait on Wayne's email. When I hear the familiar ding of a new message while brushing my teeth, I finish up and rush to the open laptop on my bed to check it.

It contains all the proper passwords and links to access all the clients' files, as well as the information on the client we are expecting tomorrow.

Tyke Douglas, the bass player for the rock band, Black Falcon, will be arriving via private transportation tomorrow morning. Tyke has been enrolled by his twin brother, Trip, with Tyke's permission. The client has had two DUIs in the past year, and reportedly has issues with prescription and recreational drugs as well.

I tap my bottom lip, curious about the guy, wanting to know more than the small report on the client tells me. I quickly minimize the screen and pull up Google, typing Mr. Douglas' name into the search engine along with his band's name. Within seconds, mug shots pop up on my screen, along with the tabloid reports on the downward spiral of Black Falcon. I flip through more photos and come across one where his eyes are closed as he strums a guitar while wearing a sleeveless shirt, displaying his vast array of tattoos perfectly. While his body appears to be absolutely banging, I'm stuck on the sadness on his face—like he's completely lost in the song he's playing.

I click on the biography link listed for Mr. Douglas, but it shows a combined history for both him and his twin brother.

TRIP DOUGLAS BIO

Character Name: Trip Douglas
Birth Date: October 14th
Place of Birth: Ashland, Kentucky
Current Residence: Paintsville, Kentucky
Height: 6'1"
Weight: 195
Hair Color: Black
Hair Length: Short
Eye Color: Green
Tattoos: Sleeves on both arms, back, and chest
Educational History: High School graduate
Work History: Drummer of Black Falcon
Quirks: Wears bandanna on his head, an identical twin
Key Adult Experiences: Achieving musical fame

Trip Douglas (born October 14th), is the drummer for the American heavy metal band Black Falcon. Best known for being the crazier of the two Douglas Twins, Trip's triple-thumping foot pedal sound has become one of the band's trademarks.

Alongside his twin brother, Tyke, Trip began playing instruments under the guidance of his musician father, but his interest in playing in a band grew once he discovered his love for hard rock music. He joined a band called *Dingy* while in high school with his brother Tyke and his best friend, Zachary 'Riff' Oliver. Later, the band was renamed to Black Falcon after the addition of the band's new front man, Noel Falcon.

Trip also enjoys extreme spots, such as dirt bike riding, rock climbing, and sky diving—making him the most adventurous member of the band. His dream is to one day climb Mount Everest.

TYKE DOUGLAS BIO

Character Name: Tyke Douglas
Birth Date: October 14th
Place of Birth: Ashland, Kentucky
Current Residence: Paintsville, Kentucky
Height: 6'1"
Weight: 190
Hair Color: Blond
Hair Length: Shaggy
Eye Color: Green
Tattoos: Sleeves on both arms, back, and chest
Educational History: High School graduate
Work History: Bassist of Black Falcon
Quirks: Frequently wears sunglasses, loves organization, an identical twin
Key Adult Experiences: Achieving musical fame

Tyke Douglas (born October 14th), is the bassist for the American heavy metal band Black Falcon. Best known for being a key songwriter for the band, Tyke's obsession with detail always seems to push the songs to a level of perfection rarely achieved by other bands.

Tyke also enjoys the arts, attending gallery openings and poetry events whenever his schedule allows—making him the most cultured member of the band. His dream to one day branch out and share his other artistic abilities with the world is something he hopes to accomplish in the very near future.

Combined Bios:

Trip and **Tyke** began playing instruments under the guidance of their musician father, but their interest in playing in a band grew once they discovered a mutual love for hard rock music. They joined a band called *Dingy* while in high school, accompanied by their best friend, Zachary 'Riff' Oliver. Later the band was renamed

Black Falcon after the addition of the band's new front man, Noel Falcon.

The band's first record, *Hell in a Hand Basket*, went double platinum, making Black Falcon a force to be reckoned with. They've released two additional albums since then, and their latest single, "Ball Busting Bitch" is currently on Billboard's Top 40.

They currently reside in Kentucky, near their other band mates.

As I read through his bio, I can't help but notice how Tyke Douglas is consistently lumped in with his brother, as opposed to giving him his own identity. Being a twin myself, I can totally relate to this issue. It's all too easy for people to see you as the same person as your twin. It's what happened with Annie and me.

I flip through the rest of the links, studying more pictures of Tyke. He's very easy on the eyes with his tall frame, tan complexion, and light hair. Even though he and Trip are twins, their hair sets them apart, making it very easy to tell the difference between them. The more I stare at the man on my screen, the more addicted I become to his profile. He's devastatingly handsome, and the thought of how attracted I am to just his mere picture scares the shit out of me.

How am I ever supposed to concentrate on helping this man when he's my own personal brand of tattooed man-flavored candy? This will prove to be a very difficult task, for sure. The best I can hope for is to find that he's simply photogenic and absolutely hideous in person.

I close my laptop and set it on my nightstand before I tug my glasses from my face and set them on top of it. I double-check my alarm clock and then snuggle down in my bed after offering up a little prayer that I'll be able to contain myself tomorrow. If Tyke is the stereotypical bad-boy rocker that he appears to be, I'll need all the help I can get to keep from jumping his bones and jeopardizing the job I've worked so hard to get.

Chapter Three

"Pain Killer" – Three Days Grace

Tyke

I rub my face as Trip pulls into the drive of Serenity Hills. "Are you completely sure this is necessary? Really, I'm fine."

He turns his head in my direction and raises an eyebrow. "Take a good look in the mirror again and then tell me you don't need help."

I sigh as I stare at my own reflection in the visor mirror; the angry bruises surrounding my left eye are instant reminders of what happened a few days ago.

I reach up and gingerly trace the wound with my fingertip. "It was an accident. I told you I'm done drinking, and that shit won't happen again."

My brother adjusts his grip on the steering wheel. "You need to stop making promises you have no intentions of keeping."

"I swear it this time. I'm done. I've had enough," I fire back, angry that he doubts my sincerity.

Trip pulls up to a circular driveway in front of a huge white house. "I want to believe that, Tyke, but I can't take the chance of you trying to hurt yourself again."

"For the last time, I wasn't trying to—" Trip holds his hand up, instantly cutting me off.

"I was there, Tyke. In the hospital when they brought you in. You were so out of it you don't remember telling me you were disappointed that you weren't dead." Trip's eyes soften. "If you won't talk to me, then you have to talk to someone—someone who can help you work through this. I feel like I'm not that person for you. Whenever we try to talk, all I seem to do is make shit worse. It would kill me if something happened to you, so please, for me, just spend some time here and get things off your chest."

I chew on the corner of my thumb. He's right. I don't remember admitting to him how I really felt that night, right before I crashed the Escalade into a concrete wall. I had been thinking I'd be better off dead, but that wasn't meant for others to hear. I don't feel that way now—at least, I don't think so. But alcohol and mood enhancers have a way of bringing out my innermost demons.

"Okay, but I promise you, I won't be here long," I tell my brother, doing my best to sound confident.

Trip smiles. "Good. I need my brother back."

The moment we get out of the car, we're met by a tall man with salt and pepper hair, wearing a gray suit, and a huge black guy with a bald head standing on the wraparound porch near the front door of the building.

54

After I take in the large arms the black guy has crossed over his chest, my eyes flit to Trip as he pops the trunk. "Are you sure this isn't a fucking prison?"

My brother's eyes snap in the direction of the two men and then he shrugs. "You're being paranoid. Looks like a nice place to me. Come on."

I grab my duffel bag from the trunk and take my guitar case, my baby inside it, from Trip before stalking toward the porch. Dread fills me already. Agreeing to come to the place was probably a big fucking mistake.

The graying man gives me a small smile and extends his hand. "Welcome, Mr. Douglas. I'm Dr. Shepherd, staff physician here at Serenity Hills, and this is Timothy, our staff nurse. I will be overseeing your medical treatment while you're here."

He moves on to shake Trip's hand. "As discussed on the phone, we have private accommodations for him at the main house and will provide the utmost professional care."

Trip sighs, like he's relieved. "Thank you. That's reassuring."

"We'll give you a moment to say your good-byes," Dr. Shepherd tells us as he and Timothy step back toward the large, white double wooden doors at the entrance, but they don't leave us alone completely.

It would be easy for me to hate my brother for forcing me to come to this place. This isn't going to be a gentle ride—more like being the captain of a ship headed straight for hell. While I don't believe I'm "addicted" to anything, I do know that my body has become dependent on my recreational drugs of choice. Every time I go for a prolonged period of time without something in my system, my body begins to go haywire, its circuits overloading and making it behave erratically. Luckily, I haven't developed the junkie shakes.

My brother wraps me in a tight hug. "I'll see you soon, man."

I clear my throat, choking back the heavy lump building there as it finally strikes me that I won't be seeing him for a while. "Okay."

Trip turns to me, his eyes sad as they flick from the floor of the porch up to me. "Guess this is it, brother. Be sure to call me every chance you get."

"I will," I say.

Without another word, Trip turns away from me and heads for his car. I stand there, watching as he gets into the driver's seat of his Mustang, firing up the engine before heading back down the drive and out of sight.

"All right, first things first, Timothy will go ahead and search your belongings and get inventory." I whip around and eyeball Dr. Shepherd as he gives his henchman orders.

I tighten my grip on my duffel bag as the nurse takes a step toward me. "Hold on just a goddamn minute. You aren't going through my things."

Dr. Shepherd holds his hands out palm up. "Tyke, I know you may not understand or agree with some of our methods—lack of personal privacy being one of them—but I assure you that we are merely looking for contraband items that could hinder the recovery efforts of both yourself and those around you. We have a zero tolerance policy here, and we search all personal items brought into our treatment center."

I cling to my bag, tucking it tightly against my chest. "Can't you just take my word that there's nothing in there?"

He shakes his head. "I'm afraid not." He extends this hand. "If you want to stay here and begin treatment, this isn't up for discussion."

Fuck.

My lungs fill with air and I shut my eyes and take a deep breath, before blowing it out through my nose. If I tell them to fuck off, and take off walking, there's not a damn thing they can do to me. This wasn't court ordered, just a Black Falcon demand—a demand that if I ignore, I can kiss my spot in the band good-bye, handing Sergio the gig of a lifetime.

What other real choice do I have?

I loosen my hold and reluctantly hand my bag over to Dr. Shepherd. The moment I let go, I shove my hands deep into my pockets, dreading the moment they find everything I've hidden in there.

"You're going to do all right here, Mr. Douglas. Following rules and protocol are key, and the sooner you understand we are only doing these things for your own good, the better our treatment program will work for you."

I simply shrug my shoulders in defeat. "Whatever. Let's just get this over with."

"Very well." He nods curtly before handing my stuff to the nurse. "Timothy, let's get started. This way, Mr. Douglas."

I follow behind the doctor and nurse as requested. We don't immediately go into the house, though; we veer off the porch toward a small building that I didn't notice. Tucked into the thick tree line, it's white like the house, and appears to be a small cottage.

Dr. Shepherd steps up onto the stoop and pulls a ring of keys from his pants pocket, sorting through them before finding the one to unlock the building. The moment we step inside, it's clear this is some sort of intake place to greet visitors, and most likely new enrollees. A small waiting room with four chairs faces the reception desk sitting in the middle of the room. Behind the desk is a small room that reminds me of a doctor's office with an exam table sitting catty-corner in the space.

Dr. Shepherd pushes the exam room door open a little wider and gestures me through. "We need to conduct a full physical exam before we get you settled into your room. Timothy will remain out here to go through your things. I must make you aware that if we find any drug paraphernalia of any type we will dispose of it in your presence. These are not items we will return to you, even if you elect to withdraw yourself from the program, because they are illegal substances."

I nod. "Understood."

Oh shit, will that nurse get an eyeful when he goes through my stuff. There's not a lot of product in there, but enough for emergencies if I needed it. Enough that the mere thought of flushing it makes me cringe.

"Coming?" The doctor's words pull me out of my haze as I realize I'm just standing there staring at Timothy as he shoves his hands into a pair of gloves and then unzips my bag.

It's too late now to stop what he's going to find, so I might as well get this exam over with.

"Yeah."

Dr. Shepherd wastes no time pulling a gown out of the cupboard and sets it on the exam table. "Strip down to your underwear and put on the gown."

The doctor exits the room without any additional instructions. I scratch the back of my neck as I stare at the fabric lying in front of me. Is this really what I've been reduced to? A man whom others deem incapable of making sound judgments on his own? A man forced to get full-body exams because people feel that he has an addiction issue? I don't fucking think so, but I'll go along with it just to secure my spot in the band.

I love that band. It's my life, and I'd do anything for it.

A couple of quick raps hit the door and then Dr. Shepherd pushes in. He doesn't meet my stare, only keeps his head down and continues to jot notes on what I assume is my chart.

"You had quite the supply in your duffel bag *and* guitar case." It's clearly not a question but a statement of the obvious.

What's really left to say after that?

I shrug. "Yeah, well, what can I say? I like to be prepared."

He glances up at me with a raised eyebrow and a semi-amused expression. "A sense of humor is a good thing to have. It's important to keep that because what you're about to go through will not be easy. It's going to be the hardest thing you've ever done in your life, but once it's over, you'll feel like a new man. I promise you that."

I sigh. "I'm sure this is absolutely the most difficult thing in the world for someone who has an actual problem, but Doc, I'm not one of those people. I can quit anytime I want to. I use it to have fun. It's not an addiction."

Dr. Shepherd leans against the counter across from me and crosses his arms over my file. "Tyke, almost every single person who comes into this exam room for the very first time says the exact same thing. Admitting you have an addiction and deciding to make a change is the first step to recovery."

"Don't worry, Doc. I'll breeze through this program. You'll see," I tell him with complete confidence. "While I'll admit that my body has become dependent on a few things I use regularly, I don't admit to having a problem."

He tilts his head. "Then why did you agree to come to treatment?"

"My band," I answer honestly. "They really didn't leave me much choice. If I didn't come here, they voted to throw me out, and I can't let that happen. Black Falcon means everything to me."

"I see." He jots a couple more things down in the chart. "Well, while you are here, Mr. Douglas, I hope that you use the time wisely, and open yourself up to the possibility that you may actually have a problem severe enough for your brother to reach out to us. He's worried about you, about losing you, and he feared he didn't have what it takes to help you because nothing he's done over the last year has succeeded. While I can't make you see the issues at hand and want to get better—that part is totally up to you—I can give you the tools and the support to begin your recovery."

He sets the chart down on the counter and washes his hands. "I'm just going to do a standard exam and go over your medical history. We'll discuss where you're getting your benzodiazepine supply. After that, you'll get dressed, collect your belongings, and Timothy will help you get settled into your room."

After about fifteen minutes of being thoroughly violated, consenting to STD testing, and witnessing a pat down of all my clothing, I'm left alone in the room to get dressed again. I quickly throw my clothes back on and head out the door. The male nurse's gaze meets mine as he sits at the desk, my things spread out in front of him. I don't care who you are, when someone else goes through your personal belongings, it ruffles your feathers.

I cross my arms across my chest and do my best not to rip into the guy for what I'm sure is just his job.

Dr. Shepherd clears his throat. "As you can see, Mr. Douglas, we've searched your things thoroughly, and we've recovered several items of contraband." He gestures to the four baggies sitting in front of my clothes. "Two bags of an unknown white powdered substance, one baggie of some sort of dried herb that appears to be THC, accompanied by several rolling papers, and one baggie of pills that looks to be benzodiazepines. As discussed, we will be disposing of these items in your presence before we clear you into the facility."

Timothy rises, his at least six-foot-five frame towering over me, and he gathers the baggies. I could tell them no—hell fucking no—but know that I can't. No sense in me getting all testy in a situation I know I can't change.

I sigh. "Lead the way."

I follow Timothy and Dr. Shepherd into a restroom behind the desk, watching helplessly as everything I need to make my time here sustainable swirls around in the toilet before being sucked down the drain.

After the empty baggies are discarded, I follow the two men out of the bathroom. Timothy sits back down and begins doing paperwork. The guy hasn't said one word to me since I got here, which is completely fucking odd and doesn't make me feel comfortable around him, but I'm grateful that I've only got one of them firing questions at me.

Dr. Shepherd folds my file and lays it on the desk. "Anything else you have on you that we didn't find? Now's the time to come clean without any judgment."

I shake my head. "Honestly, everything I brought with me was either taped inside the guitar, which you obviously found, or in the duffel bag."

"Good. We really want to focus on the twelve steps of recovery with you, Mr. Douglas. Whether you realize it or not, you've already started the program by completing the first three steps in order to get here—acknowledging your addiction and deciding to change, exploring your rehab treatment options, and finding the support that you need."

I furrow my brow. "But I didn't pick this place. My brother did."

He nods. "Yes, but it was ultimately your choice to come here. Knowing your brother will support you helped make you comfortable, I'm sure."

"I guess, but Doc, I have to be honest with you—I really don't have a problem. I like to party, but that's nowhere near having an addiction issue. I'm only here to keep my spot in the band," I tell him.

He raises one eyebrow. "Noted, but I hope you are here to take a hard, *honest* look at your life and the direction it's going. We can only help you as much as you'll allow us."

His words play over in my mind. While I know what he's getting at, he doesn't get that, unlike most people that waft through his door, I don't have a problem. I'm not an idiot, and I sure as fuck am not in denial about the shit I do.

After a short pause with no words passing between us, the doctor requests that Timothy show me to my room so I can settle in. I follow the nurse out the door, and we head back up toward the house carrying my duffel bag in my hand and my soft guitar case slung over my shoulder. One thing I will say for this place: it's quiet. It reminds me a lot of the land I grew up on in Kentucky. Large hills covered in thick trees surround the open area where the main house sits, and small cabins spread out about fifty yards back from the main house.

I wonder for a split second who gets to stay in those before I ask, "Any chance of me getting a cabin?"

"No." It's a stern answer, given by a deep rumbling voice in such a way that I know there's no chance I'm finagling it into a yes. So, I don't even bother trying.

This place is going to suck so badly.

The moment we step up on the porch, the front door opens, and the most beautiful creature I've ever seen steps through it. Her eyes are so blue they remind me of a crisp summer sky, and I can't tear my gaze away. Her jet-black hair only accentuates the heavenly color of her eyes, while her curvaceous body causes me to lick my lips. She's like the perfect mix of heaven and hell—angel and sinner rolled into one.

The musical laughter coming from her has my eyes drifting to her full, pouty mouth. What I wouldn't give for one night with her. The things I could do to her to make her scream my name from that mouth. I could throw her my best pick-up line to try to make that happen, but I fight the urge. This is neither the time nor the place to pick up a woman.

The moment her gaze lands on me, I lose my breath. Every fiber within me halts, and I am fixated, unable to move away from her. Her lips curve into a natural smile as her eyes give me a quick once-over.

Holy fuck. Being here might not be so damn bad after all.

The vixen extends her hand. "You must be Mr. Douglas. I'm Dr. Mead."

I raise my eyebrows, and my eyes widen as I take her hand in mine, feeling the smoothness of her skin. "You're a doctor?"

Her cheeks redden, making her even more fucking attractive. "I'm an addiction therapist."

I bite the corner of my lip and allow my eyes to wander down her body, not making any attempt to hide the fact that I like what I see as I study the way her sundress molds to her. "I'll definitely be looking forward to my treatment now."

She shakes her head while rolling those magnetic eyes of hers, doing her best to pretend to be annoyed by my comment, but I know she's full of shit—her continual blush is giving her away. "I'll see you in group, Mr. Douglas."

I turn and watch her saunter away, enjoying the view of her hips swishing from side to side as she heads off the porch toward one of the cottages.

She likes me hitting on her. I know it.

"Come on, Romeo," Timothy says next to me, causing me to chuckle.

"That's the first complete sentence you've said to me since I got here. I was beginning to think you were mute," I tease, but my eyes remain glued to the hot little doctor's ass.

"You've got other things to focus on," Timothy says as he opens the front door. "What you've got to go through the next couple of days won't be pretty, and I doubt hitting on the woman who is here to help you through it is the best idea."

Reluctantly, I pull my gaze away from the woman and pat Timothy on the shoulder as I pass by him to get inside. "I told you guys. I don't have a problem."

He shakes his head, leading me up the stairs. "Remember that when you're detoxing so I don't have to remind you that an addiction is what's made you feel so bad."

Once we get to the top, he points to the hallway to the left of the stairs. "Women's quarters. That's off-limits to you." He gives me a stern look, and I raise my hands in surrender. "The right is men only. You're the second door down that hall, on the left. Go unpack and then come down and find me, and I'll give you the tour of the grounds."

I adjust the strap on my shoulder. "Will do."

When Timothy turns and heads back down the stairs, I have the sudden urge to salute him like he's a fucking drill sergeant. That guy is definitely no fun.

I push open the door to my room and quickly discover that I have no way to lock it behind me.

Talk about no fucking privacy.

The room is a hell of a lot smaller than I'm used to, a twin bed and small dresser with a television on top of it taking up most of the space. A tiny closet just deep enough to hang my clothes in faces the foot of the bed. Most hotel rooms I've stayed in lately are mansions compared to this place.

I lean my baby against the empty corner and then plop down on my bed. I scrub my hands over my face, and all I can think about is what I wouldn't give for some weed to help take the edge off this situation. It's been the only thing that's kept my nerves calm over the last few years, since we started making music full time. People always believe being a rock star is so easy, but they have no clue just how much work goes into coming up with new material, doing appearances, and dealing with all the bullshit tasks the label makes us do. When all that piles up on a band that has the kind of turmoil we do, it's enough to put anyone on fucking edge— which is why I don't see why me dabbling a little hurts. I do it to stay mellow. The guys just don't fucking get it.

I lie back on the bed and shut my eyes, suddenly tired and annoyed with the entire situation. What in the hell am I doing here? This kind of place isn't for a guy like me.

Just as I'm about to fall asleep, someone begins to pound on my door. "Downstairs for dinner, Mr. Douglas."

I sigh deeply. I knew that guy was going to be a pain in my ass.

Chapter Four

"Buttons" – Pussycat Dolls

Frannie

Oh shit.

Tyke Douglas is just as freaking sexy in person as he is in the damn pictures. This is so not good.

Those green eyes of his, paired with the sexy-as-sin tattoos covering his delicious forearms could get me into so much trouble.

"Sweet bejesus!" Kimmy's voice startles me as she meets up with me on the path heading toward the cottages. "Did you get a load of that piece of man meat? I don't think we've ever had anyone as fine as Tyke Douglas here before."

I lick my lips and try to be as professional about the situation as I can, all the while pretending that my pulse isn't still beating wildly out of control. "Yes, I guess he is quite handsome...if you're into that whole 'tattooed bad-boy' thing."

Kimmy cackles beside me. "Who *isn't* into that? Any woman who says they aren't is a damn liar. There's no way any single woman wouldn't take one look at that and not fantasize about screwing him seven ways 'till Sunday. You can tell me what you really think of him—I can totally keep a secret."

It's tempting to gush over his hotness with Kimmy, but I know better than to let my guard down with someone I barely know. It's too risky. If anyone ever found out exactly how attracted I am to him, I'd surely be fired on the spot.

I shrug. "Honestly, Kimmy, he isn't my type."

She sighs longingly next to me as she toys with a strand of her long blond hair. "If you say so, but Frannie, you are most definitely *his*. Did you see the way he was looking at you? I swear he was going to try to jump your bones right there in front of Timothy."

"You saw that, too, huh?"

She nods. "I watched it all go down from the doorway as I started following you out. Be careful, girl. A woman can only resist so long when a guy like Tyke Douglas sets his sights on her. But I don't doubt a night with him would be worth risking everything for."

I pat her shoulder. "Don't worry. I promise he has no effect on me whatsoever."

"If you say so. I'll see you at dinner," she calls as she trots off toward her cabin, which is conveniently next to mine.

I hate that this is only my second day here and already I'm allowing a man to get to me. No matter how much my body may crave him, I have to fight it.

I fold my arms across my torso. "Be strong, Frannie. He's just an absurdly sexy man. You can totally ignore that fact and remain completely professional."

I square my shoulders, finding a new sense of self-pride as I step up on the stoop of my little cottage and unlock the door. I will not flush my job down the drain over a handsome face and a seriously toned body. There's too much riding on me getting my act straight just to piss away my very first job opportunity. This job has to work. It's all part of my plan to become a better person—someone my parents will be proud to call their daughter again. They haven't really spoken to me much since Annie died. It's like the good daughter is gone and now they're stuck with me—someone who's exactly the opposite of their ideal daughter.

After a quick shower, I decide to wear a blouse that reveals no cleavage whatsoever and a pair of Capri pants. Even though the memory of Tyke's eyes roaming down my body, staring longer than necessary at my chest, causes my belly to tingle, I can't allow that to keep happening. So, from now on, I'll only wear the most conservative outfits I brought. There's no sense in putting myself in a vulnerable position. That's part of the twelve steps we teach all recovering addicts. No matter what they are struggling with, avoid putting yourself in situations where you might be tempted to fall back into old patterns.

After I double-check my appearance in the mirror, I head to the main house for dinner. So far, I've thoroughly enjoyed having dinner with the clients. It's given me an opportunity to observe their behaviors and get to know them before I start my first official day of counseling with them tomorrow.

This morning after breakfast, I met with Wayne in his office. He explained that they now have more clients than they've ever had at the facility, and he no longer has enough time to counsel all of them on his own.

That's where I come in.

We went over the files of all the existing clients here at Serenity and discussed their treatment plans. Wayne is giving me a lot of responsibility already, telling me that I'll be leading some group sessions, as well as giving me a few additional files for the one-on-one sessions I'll be taking over.

I'm excited for this opportunity. It's a test, I'm sure— to see how well I'll do here before he gives me a full caseload. I'm ready to prove, not only to him, that I can do this, but to myself, too.

The moment I step up through the back door of the main house, I'm hit with the delicious aroma of dinner. I inhale the tangy-sweet smell into my nose, and my mouth instantly begins to water.

Sue stands over the stove stirring something in a big pot as I pass by. "Wow, Sue, that smells amazing. What is it?"

She turns to me and smiles. "It's ham covered in honey and brown sugar glaze, topped with pineapple."

"I can't wait to try it. I'm going to get so fat working here. I've never been fed this well," I tease her.

She chuckles. "A little bit of meat on a woman has never killed anyone."

I lean against the counter and watch as she dumps the gravy from a pot into a few serving boats sitting on a metal tray. "How long have you worked here, Sue?"

She scrapes the rest of the steamy liquid into the last boat and twists her lips. "Since it opened, which has been about ten years now."

I step around the counter and begin helping her load the serving cart. "Any pointers you can give me? Anything I should know in order to keep my job here?"

She sets the last of the salads onto the cart. "It's really a pretty nice place to work. Dr. Shepherd and Timothy tend to have the roughest job detoxing the clients when they first come in. The rest of us get to be more friendly with the clients—some a little too friendly, if you know what I mean."

I laugh and the memory of first meeting with the clients pop into mind, and the handsome activities director who seemed a little too friendly with our resident pop singer. "You mean Randall?"

Sue nods. "You've been here one day and have already picked up on it. You're going to do all right here, Mrs. Mead."

"Please, call me Frannie, Sue. Mrs. Mead is my mother, and I am most definitely not married," I say, earning a laugh from her. "Has he ever..."

I try to stop myself from digging into someone else's business, but the beginning of my thought is already out there and there's no taking it back.

"Messed around with a client?" Sue furrows her brow as she considers the question. "I don't think so. He's probably been tempted, but he knows Dr. Shepherd has a zero tolerance for fraternization with the clients. He'd surely lose his job if he did."

"Noted. Not that I would ever have any kind of relationship with a client, though."

Sue sighs as she wipes her hands on a dishtowel. "That's what they all say, but I've seen it happen more times than I can remember. The therapist before you had an affair with a football player that we had here at the facility for a while."

"Really? What happened?" I ask, extremely interested in where this conversion seems to be heading.

"Timothy caught them in the therapist's office. Apparently, he walked in during a session, and she was counseling the client in more ways than one on her couch." Sue waggles her eyebrows, and I burst out laughing.

"Remind me to never sit there."

It's easy for me to joke around with her and act like I would never be caught in a situation like that because it's easier than revealing the truth about myself to someone who won't understand. I'm an addict myself, but my drug of choice isn't anything crushed, shot, or snorted. It's better if I put on a facade and pretend that I'm a very conservative woman—a little prudish. It won't make my coworkers here suspect that every moment I'm around men I'm attracted to, I'm in danger of relapsing into my old ways.

Sue steps back and appraises the cart that we've just loaded. "I think that's it. Thank you for all the help."

I dust my hands off. "Anytime. It was good chatting with you."

I push through the door of the kitchen and make my way into the huge dining room. Every time I come in here, I think of those old movies where the mansions have humongous formal rooms, each detail of the place screaming that the owner is made of money.

Several clients mill about the room, paying no mind that I've even entered as they continue to talk among themselves. In the short time I've been here, I've already sort of learned the hierarchy—Josie Sullivan has to remain the center of attention at all times, while the rest of the clients take a backseat. Wayne tries to combat this by reminding her constantly of the rules he's set in place about respecting everyone, and allowing others an equal chance to express their feelings and thoughts. Randall fawns over Josie, giving her a little extra affection when he thinks no one is looking, but I can tell he's not in love with her or anything. I've noticed the way his eyes linger on me a little too long from time to time. I know guys like him. Totally hot and one hundred percent player—the kind of guy I need to steer clear of.

I make my way to the seat where I've been sitting for the past couple of days, to the immediate right of Wayne, who sits at the head like our leader. Before I have the chance to pull the chair out myself, it slides out for me. My gaze instantly lands on the large thick fingers wrapped around its edge, before my eyes trail up the toned, tattooed forearms of none other than Tyke Douglas. The wicked gleam in his eyes is much too appealing, taunting me to give in to his subtle advances and flirt back.

I swallow hard and tip my chin up, doing my best to act like being this close to him doesn't bother me one bit. "Thank you, Mr. Douglas."

Even the slow nod he gives me is sexy. "Dr. Mead."

Sliding into the seat, I feel it scoot in behind me, his thumb grazing my shoulder. Goosebumps erupt all over my skin at the thought of Tyke's proximity. The feeling doesn't let up because moments later he takes the seat directly beside me.

I risk a glance at him just as he unfolds the cloth napkin from the table and then smoothes it over one leg. I find myself mesmerized by the way his thick fingers move so gracefully across the material and my gaze lands on his crotch, a visceral reaction to the idea of what could possibly be under those snug jeans causing me to bite my lip.

A deep chuckle snaps me out of my daze, and I quickly look away, refocusing harder than necessary on the silverware in front of me.

I go to work, straightening my fork next to my knife, and feel his hot breath on my neck as he leans in and whispers, "See something you like, Doc?"

Still unable to look at him, I shake my head, feeling my hair slide across his face. "No."

"Did you say something, Dr. Mead?" Josie asks from across the table, and I'm instantly mortified that I said anything out loud.

My cheeks heat, and I know without a doubt they're rosy red. "No, Josie, I was just thinking out loud."

She raises a perfectly plucked eyebrow at me. "Okay..."

For a moment, I worry that I'll have to explain myself further, but thankfully Randall sits next to her and Josie forgets me almost immediately.

I snap my gaze to Tyke and narrow my eyes, the urge to let him know that he's not going to possess any power over me whatsoever overwhelming. No amount of smooth talking will make me change the rules I've set for myself. I'm going to remain celibate, no matter how much it freaking kills me.

"No more of that will be tolerated, Mr. Douglas," I tell him sternly, which only makes his smile widen.

Dear God. Why does he have to have such a sexy mouth? This isn't fair. How am I expected to live so close to this man if he continues to pursue me in such a forward manner?

Tyke rests his arm on the table and grins crookedly. "We'll see."

I open my mouth to scold him, but before I have the opportunity, Wayne's voice startles me. "Good evening, everyone."

I turn toward the door just in time to see my boss strut into the room in yet another fabulously pressed and extremely expensive-looking suit. It's almost as if everyone answers in unison because a chorus of good evenings rings around the room.

Wayne takes his seat next to mine. "Dr. Mead, I trust you've met our newest resident?"

I place the napkin on my lap just as Sue pushes her cart full of salad into the room. "Yes, I've had the pleasure twice now."

Tyke chokes on his water next to me, but I refuse to acknowledge his response to my choice of words. When I said *pleasure*, in no way did it have any sexual connotations.

Wayne, on the other hand, begins to eat his salad, paying no mind at all to the smartass next to me. "Good. I would like you to head up his first session after dinner. Would that be all right with you, Mr. Douglas?"

Tyke's eyes flick to me, and then he gives me a dazzling white smile. "I'd love a little one-on-one time with her."

75

Oh, God. Heaven help me. This man is going to be trouble.

The kind I have a very hard time resisting.

Chapter Five

"Man in the Box" – Alice in Chains

Tyke

Dr. Mead takes the seat across from me and crosses her smooth legs, which immediately catches my attention. My gaze travels from the tip of her black stiletto all the way up her toned, tanned calf, stopping when I get to the hem of her short skirt, stretched tightly across her thighs. All I can think of is getting down on my knees in front of her and tracing the length of those sexy legs with my hands to discover what material her panties are made of. I bet they're lace. An image of a red lace thong pressing against her pussy pops into my mind and my dick twitches.

Fuck.

I move in my seat and fight the urge to adjust my semi-hard cock right in front of her. I have to stop thinking of her like this. This woman is a fucking professional. She's not going to fuck me on a whim, no matter how much I turn on the charm. Besides, she's my doctor for fuck's sake, and my way back into the guys' good graces.

"Mr. Douglas, you may call me Frannie. I find that the less formality, the more beneficial it is in helping us connect on a more personal level, since the things we discuss in my office are very sensitive in nature. I want you to feel comfortable with me and allow yourself to open up. It's the only way to dig deep into the true root of the issues you're here to work out." Frannie takes the reading glasses that are clinging to the neckline of her shirt and carefully unfolds them, before slipping them onto the bridge of her nose. "Would you like to start by telling me a little about yourself?"

I furrow my brow. I hate talking about myself. It always feels so lame. Put me in an interview where we talk music and I can spout that shit all day long, but getting personal is an entirely different beast.

"I'd rather talk about the possibility of me and you happening."

She sighs. "Mr. Douglas—"

I hold my hand up. "Call me Tyke, and never say never. I'd hate for you to lie to yourself."

"I'm sure you're used to women throwing themselves at your feet, Tyke, but that's not going to happen. I'm here because I am your therapist, not because we are going to develop a sexual relationship. The only issues we need to discuss are about why you are here. There will be nothing else discussed in this room."

I scrub my hand down my face. It's obvious I had the vibe I felt between us all wrong.

"I'm not sure where you want me to start or what you want me to say," I answer honestly. "I've never been in *therapy* before."

Frannie makes a note on the tablet in front of her before her gaze returns to me. "It's not what *I* want you to say. You have to begin opening up to me in order for treatment to work. The best way for that to happen is to start small. For instance, tell me about your family, and where you grew up."

I rub my clammy hands against my jeans. That's easy enough. "I grew up in a small town here in Kentucky. My parents are still married, but I don't see them often, and I have a twin brother named Trip."

She nods. "Trip is also in Black Falcon with you, correct?"

"Yeah."

"Have you two always been close?"

My mind wanders back to when we were kids. Every event I picture, I see Trip standing right next to me. "Yes. Since birth we've been inseparable."

Her pretty pink lips twist. "Until now."

I pick at the leather cuff on my wrist and shrug. "That's not what this is all about."

Frannie pulls the black-framed glasses away from her face, revealing a clear shot of the most beautiful blue eyes I've ever seen. "I don't mean to sound as if I have already pinpointed anything. I just want to get to know you—to understand what you're feeling."

I stare down at the thick leather cuff again. "Even I have a hard time understanding that sometimes."

"What do you mean?" The softness in her voice wraps around me, making me almost believe she actually cares.

"I...it's just, I've never been great at telling people what's really on my mind. Talking *feelings* has always been difficult for me."

She uncrosses her legs and then crosses them in the opposite direction. "But aren't you the predominant songwriter for your band?"

I quirk an eyebrow, and my mouth pulls up into a half smile. "You've been researching me?"

A simple shrug and the slight blush staining her cheeks tells me she's definitely looked me up. "I wanted to be prepared. Songs usually convey the emotion its writer is feeling at the time. Knowing facts like you've written most of the songs tells me that you've been able to express yourself through music in the past."

I pull my lips into a tight line as I consider what she's saying. I guess I've never really thought about it, but she's right. Thinking back on most of the songs I wrote completely alone, the lyrics have always evolved from something that was going on in my life. Maybe she's on to something, but it still doesn't mean I can completely open myself up to a stranger when I'm not even sure what the fuck is going on with me.

I sigh. "Maybe that's true, but that sure doesn't help right now. What's all this have to do with me talking to you, anyhow?"

She levels her gaze on me. "Why not use music to express your emotion?"

I laugh. "You mean like sing to you? No way. That's ridiculous."

She raises her brow. "Is it?"

"Yes," I tell her simply.

Frannie stands and walks over to her desk and grabs a black notebook from a drawer. She comes back and stands before me. "Here."

I take the notebook from her outstretched hand. "What exactly do you want me to do with this?"

She remains standing in front of me. "Since you seem to find it difficult to express emotion through traditional channels of communication, let's try something different. If a song comes to mind that touches you for any particular reason, write it down, and we'll discuss it."

I twist my lips, attempting to hide my smirk as I rise from my seat. "I'd much rather *you* touch me."

"Tyke—"

I raise my hands in surrender. "I wish I could say I'm sorry, and that it won't happen again, but I'm afraid lying to my therapist is bad karma."

Frannie shakes her head. "Please try and write your feelings in the notebook. It'll give us something to talk about when I see you again in five days or so."

I tilt my head. "Five days? I thought we'd be seeing each other on a daily basis."

A small frown crosses her beautiful face. "The last thing you'll feel like doing for the next three days is talking to me about your feelings. Detoxing will not be pleasant, and you won't be able to focus on anything else."

I fight the urge to roll my eyes again. Why does everyone and their fucking brother keep saying that? "Don't worry, Frannie. I'm no crackhead. I'll be the same as always for the next few days."

I fully expect her to answer me, but she doesn't say another word, just simply sighs again, and leads me toward the door. "I'll see you once you're able, Tyke."

When I leave her office, I catch myself shaking my head. Everyone always fucking doubts me. I hate that shit. I'm about to show everyone that I'm the one in control of my life and body, not some substance.

I toss and turn in the small twin bed in my room all night; the craving that usually creeps in late at night when I have too much idle time to stress over the ultimate demise of the band coming at me in full force. Thanks to Timothy and Dr. Shepherd flushing all my benzodiazepines and oxycodones, along with everything else I brought, down the toilet right in front of me, I have zero chance of scratching that stupid itch for a high. But still, it's not anything I can't handle. I'm still in control.

A loud knock on my door jerks me awake, and I squint at the morning sun pouring through my window. "Mr. Douglas, breakfast in ten minutes."

I groan at Timothy's voice, wanting no part of getting up yet. "I slept like shit, and I'm not hungry."

"There's no sleeping in, either." I toss my pillow across my face and will Timothy to just go away. "I'll be back in ten minutes to assist you if you aren't downstairs."

"Jesus. This is a fucking concentration camp," I mumble to myself before sighing and tugging the pillow away from my face.

The dark hardwood is cool against my bare feet as I make my way over to my duffel bag and pull out some clean clothes. I eye the notebook Frannie gave me, lying on the dresser as I tug my black T-shirt over my head.

Think of songs that express how I feel, huh?

I grab the pen on top of the notebook and grip the cap between my teeth, pulling the pen free. I stare at the blank page that's just begging for some words to be scratched on it. I glance around the small room, suddenly feeling very trapped in this place. Alice in Chains' "Man in the Box" pops into my head, and I begin to hum the iconic intro and sing the words to the song, wondering if the front man of that band, Layne Staley, felt trapped in his own prison when he was writing that song.

I smile as I close the notebook, not elaborating on the lyrics of the song, simply writing the title and the band down. I'm sure that's not exactly what Frannie had in mind when she asked me to document my feelings through the use of songs, but hey, at least I'm fucking participating in her little assignment.

I open the door to my room just in time to see Timothy, arms poised, ready to knock on my door once again to no doubt help me find my way to breakfast like he threatened moments ago.

His eyebrows shoot up in surprise the moment I step past him and clap him on the back. "Heading there now, big guy, and as you can tell, I'm fit as a fucking fiddle—told you guys that I didn't have an addiction problem."

He sighs as he follows behind me. "Being hooked on benzodiazepines is no less threatening than any other addiction, Mr. Douglas. Anti-anxiety medications are powerful medications. It can take twenty-four hours for the first effects of withdrawal to appear. I'm guessing you dosed up before coming to us yesterday, so you'll be jonesin' for your next fix soon. But we'll be here to help you through it."

I open my mouth to protest again, but quickly close it because I've said it enough times to know now that, no matter what I say, they're going to believe what they want—that I'm an addict. It's why I'm here. Everyone working here, including Frannie, has lost sight of the fact that drugs can be used purely recreationally.

The moment my boots hit the first floor, my mouth begins to water and it's not because of the delicious aroma of buttermilk pancakes wafting through the air. Frannie stands in the dining room, talking to a short balding man. She's laughing again, and her face bears the same carefree expression she wore the very first time I spotted her—the one that drew me to her and made me crave the time in my life when I was that happy. She's truly an exquisite creature; one I shouldn't be thinking about the way I am. Frannie is off-limits. That's been made clear to me by not only her, but the staff as well. That still doesn't deter me. If anything, it only increases her allure.

She turns to me, smile still on her face, and says, "Good morning, Tyke. You look well this morning."

I grin, knowing she, along with the rest of the crew here, fully expected me to be brought to my knees this morning, but I'm glad to prove them all wrong.

"Told you I'd be fine today."

She tilts her head and examines my face like she's ready to argue with me, just like Timothy did only moments ago, but she doesn't. "Well, maybe I will see you today then."

"Looks like it."

I wink at her as I pass by her and head into breakfast.

Chapter Six

"Red" – Taylor Swift

Frannie

The green and orange sweater that Arnold, my nine thirty session, is wearing completely distracts me. First of all, it's September, and while the constant beating heat of the summer has begun to drift into the crisp feeling of fall at night, it's still too damn hot for a sweater.

I study Arnold's features as he prattles on about never being liked in high school. It's what he believes has led to his addiction issues. His short stature, coupled with his obvious beer gut and balding hairline, makes it hard for me to picture him as ever being young enough to be a teenager.

"The turning point is when I asked Lesley Peacock to the Junior Prom. When she turned me down, I couldn't get over it," Arnold explains as he continues to shrug his shoulders over and over as if he, himself, isn't exactly sure about the story he's telling me. "I think she broke my spirit, and I turned to drinking to cope."

I'm not buying that. I know it's not professional, but I want to roll my eyes. "Arnold," I interrupt. "Are you saying that *that* one moment was *impossible* to get over? That one simple rejection sent your life onto the path of self-destruction? There's nothing a little deeper that haunts your mind every day? Something you turn to alcohol to forget?"

Arnold's lips pull into a tight line as his eyes drift up toward the ceiling. "Nothing that I can think of, Frannie."

I glance down at my cell on my desk, noticing a new text message. "Our session time has come to a close. What I would like for you to think about is if there's something else that bothers you, other than a girl turning you down for a date. Something else you try to escape."

He nods and stands. "See you tomorrow."

The moment he leaves the room, I swipe my finger across the screen of my phone. My eyebrows shoot up when I see that the text is from my mother, asking for me to call her. Something must be wrong because I rarely hear from her. She's either too busy donating her time to one of her multiple charities, or caught up in planning some over-the-top affair at the country club she and my father are members of.

I press the green phone symbol and wait as two rings pass before Mother answers. "Frannie, darling, thank you for returning my call so quickly. What are you doing this weekend?"

My lips pull into a tight line. Has she forgotten so quickly that I've recently moved? "I'm in Kentucky."

She sighs heavily into the phone. "What are you doing in that god-awful state?"

It's with that one sentence she confirms that, once again, she has paid no attention to what's going on in my life. "I took a job here, remember?"

"Oh, yes, that's right." I can tell by her exasperated tone that she still doesn't understand why I felt the need to go into a career field that doesn't exactly meet her standards. "Your weekends are still free though, yes?"

"Yes, but—"

"Perfect!" she exclaims, completely cutting me off. "I need you to housesit this weekend. Your father is flying to London on business, and I've decided to go with him. You know how I love that city, and I simply can't resist going even if it's only for a couple days."

I furrow my brow. "That sounds great, but I don't understand why you're calling me."

"Penelope already requested the weekend off, and there's just no one else I trust to take care of Spencer and Ruby."

I roll my eyes as I think about my mother's obsession with her Cavalier King Charles Spaniel dogs. She treats those dogs better than she ever treated Annie and me. My sister would always laugh when I would complain that those stupid animals weren't my siblings like Mother would refer to them as. Even if they are undeniably cute. "Give mother a break, Frannie," Annie would say. "They've actually softened her up." Annie would only laugh harder when I would mumble that her twin daughters should've been the ones to unfreeze that icy heart of hers.

Needless to say, I'm not a fan of how much Mother loves those dogs.

"Can't one of the other staff take care of them since Penelope is off?" I ask.

"Frannie, you know I don't just trust my babies to anyone. I'll need you to come home for the weekend and take care of your brother and sister."

Ugh. There it is again. I swear to God the woman is delusional.

"I can't," I tell her simply. "That's a long train ride and—"

"Oh, Frannie, don't be silly. We'll send the jet to pick you up and take you back," she says in a nonchalant tone.

"Mother, you know I don't do planes since..." I feel the emotion pique in my voice, and I choke it back.

"Pish-posh. You can't let what happened to Annie stop you from living your life. It's been four years, Francine. It's time to move on." My mouth gapes open at her words.

Am I the only one who loved my sister? How can she act like being up in the air, helpless, under some random pilot's control, isn't a big deal after her own daughter died in a plane that went down somewhere over the Atlantic. The search went on for a couple of weeks, but all they found was part of the wing. The rest was never recovered.

There's so much I want to say to her—no, to scream at her—about how I don't understand how she's not broken by Annie's death like me. Unlike Arnold, I can say with the utmost certainty that the moment I knew my sister wasn't coming back—that her body was likely deep in the dark water abyss, never to be seen again—I lost it. Things that mattered once before—parties, finding a husband, having a family—no longer registered. Zero attachment to anything became my new motto, one that led to me having numerous, purely physical relationships with men. I never want to feel the kind of pain I felt from her loss ever again.

But there's no way I can explain all that to my mother. We might as well be from different planets when it comes to understanding one another's feelings about what happened to my sister. There's no use talking to her about it because she'll never understand what I've lost.

"Frannie? Hello? Did you hear me?" Mother's voice cuts through the haze of my thoughts.

"I'm here."

"Well? What time would you like the jet there Friday to pick you up?" she asks, and I detect a hint of impatience in her voice as she waits on my answer.

"I'm sorry, Mother, but I won't be able to make it this weekend. You'll simply have to find someone else."

"Francine—"

"No time to chat, my next appointment is due any time now. Goodbye, Mother."

With that, I simply end the call, allowing no time for her to make me feel guilty for telling her no.

My finger slides over the phone, hunting for the one picture of Annie that I keep close. I stare at her vibrant smile, so full of life, and my eyes begin to burn as tears well up in them. There are so many things we planned to do together that will never happen now. How can I go on pretending life is fucking perfect when the one person in this world who felt like my other half is gone? The one person I shared everything with.

Sometimes, when I allow myself to think of her too much, I can't hold back the pain. Hot tears slick down my cheeks as I try my best to hold in my sobs and not lose what little bit of control I still have.

My office door opens, startling me. I swat at the tears streaking down my face, attempting hide the fact that I'm teetering on the edge of yet another nervous breakdown while thinking about Annie.

Tyke's green eyes lock with mine and concern instantly etches on his face. "Are you okay?"

I sniff. "Yeah, I'm fine."

He closes the door behind him and takes a hesitant step toward me. "I've always been told when a woman says she's 'fine,' it means just the opposite."

I shake my head. "Things going on with me aren't really open for discussion."

From the slight tilt of his head, I can tell that he's trying to figure me out. "Why?"

When he moves toward me, I step back, bumping into the desk. He's close enough that the heat of his body radiates off him, causing a tingle to creep up my spine. I shouldn't like being this close to him, but I do.

Too damn much.

Slowly he raises his hand to my face, and with the pad of his thumb, he brushes a lingering tear from my cheek. "How can you expect me to open up to you about my feelings when you won't even tell me what's made you cry?"

His thumb leaves a trail of fire in its wake, my skin begging him to touch me everywhere. But no matter how much my body craves his closeness, it can never happen. He's off-limits.

He's a client, for Christ's sake.

The moment he cradles my face in his hands I begin to panic, knowing what would happen if I allow this kiss to occur. Is another random tryst worth losing this job? I've worked so hard for this, and not only would I be letting myself down, but I know Annie would be pissed at me, too. Even knowing all that, I can't deny the attraction I feel toward him.

Tyke's lips part slightly as he begins to lean into me. I place my hand against his chest. "We can't do this," I whisper.

His gaze locks with mine. "I know."

I'm not sure if it's the strain in his deep rumbling voice, or the fact that I'm emotionally vulnerable that makes me momentarily lose my resolve, but something comes over me and my hand against his chest relaxes and I fall into him a bit. Tyke seizes the opportunity and presses his lips to mine, my eyes closing of their own accord, my mouth betraying me by opening and allowing his tongue to slip inside. A low groan emits from the back of his throat as he wraps one arm around the small of my back and pushes his body against mine.

"You taste like sunshine," he says between kisses.

My knees nearly buckle at his words, and I thread my fingers into his blond hair. This only excites him more. Tyke grabs my waist and hoists me onto my desk, pushing his hips between my legs, his erection straining through the coarse material of his jeans as he rubs against me and his kiss turns hungry.

I could give in right now and escape. His touch feels so good, it's almost enough to make me forget where we are.

Almost.

I shove my hand into his chest, pushing him backward. "No. We can't do this. I'll lose my job."

Tyke's lust-laden gaze meets mine as his body stills. I fully expect him to try to convince me that we won't get caught, but he doesn't. He simply steps back and straightens his T-shirt while he nods. "I don't want that to happen, but you can't blame me for trying. You're so fucking sexy, and your eyes...God, so damn blue— they're intoxicating. I think I could stare into them forever. I guess I just couldn't help myself."

I bite my lip and stare at him as I hop off the desk. "We have to stay professional. This kind of thing can never happen between us again. No matter how much we both may want it to."

That earns me a crooked smirk because I've just admitted that I want him. "I promise to be on my best behavior from now on, Doc."

He grabs the notebook I didn't realize he'd brought with him off my desk and saunters over to the couch. I know I shouldn't, but I can't help checking out his ass while his back is to me. That man is something— definitely a lot more suave than I'm used to. And his kiss...dear God. If just his kiss can tempt me to throw caution to the wind and nearly fuck the career I've worked so hard for, I can only imagine what sleeping with him would do to me.

Probably destroy me, and ruin me for all other men.

The moment he pats the seat next to him on the couch, my back straightens. There's no way in hell I can be that close to him while being this turned on and expect things to stay innocent.

I grab my tablet, along with my glasses, and take the seat across from him.

He chuckles. "I suppose that's safer."

Blood rushes to my cheeks, no doubt showing off a fierce blush. "I think distance is best."

He repositions himself, stretching his long legs out and throwing his arm casually across the back of the couch. "So what are we talking about today, Doc?"

There are so many things he and I could be talking about, but right now, I need to focus on the reason he's here. My eyes flit to the notebook balancing on his left thigh. "I'm assuming you've written something down, since you've brought it with you."

He taps his thumb on the cover a couple times and then shrugs. "Just one song."

I slip my glasses on, ready to take some notes. "Care to share what it is?"

"'Man in the Box' by Alice in Chains. I know that's probably not exactly what you were hoping for, but it was all that I could think of."

I ponder over the song he's just given, trying to recall in my brain the lyrics, but nothing comes up. "I'm sorry. I'm not familiar with that song. Can you tell me a little about what it's about?"

Tyke smirks. "Not a metal fan then, huh?"

"Not really, no, but I know that's what Black Falcon plays." I blush again, knowing full well, after all my research that it's the type of music he plays.

He picks at the thick leather cuff on his wrist. "It's cool if you're not a fan. Metal isn't for everyone, I suppose, just please tell me you're not one of those chicks who's into the bubblegum sounding top forty hits. That would break my fucking heart."

I laugh. "If you're talking about all the music that sounds like it could be on the Disney channel then, no, but I won't say I'm a pop hater. I like anything with a good beat, but I'm more of an alternative girl."

That earns me a smile. "Alternative? Nice. I can work with that. I've been really diggin' the Artic Monkeys lately."

"I love them," I say, excited that someone else appreciates the complex sound of that band. "'Do I Wanna Know' is one of my absolute favorite songs."

That causes him to raise one eyebrow. "That's a pretty deep song. Does it make you think of anyone when you listen to it?"

I instantly shake my head. "No. What makes you ask that?"

"That song is basically about a guy who is so lovesick he doesn't know what to do with himself. I was curious if I need to be concerned that you're already in love with someone else, and you turning me down a few minutes ago had more to it than just the off-limits factor. I like to know exactly what I'm up against."

My stupid blush rushes back to my cheeks in full force as his eyes stay locked on mine, waiting for my answer. The heat of his stare is almost too much to take, and I'm tempted to drop my eyes away from his gaze, but I don't. I want him to know that I'm in control of the situation going on between us.

After a long moment, I sigh. "There's no one else, but—"

"That's good to know," he says, seemingly delighted by the news.

"I meant what I said before. Nothing can happen between us."

He holds up a hand and tries to fight back a grin, like he knows no matter how much I resist, my giving into his advances is inevitable. "Strictly professional, I got it."

I push my glasses up the bridge of my nose and say, "Good. Let's get back to the song. I'm going to guess it's about a man being trapped."

Tyke nods. "Yeah. After being basically on lockdown in my room last night and ordered to be on time for breakfast, I feel a little closed up in this place."

I make a note about checking into the daily routines of the clients a little more with Wayne. "What did you do when you went up to your room last night?"

"You want to imagine me in my room? Sleeping in the buff, perhaps?" His teasing tone doesn't go unmissed, and I shake my head again at his crassness.

"I simply meant do you feel that you're not getting adequate time to reflect on the day and unwind?"

"I never get that. Doing what I do for a living, there's always somewhere to be, or something to be doing. I typically keep going until I pass out," he answers.

"Pass out?" I question.

Tyke rolls his eyes, not missing what I was getting at. "From exhaustion."

I frown. "That's a shame. What good is it to be so successful if your life is no longer your own?"

"It is what it is, Frannie. Sacrificing your personal life is sort of expected in the music business."

I knew musicians were always busy, but hearing it from him directly that he basically has no life other than his job makes me sad for him. "Why do you continue to do it if you're not happy?"

"I love making music. It makes me happy. All the bullshit that goes along with it is what I hate. Once music is in your skin, it's impossible to just scrub it away. It sticks with you, and like it or not, you'll never be able to walk away, even if you want to. Just the thought of not being able to do this for a living makes me so fucking anxious that I can't breathe."

I make another note, beginning to understand where his addiction began. "So when the business side of the music came into play, adding pressure to your creative process, is that when you first began taking benzos?"

He fidgets in his seat, clearly uncomfortable with me getting down to the nitty-gritty so quickly. "I think so. It all began when I went to see my doctor and mentioned that I constantly felt anxious that something was going to happen with the band, that everything we've worked for would be yanked away from us."

"And he wrote you a prescription for benzodiazepine to help calm your nervousness about the inability to control the outcome of your future?"

He nods. "Yeah. And then once I started taking them, I liked the way they made me feel. The way they helped me forget sometimes that the band falling apart is always a possibility."

"So what led you to the point in your life where you determined that benzodiazepines alone was no longer enough of an escape?"

He rubs his palms up and down his thighs, along the material of his jeans, as he stares down at the floor. "I'm not sure exactly. I think everything began gradually. A bump of cocaine here and there, topped with the alcohol that we always partied with . . . I don't know . . . I like the feeling of not worrying."

My heart breaks for him. While I might not have turned to drugs to help mask the pain I felt after Annie died, I did turn to the one thing I found helped take my mind off it. "I can understand wanting to forget for a while."

His eyes flick up to mine, and I can see the relief in them. "You can?"

I nod, feeling myself teetering on the edge of professionalism. Exactly how much of my own personal life should I be revealing to him? "I think everyone reaches a point in their lives when they want nothing more than to forget something, or forget the possibility that a good thing can go terribly wrong at any time."

"You've felt that way?" he asks, his need to know the answer burning in his eyes. It's like he wants confirmation that he's not alone in struggling with the crazy feelings going on inside him.

I know it's not professional, but I think sharing might be the only way to make him understand that everyone feels the way he does from time to time. "Yes, for a long time. My sister—my twin—died, and it's a pain I've been running from for nearly four years."

He licks his lips slowly as he digests what I've just told him. "What's that like? Losing your twin?"

I sigh as the familiar pain grips my heart like a vice as I think about Annie. "I imagine losing anyone you love is probably hard, but in my mind there's nothing that could be harder than losing my sister. She was the one person who understood everything about me, the one person who knew all my secrets and understood my crazy personality. It's hard not having her in my life anymore. Annie" —I take in a ragged breath— "she was my other half, my soul mate, someone who can't be replaced."

I fully expect him to pepper me with more questions, but instead he returns his stare to the floor. I wonder if any of what I just told him makes sense.

I open my mouth to continue to push him for more about his reliance on benzodiazepine to forget, but close it the moment there's a knock on my office door. "Excuse me a moment."

I rise from my seat to answer the door, laying my notepad and pen on the couch next to Tyke.

I find Kimmy standing on the other side, wearing a hot pink top and jeans, chomping on a piece of gum. "Hey, Frannie. I've got to go into town to pick up some cleaning supplies in a bit. Do you want to come with me? It's the perfect time to get out of here for a while."

I glance down at the wristwatch I have on and nod. "Sure, our session time is up anyway. Let me wrap up, and I'll be ready in a few minutes, okay?"

She nods. "Sure thing. I'll wait for you on the porch."

I close the door behind her and turn my attention back to Tyke, who is standing in the middle of the office now, watching me curiously, like he's seeing me for the first time.

I interlock my fingers in front of me. "Sorry about that. I don't mean to rush you or anything. If you need more time, I can—"

He shakes his head. "It's okay. Go. I've got a splitting headache anyhow. I should probably go and lay down."

This is it, I bet. The beginning to the detox he's been so adamant that he's not going to experience. "All right. I'll see you again when you're feeling well enough to continue our sessions."

He rolls his eyes. "It's just a headache. I'll be back tomorrow."

I give him a small smile. "Okay, then."

Tyke doesn't say another word, just walks past me and out the door.

As soon as I'm alone, I drop my head into my hand and rub my forehead. I hope I can help him. There's always that little bit of niggling doubt in my head as to whether I'm cut out for this job or not. Can I really help people who have addictions when I still struggle with one myself? An addiction that's become a whole lot harder to fight since I succumbed to that kiss? I should've known better and never allowed him to get so close. His physical presence just does something to me that I can't explain. The moment I laid eyes on him, I knew he'd be my biggest professional challenge, but I didn't anticipate the personal challenge as well. No matter how much I want him, I have to remain focused on the reason he's here and try to help him overcome the darkness that threatens to envelope him.

I slump down in the chair next to the couch and reach for the notepad, my gaze pausing on what Tyke's left behind.

A single green guitar pick.

I hold the thin piece of plastic between my fingers and examine the words he's written on the back.

Thank you.

I fold my fingers around it and clutch it to my chest as pride washes over me.

I'm doing this.

I'm getting through to him.

Chapter Seven

"Behind Blue Eyes" – Limp Bizkit

Tyke

Climbing the massive staircase back to my room takes forever. The pounding in my skull began when Frannie and I were talking in her office. Through most of our time together, I could ignore the constant thumping, but now it's almost unbearable.

My door swings open with ease and I collapse on the twin bed, facedown. Sweat pours out of me and drenches my shirt. I must be coming down with something. It feels like the fucking flu. This is not the most opportune time for me to be sick.

I rub my forehead and then fling the sweat from my fingers when it hits me.

"Fuck. Am I really fucking detoxing?" I mumble to myself.

But as my entire body trembles, I already have my answer.

Detoxing:

Day One: It's not pretty.

Day Two: Definitely not fucking pretty.

Day Three: Still bad, but nowhere as bad as yesterday.

Day Four: Almost there, but my anxiety levels are through the fucking roof.

Day Five: A New Leaf

I stare at myself in the mirror and wonder at what point in my life I decided to give so much power to some little goddamn pills. It makes me wonder if I had known that I would end up needing help to get off them a couple years ago, back when I started taking benzo medications, would I have ever taken them to begin with? I wish I could honestly say that I wouldn't have touched them with a ten-foot fucking pole, but I don't know if that would be the case.

Without them now, things are clearer. I can definitely see the demise of the band happening. The leading cause at this point is me, but I know now that it wasn't just the drug haze. I haven't simply imagined that Black Falcon has started going in different directions, because that shit is fucking true, and the guys need to accept their roles in the band falling apart, too.

The hard table is cold against my skin as I sit on it while Dr. Shepherd examines me. He takes his time, taking my blood pressure and then pulse, before he flashes a small light into my eyes.

"Go ahead and follow the light with your eyes, Mr. Douglas."

I do as he asks, and he clicks the light off before placing the instrument back in its holder on the wall. "Everything looks good. How do you feel?"

I take a deep breath. "I'm grateful that I don't feel like ass today."

Dr. Shepherd chuckles. "Well, I suppose that's a start. I know that the last few days have been difficult for you—"

"That's the fucking understatement of the century," I mutter, cutting him off.

He continues like he didn't even hear my smartass remark. "But think of it as crossing the first big hurdle in your recovery. During what you've just been through, most people give up and quit—unable to take the sickness that goes along with ridding the drugs from their system. Now that you're clean, the rest is up to you and your willpower. You have to fight to stay that way."

I nod, knowing that if I start fucking up again, it's no one else's fault but mine. I make the decision. I make the call.

Dr. Shepherd tucks my chart under his arm. "Today I want you to join in group therapy."

I raise my eyebrow. "Group? How is talking to a bunch of complete strangers going to help?"

"Most clients find it beneficial to listen to the stories of others. A lot of the time, it helps them to realize that they're not alone—that addiction knows no gender, color, or age. It can happen to anyone, so there's no reason to feel isolated."

I want to argue that I've never felt alone, but the truth is that loneliness is all I've felt over the past couple of years. Not to sound like a whiny bitch, but it's hard to watch everyone around you move the focus of their life to something else while you're still trapped in the same routine. It's not that I'm jealous that the rest of the guys in the band have done that, I just feel left out—like the band, and me, don't matter to them anymore. And that scares me more than anything.

It's been easier than I thought to admit that to myself in the last twenty-four hours, but that doesn't mean I'm ready to talk to a group of complete fucking strangers about it.

I rub the back of my neck. "I don't know."

"You don't have to speak in group unless you want to," he assures me. "It's okay to just go and listen, and when you're ready, jump in."

As much as I want to avoid the situation, I also want to prove to everyone that the new, clearer thinking me is not always a difficult person. "Okay."

"Great." Dr. Shepherd smiles encouragingly. "I'll make sure Dr. Mead saves you a seat."

My ears prick up at the sound of her name. I haven't seen Frannie since the day I overstepped the boundary and kissed her, the image of her blue eyes, focused on me when she had tears in them, burned into my brain. It was the one picture that kept flashing in my mind as I went through the pure hell of detoxing. I know she's here to help me, but I just can't shake the feeling that, for some reason, I can support her in return.

I nod, suddenly excited about this group thing. "Great."

Dr. Shepherd grins. "That's the right attitude, Mr. Douglas. It's good to see you positive and on the road to recovery."

I hop off the table, and a thought comes to mind. "Do you think it'd be okay if I took my guitar and found a quiet place out in the garden to work on some songs?"

"That's perfectly fine. It's good to focus on something else besides being here. I'll see you at dinner."

A little while later, I make my way back to my room and grab my baby from the corner, slinging the soft case around my shoulder and heading outside. It's been a while since I've written anything. Riff was right when he said I didn't have a fucking clue what was going on with the new album, and that bothers me. It tells me that I allowed the drugs to come between me and my music, and that's one thing that I never thought possible. But it happened. Drugs became the most important thing in my life. But not anymore. I'm getting myself back on the right track.

Starting today.

Walking down the path toward the cottages that the staff live in, I spot the most tranquil-looking fountain. The water coming from the bucket of the stone woman in the middle spews into the body of water surrounding her, and the sound is almost rhythmic.

I glance around, seeing four benches surrounding the fountain mixed in with a wide array of flowers. If there was ever a more tranquil place on earth, I'd like to see it.

I lay my case on a bench and then unzip it, reaching inside for my Martin. This carefully crafted piece of wood has been in my family for years. It belonged to my grandfather, who taught Dad to play on it, who in turn taught Trip and me. This isn't just any guitar to me. It's a little piece of home.

I hold it by the neck until I make it to another empty bench and sit down, the strings ringing out in perfect tune as I run my pick over them. My calloused fingers mash against the frets and I begin to play the first song that comes to mind, "Behind Blue Eyes."

I close my eyes, singing the words while picturing Frannie's face. The sadness I saw in her eyes makes me wonder if she feels the loneliness, too—the kind where, although people surround you, it's still like being alone.

There's so much in this song that I can relate to. The lyrics roll through me, working their way into my chest, and wrapping around my heart. With each beat, the pressures that I've been struggling to forget come at me in full force. The line about being hated and no one understanding my loneliness really hits home.

My life is so fucking screwed up.

I rock in time to the music and moisture builds under my closed eyelids, the tears threatening to push their way out and expose my sadness to the world.

I sing the last line and play the last riff, sighing as I open my eyes.

My heart does a double thump in my chest the moment my vision comes into focus, and my eyes land directly on Frannie.

She stands behind the bench rubbing her bare arms, studying me with those same eyes I was just singing about—sad ones.

I clear my throat, suddenly uneasy that she's caught me at such a vulnerable moment. "I didn't know anyone would be out here."

Her pretty pink lips twist. "I'm sorry. I didn't mean to spy on you. It's just your singing...it was...wow. You're amazing."

The kindness in her words makes me smile. "Thank you."

Without an invitation, she walks over and sits next to me on the bench. I raise one eyebrow, questioning if sitting so close to me is suddenly allowed, but she just rolls her eyes at me. "We can behave, right?"

I nod, but know that given the opportunity, I'd kiss her again. No hesitation.

"Good," she says and then folds her hands in her lap. "Will you tell me what you were thinking of just now, when you were singing?"

My entire body tenses. Shit. I guess she did see that. The only thing I can do now is pretend like I don't know what she's talking about. "What makes you think I was thinking about anything? Can't I just be really focused on the song?"

Frannie tilts her head, allowing her dark hair to fall over her shoulder. "I saw you," she whispers. "No one can sing with that kind of feeling without something coming to mind."

I break away from her gaze, debating what to say next.

"Please, Tyke." She places her hand on mine that rests on the top of the guitar.

For some reason, the simple act of her touching me makes me want to spill my guts to her, but I'm afraid if she knew what was really on my mind, she'd freak the fuck out and treat me just like any other patient. And I don't want that. I don't want to be looked down on, which is why the things I really feel will always need to be locked away. But I can tell by the way she's looking at me that I'll have to give her some part of the truth to appease her curious mind.

I take a deep breath and then return my gaze to her. Looking her dead in the eye, I say, "You. I was thinking about *you*."

Frannie sucks her bottom lip in and then pulls it between her teeth slowly as she considers what I've just admitted. "Me?"

"I can't get the thought of us out of my mind. Your eyes..." I raise my hand and touch her cheek. "Your eyes haunt me."

She blinks a couple of times. "Behind blue eyes...you were thinking about when I was crying?"

"Yeah, I mean, you looked so sad. You looked like how I feel sometimes," I admit to her rather easily.

She tilts her head. "Do you feel that way often?"

I sigh and scrub my hand down my face. "I know what you're getting at, Frannie. I'm not suicidal. Not now. No matter what that file says about me."

"So when you crashed your car—"

I cut her off, explaining the best I can. "Have you ever felt like you were nothing? Like you were so inconsequential that it didn't matter if you even lived anymore?" Tension strains my already shaky voice. "That's what landed me in here, Frannie. Black Flacon is falling apart, and it's fucking killing me. I'll be lost if I lose my music.

"The guys in my band were right. I have a problem. If I hadn't been totally blitzed out of my fucking mind the night I crashed, I wouldn't have been so reckless. I'm usually the cautious one—the worrier—but I can't sit here and lie to you and say the thought of leaving everything in this fucking world behind hasn't crossed my mind a time or two. And you know what? I wouldn't have even cared if I hurt anyone else by doing it. I can see now with a clear head that I *do* have a problem."

She grips my hand tightly in hers, a small gesture that speaks volumes. She does understand. "When something you love so much slips away from you, it's hard to go on. I understand that more than anyone else. I'm still healing from the loss of my sister, but the one thing that has helped me the most is finding a new focus. For me, it was school and learning how to help other people."

Frannie stares at me for a long moment, gauging my reaction. When I don't immediately respond, she closes her eyes and takes a deep breath. "I know what it's like to want to lose yourself."

I stare at our connected hands while the same thought runs through my mind over and over, pushing me to tell her how I'm feeling. "I wish you weren't my doctor so I could kiss you right now."

When my gaze meets hers, she whispers, "I wish that, too."

There we sit, at an impossible crossroad. Our desire for one another evident, but our circumstances preventing us from ever acting on it. The most beautiful woman in the world who seems to completely get me is off-limits, and I already know simply being around her without touching her is going to be pure fucking hell.

I pull her hand to my lips. "Maybe someday, when I'm out of here, our dreams will become reality."

Her breath catches the moment I kiss her skin, and I know she feels it, too—the overwhelming desire to be something more. "Tyke—"

"Don't," I plead. "Don't tell me again how we're never going to happen."

"No matter if you're out of here or not, a relationship between us would never work."

"Why?" I tilt my head. "If something is meant to be, it will happen. Like us. I don't know why, but I have this gnawing feeling in the pit of my stomach that we met for a reason."

She sighs. "We did meet for a reason."

"I'm not talking about what landed me in here, Frannie. I'm talking the big picture here. I don't know why, but I feel like we can help each other, like we're—" I stop myself from saying what's on the tip of my tongue because it sounds totally lame and semi-creepy.

"Like we're meant to be?" she questions, a hint of a smile on that sexy mouth of hers.

I shrug, embarrassed. "Sounds fucking ridiculous, right?"

She gives my hand a gentle squeeze. "No, it doesn't. I can't tell you how often I've thought of you the last few days. Especially at night, when I'm alone."

A fiery blush assaults her cheeks, and I know exactly just how she was picturing me. My cock jerks in my jeans at the memory of how close we were to saying "fuck it" in her office and just going for it. The thought of how it felt when her mouth melted with mine causes my stomach to flip with anticipation, instantly wanting to feel that once again.

I lick my lips and stare into her eyes as her lips part. She wants me to kiss her. She's practically begging me for it as she leans into me. All I would have to do is inch forward and it would be all over. We'd be crossing a line, but I think it'll be worth it.

I reach up and stroke her cheek. "You don't know how bad I want you right now."

She leans into my touch, batting her eyes. "Not as much as I you."

That's when I lose it and cross the line. I know I shouldn't, but after hearing that she wants me too, it's impossible to resist the taste of her mouth. I lean in and crush my mouth to hers, enjoying the taste of her sensual lips. Carefully, I set my guitar down, and then cradle her face in my hands.

"This is wrong," she murmurs between kisses as I pull her onto my lap.

"I know," I agree but flick my tongue into her mouth.

She hikes her dress up and straddles me, and God, I know this is wrong but I don't have the fucking willpower to stop it. I want her too damn much.

I begin to work on the buttons on the front of her dress and she wraps her hand around my wrist. "Not out here. Not in the open."

She pushes herself off me and begins to walk backward into the thick forest surrounding us. I watch as her eyes beacon me to follow. It's then I know.

I would follow her anywhere.

Chapter Eight

"Desire" – Meg Meyers

Frannie

When Tyke's hand meets mine, I can tell by the look in his eyes that he's just as hungry for this as I am. I know I'm breaking every single rule I set for myself, but there's something about him that I just can't resist. The thing is, even though I don't know him extremely well, this doesn't feel like it's just about sex. We actually have a connection. Most men I've had random moments of passion with I didn't even know their names, let alone have them open up to me the way Tyke has.

I know he still has an addiction issue, but hell, I can't fault him for that. Look at me right now, falling back into my old ways, seeking comfort in physical intimacy, even though I'm risking everything for it.

I pull him further into the trees until the sun is no longer shining down on us, just merely squeaking through the autumn leaves.

"How much farther do we need to go?" he questions.

"Far enough that we won't be caught," I answer. "No one can ever know about this."

Hopefully, one time with Tyke will be enough to curb this damn craving. If I can just fuck him and get it out of my system, maybe I can focus more on my actual job, rather than allowing him to take up all the space in my brain.

We come to a stack of flagstones: solid and appearing almost like a small table, made by nature. I pull him over to them, and he swiftly picks me up and sets me down on the rock. It's cool against my skin as his skillful hands slide my dress up, revealing the bare skin of my thighs.

He leans in to kiss me again, and I press my index finger to his lips. "Promise me, this stays just between us."

The heat of his stare overwhelms me as he tilts his head and runs his tongue along the side of my finger and when he bites the tip, my panties nearly incinerate on the spot. Dear God. Where did this man learn to be so damn sexy?

"I swear. If you don't want anyone to know, then this stays our secret," he whispers before he leans in and kisses the tender flesh below my ear. "I want you. I'll follow whatever rules you want."

With those words from his lips, every ounce of rational thought flies out of my head and I let go, giving into my body's desires as I pull back and then crush my lips to his. My fingers thread through his thick blond hair, and I whimper the moment his tongue clashes with mine.

His hands slide under my dress as I wrap my legs around his waist and grind my pelvis against the hard length in his jeans. His kiss sears me and warmth spreads over the entire length of my body, the material of Tyke's dark red T-shirt crumpling in my palms as I clutch it hard and tug it over his head.

When my eyes drift down to his body, I lick my lips in anticipation. His chest is toned, tanned, and beautiful. It reminds me of one of those naked male sculptures that only few men in this world actually resemble, the pronounced "V" that makes women lose their minds on full display as it dips down into his jeans, pointing me in the direction I should go next.

I move my hand down to the button of his jeans while he pulls on the straps of my dress, exposing the tops of my breasts. His head dips down and his lips caress the soft skin on my chest while his fingers work down the lace of my bra. My nipples pucker as soon as the cool air wafts over them.

"So goddamn beautiful," Tyke murmurs, before closing his mouth around the taut pink skin.

As we continue to tear away each other's clothing, the sound of both of our panting fills my ears. We take turns exploring, kissing, and tasting each other's flesh until we are both down to just our underwear. Tyke grabs the sides of my panties and drags them down my legs, leaving me completely naked before him. He hooks his arms under my thighs and pulls my hips to the edge of the rock, dropping to his knees and resting my legs on his shoulders as he uses his fingers to splay open my most sensitive flesh and then plunges his tongue inside.

The warmth of his mouth on me causes my entire body to writhe. My hips rotate while my head drops back. "Oh God," I pant.

My pleas of desire only excite him more as his tongue continues to lap my folds before sucking on my clit.

"Tyke," I half whisper, half moan his name as I jam my fingers into his hair.

It doesn't take long for that familiar euphoric feeling of an impending orgasm to rush through my body—the same feeling I turned to in order to forget, at least for a while.

Every nerve ending in my body ignites as I let loose and fall into the bliss of pure ecstasy. I writhe beneath him as he continues to kiss a path up my stomach and then to my breasts. Finally, his lips connect with mine and our mouths meld together, my arousal still evident as our tongues intertwine. If it wasn't happening to me right this very second, I would never believe that, even after an orgasm I could still be this turned on. I don't think I've ever craved a man inside me as much as I do Tyke Douglas.

I press my pussy against his crotch and rub myself against his cock, still restrained by his boxer briefs. "I want you."

He inhales sharply through his nose and then blows his hot breath across my lips. "I want you, too, but I don't . . . we can't . . . *fuck.*" He drops his forehead to my shoulder, defeated. "I don't have a condom."

I let out a deflated breath, but the need for him still throbs deep within me. I debate for a long moment, worried that we may never get another chance to be alone. "Have you been tested lately?"

He raises his head and stares at me. There's no mistaking the wheels turning in his brain as he tries to figure out where I'm going with this question. "Dr. Shepherd tested me for everything the first day I came in, and I got a clean bill of health. Have *you* been tested?"

I nod. "I get tested after each sexual partner I've had."

I feel a twinge of guilt for not telling him exactly how many times that's been, but considering he's a rock star, I'm sure his numbers are still higher than mine.

"Look, Tyke, we're both adults and have been tested. I'm okay with no condom if you are, as long as you pull out. I'm not on any birth control."

He lifts one eyebrow. "You're not a virgin, are you?"

"No," I laugh. "Far from it."

He grins. "Good. The last thing I want is some psycho, over twenty-five virgin becoming obsessed with me for taking her most prized possession."

I roll my eyes. "That ship has long since sailed."

He laughs with me for a moment before becoming deadly serious again as he presses his still hard cock against my wet flesh. "Okay. One time. I'm in no fucking shape to be a father right now."

"Agreed," I add and earn what I can only describe as a look of offense on Tyke's face. "Not that I'm saying you're not father material. I just mean me. I'm not ready for kids, either." I quickly rush to make him understand what I meant.

He kisses my lips. "I knew what you meant. I'm just fucking with you."

I bite my lip as a surge of bravery shoots through me and I tell him, "I'd rather you just be *fucking* me."

He growls as he cups my breast in his hand. "That can most definitely be arranged."

The playful tone in his voice is soon replaced by a wicked gleam in his eyes—one that tells me he's most definitely ready to fulfill my last request. With a swift movement of his hand, the gray briefs disappear and his thick cock springs out. I reach between us, eager to touch and explore his beautiful body. His flesh is warm and silky as my fingers run along the length of his shaft.

I know it's completely ludicrous to call a cock stunning, but it's the only word that comes to mind as I gaze upon this magnificent man before me.

I lick the palm of my hand and then wrap my fingers around his cock, giving it a few long strokes. Tyke's head falls back, and his mouth drifts open as I work him.

"Shit," he murmurs as he licks his lips then brings his face back up so he can stare at me with his lust-coated eyes. He reaches out and flicks his thumb over my still erect nipple. "You don't know how good your touch feels."

I bite my lip as the memory of how damn good he made my body feel floods me, and instantly, I crave that euphoria again.

"I think I have a pretty good idea," I say, edging closer to the end of the stone and guiding his cock up and down my folds, making impact with my clit each time.

Tyke sucks a quick breath through his teeth. "Jesus. You're still so fucking wet."

I lean in and lick his parted lips. "It's because I want you inside me so damn bad."

He crushes his mouth to mine as he thrusts his hips forward and the tip of his cock teases my entrance. "This? Is this what you want?"

My thighs spread wider, and I grab his ass. "Yes."

"Need it?" he questions, inching forward.

"Oh, God, yes." Even I can hear the pleading in my voice as I beg him to give me more. "I do."

He trails his nose along my jawline. "Tell me what you want me to do to you, Frannie."

Chills shoot down my spine as my entire body covers with goose bumps. I don't remember ever wanting a man this much. No one has ever brought me to the edge and allowed me to teeter on the cliff of desire as long as Tyke has, and, *God*, the anticipation is killing me.

"Say it," he coaxes. "I want to hear the dirty words coming out of your sexy mouth."

"Fuck me, Tyke. I want you to fuck me," I whisper against his lips.

As soon as the words touch the air, he thrusts his dick inside me. My pussy immediately clamps around him, holding him there.

"Fucking heaven," he breathes, moving at a deliciously slow pace. He drops his head and rests his forehead on my shoulder. "I don't know how long I'm going to last because it feels too—damn—good."

I run my nails down his back, and he looks up to lock his gaze with mine. "Then fuck me hard and make it fucking count."

My words must ignite something within him because he snakes his arms under mine and grips my shoulders, locking me into place. His thrusts pick up speed. "You like it hard?"

"*Yes*," I hiss.

I close my eyes, loving the way every inch of me is on fire for this man. The sound of our skin slapping echoes around us in the otherwise quiet forest, turning me on even more.

He fists my hair, pulling my head back, forcing me to look at him. "Watch me while I fuck you. I want to see you. I want to look in your eyes when you come with me inside you."

The constant rhythm of him driving into me as deep as he can causes that familiar tingle to erupt throughout my body. I pant, and the urge to give in to the feeling and close my eyes rushes over me, but Tyke's hold on me reminds me he wants to see me fall apart.

My mouth drifts open and a low moan rolls out of me as my second orgasm hits me hard. "Oh God. Tyke, yes."

"That's right, baby, come for me. Remember it's me who makes you feel like this," he chants as he watches me come undone before him.

His thrusts become more rigid as he pounds into me, seeking his own release while I'm still on my high. A string of unintelligible curses fly from his mouth as he comes hard.

"Shit," he yells as he realizes he's coming inside me.

He pulls his cock out just in time for me to watch one small shot of thick white come shoot onto the outer lips of my pussy. It's hard to tell, but it looks like there's some oozing out of me as well.

He grips a handful of his hair and stares down at his come dripping out of me. "Fuck. Jesus. Frannie, I'm sorry. I didn't pull out in time. I was just so caught up in feeling you. If something happens, I want you to know I'll take care of it."

I shake my head as I hop off the rock—the lust-filled moment I was just living suddenly darkened by the reality of what has happened.

I grab my underwear off the ground. "It's okay, Tyke. What are the odds of anything happening, right? It was an accident. One we won't let happen again."

I know it's a lame attempt to console him. He's no idiot. He knows just as well as I do what we just did is legitimately concerning.

He nods as he watches me put my clothes back on. "Still, if you get pregnant, you tell me. We'll take care of it."

The word *abortion* rolls around in my brain for a moment. While I'm not against a woman having the right to choose what to do with her body at all, doing that just isn't for me. I always told myself when I was fucking around before that if that happened with a man I didn't know well or wasn't in a good relationship with, I would give up the child for adoption. But there's no need to go into any of that with Tyke.

I finish the last button on my dress just as Tyke buttons his jeans. His green eyes are filled with concern as he watches me, waiting for me to agree to the abortion if a pregnancy does happen.

I debate whether to tell him my true feelings about the situation but decide against it. At some point, he'll leave this place, and what happens to me will be none of his concern.

"You'll let me know, right?" he questions again.

I pat his chest as I walk by him. "Sure."

That's the last thing I say as I walk away, leaving him standing in the middle of the deserted woods, alone.

Chapter Nine

"The Morning After" – Meg Myers

Frannie

The lavender soap lathers easily against my skin, cleaning every trace of Tyke Douglas from my body. On one hand, our stolen moment together in the woods was one of the most exhilarating experiences I've ever had. We shared a true connection, unlike anything I've ever felt before. On the other hand, being hit with the harsh realization that the act was "just sex" has never happened to me like that before. Sure, I've had countless, meaningless trysts with random strangers, but never have I felt immediate regret for allowing myself to get so out of control. I shouldn't have had sex with him without a condom. I'm fucking smarter than that. I don't know why I allowed it to happen.

Well, that's not strictly true. I'm attracted to him, and God, him singing a song about me—I lost all resolve. I wanted him right then and there. To hell with the consequences.

I rinse my body clean, dry off, and then quickly dress in a black dress suit. Tonight, after dinner, will be my first group therapy session including Tyke. I don't know how I'm going to hold it together when I see him. My stupid emotions are everywhere. The attraction I was hoping would go away after I allowed him to ravage my body is still there, if not stronger than before. What happened out in those woods can never happen again. It's too big of a risk, not only to my job, but to my heart, too.

Every woman has an ideal man, a dream man, and Tyke Douglas is exactly that for me. He's sweet, amazingly talented, and insanely sexy. On top of that, knowing that he thinks about me, actually caring that I'm sad . . . there's absolutely no resisting that package. I'll need to keep my distance, no matter how much I'm tempted.

Once I'm presentable, I step out of the cottage and make my way up toward the main house. When I'm only a few feet away, I hear a door close behind me and Kimmy's voice calls for me to wait up.

I turn in time to see Kimmy bounding up to me, wearing yet another adorable outfit that gives her the appearance of being younger than she actually is.

"Hey, Frannie. What'd you spend your afternoon doing?" She matches my pace as I continue on to the house.

"Nothing much. Hung out in my room mostly." Lying to her about my afternoon is absolutely vital. "How about you?"

She shrugs. "I stayed in the main house and read a book. Not having cable sucks. I miss reality TV."

I nod. "I've noticed there aren't any televisions on the property. Why is that?"

"Dr. Shepherd says he wants to eliminate as much negative drama from the clients as possible, since some of them are famous and all. But, if you ask me, not allowing TV is dumb, especially considering he doesn't confiscate their phones." She pops her gum as we step up onto the porch.

"You're right," I agree. "It's not like they can't Google themselves—if their phones actually get service here. I've noticed mine is spotty at best, and I drop a lot of calls."

"It's these damn mountains. They make it impossible to get a lot of things out here." She steps up on the porch and then heads toward the side of the house.

"You aren't coming to dinner?" I ask, wondering where she's going.

She shakes her head. "Nope. I'm going in to use Dr. Shepherd's computer. It's a school night for me."

I smile, remembering that she told me when I met her that she was taking online classes while she worked on getting into design. "I'll see you later then. Have fun studying."

Walking into the kitchen, the spicy scent of grilled meat floats around me and I lick my lips as the aroma fills my nose. "Hey, Sue. Need some help?"

She smiles as she looks up from the chocolate cake she's frosting. "Hello, Frannie. Thanks for the offer, but I'm just about finished. Hope you're hungry."

"Starved," I tell her with a smile as I pass through on my way to the dining room.

Most of the clients are already seated at the table. I scan the faces and find myself disappointed that Tyke's not here yet. The urge to kick myself comes over me. How stupid am I to be so excited to see him again. I *just* vowed to stay away from him.

"Hey, Dr. Mead," Randall says, nudging the chair beside him. "This seat is open."

A small amount of relief floods me. Sitting here guarantees that I won't have to sit next to Tyke. I squeeze into the seat between Randall and Arnold. Like a gentleman, Randall stands to push the chair in behind me.

"Thank you," I say, watching as Josie, sitting on the other side of Randall, shoots an evil look in my direction.

Clearly, she thinks I'm encroaching on her territory.

Seconds later, Tyke enters the room and sits in the same seat he's been at since his arrival. He's eaten all his meals sitting next to me, so far. His confused green eyes rake over me. After the way I left him standing in the woods, I don't know why me moving to another seat surprises him. We had sex—a one-time thing. There's no need to keep up the charade of being close when we both know there's no real future.

Randall turns toward me with a polite smile. "So, Dr. Mead—"

"Frannie, please," I quickly correct him.

His smile widens. "Okay, Frannie it is, then. What I was about to ask is if you have any big weekend plans two weeks from now?"

I shake my head. "Not really."

"Do you like art?"

"Yes. I appreciate art in a variety of forms." My mind automatically drifts back to Tyke singing and how beautiful that was. He is truly an artist.

"Well, as you know, I'm the activities director, and from time to time I like to plan outings for the clients. There's an art gallery in a city that's not too far from here, and I was thinking it would be nice to get out. Would you be interested in being the second chaperone?"

The idea of leaving the property for a while is enticing. "I'd love that."

"Great." Randall drums his fingers on the top of the table in a fit of glee and then addresses the rest of the table. "Everyone? Can I have your attention?"

The small chitchat at the table stops and everyone focuses on Randall—everyone but Tyke, who's staring directly at me. His eyes bore into me as he tilts his head toward the seat next to him. I give my shoulders a slight shrug and pull my lips into a tight line.

I know he wants more of an explanation than that. Hell, if I were him, I would, too. But what can I tell him? Thanks for the sex? Maybe now, since we've acted on our desire for one another, we can focus on being strictly professional? He doesn't want to hear that. He probably won't even care.

"In two Saturdays, we are going out as a group to the art gallery. For those of you who would like to go, please see me after dinner and express your interest," Randall announces. "For those of you who do not wish to go, Dr. Shepherd and Timothy will be here on staff so that you may stay behind for independent reflection."

The clients' excitement is evident. They must like getting out of here from time to time, since most of them are here for at least a month or more.

For the rest of the meal, I feel the tension emanating from Tyke. Every time I look in his direction, his eyes are fixed on me. If he's not careful, people are going to figure out something is going on between us and start prying, asking questions, and I'll be forced to lie.

No one can ever know what we did.

When everyone is finished, Randall stands, and the clients immediately flock to him. Excited murmurs fill the room as everyone rushes to tell him they want to go.

I stand and head for the foyer, needing to prepare for the group session I'm about to lead. When I get to the room, the door closing behind me startles me. Quickly, I whip around and my heart thumps against my ribs.

Tyke stands a few mere feet from me, a perplexed expression on his face. "Do you want to tell me what the hell that was about back there?"

I shake my head and turn back toward the table, focusing on the handouts I prepared for the session earlier in the day. "I don't know what you mean."

Unsatisfied with that answer, he steps next to me and grabs my wrist, turning me, forcing me to look at him. "Yes, you do. What's with the cold shoulder? I thought we had things figured out?"

I narrow my eyes and jerk my hand away from him. "Look, Tyke, I'm not interested in being your fuck-buddy while you're stuck here. We had sex—one time. It's not going to happen again."

He shoves his fingers into his hair and sighs. "I don't think of you that way."

I want to believe that. To feel that I'm more to him than just some easy lay. After seeing how much emotion he put into that song he sang about me, it seems like I mean something to him.

"How *do* you think of me then?" I ask before I even realize I've said the question out loud.

He licks his lips and takes a determined step toward me, my hips fitting perfectly in his hands as he pulls me against his chest. "You've taken up every spare inch in my brain since I got here, Frannie."

I take a deep breath. "Don't tell me lies, even if they're sweet. You don't have to do that with me. If you just want sex—"

He tips my chin up with his index finger. "I don't."

"Don't," I repeat and then close my eyes unable to look at him. "Don't say things you don't mean. I know what this is. I've been in situations like this before."

He tilts his head. "Why?"

I flinch back and do my best to evade it. "Why what?"

"Why do you think I'm just using you? Don't you feel it?" he whispers, and the warmth of his breath floats across my lips. "The connection we have is insane. There's no faking that. What's happening between us is more than just sex, Frannie."

While I've felt an array of emotions for Tyke Douglas, the invisible rope pulling us together is just too strong. "Tyke..."

"There's no need to deny it. It's written all over your face that you feel the same way."

I shake my head. "It doesn't matter. Soon you'll be gone, back on the road, and where will that leave me? If we get caught, I'll be jobless. I'll have nothing, and you'll have moved on and all this will have been for nothing." Tears threaten to spill from eyes as I explain our reality to him. "There will never be an us. Ever. It's not worth the risk."

"So that's it? You're done? Just like that? Can you really walk away from this—from the possibility of an 'us'?"

"Tyke, what choice do I have?" The quiver in my voice tells me I won't be able to hold the tears back much longer.

"You always have a choice, Frannie." He steps back and grabs his chest with both hands, fisting the dark fabric of his T-shirt. "Choose me. We'll leave this place together."

"I've worked too hard. I can't—I won't—walk out on a career for a man I barely know."

My heart squeezes in my chest as I see how desperate he is to hang on to what little bit of a relationship we've started, and how much my harsh words are a slap in the face. As much as I wish we could have a fairy tale romance, I know this is reality and happily ever afters don't happen to broken people like us. It's best to cut things off now, before we get in any deeper. "Besides, you're not ready to run away from here. You still need help."

His face contorts with pain as he steps back from me. "You still think I'm a druggie, and yet you fuck me?" He turns away from me and locks his fingers behind his head. "So we're done? Just like that? Got what you wanted and now you're ready to bounce? You're just like everybody else in my life. You used me."

"Tyke." I reach for him but quickly pull back, knowing that while it makes me a cruel bitch to hurt him like this, it's the right thing to do.

For both of us.

He closes his eyes and takes a deep breath. The second he exhales, a look of clarity shines in his eyes. They meet mine. "Fine. If that's how you want it, I won't bother you again."

My lower lip trembles as I pretend to be unfazed by his decision, lifting my chin defiantly. "I think it's best for both of us to remain strictly professional and pretend that we never allowed things to—"

He holds up his hand, and his expression contorts once again. "Distance. I got it. Consider this afternoon forgotten."

I hate that I'm hurting him, but I don't know another way to end this before we get too deep and I allow my heart to be crushed. I promised myself I would never care for anyone again. I don't want to ever feel the pain that comes when a person leaves you forever. But the way he's looking at me...it's almost too much to bear.

The door opens and we immediately step away from each other. The rest of the clients filter into the room, and I'm suddenly paranoid that they'll be able to feel the tension in the between us.

Tyke walks over and takes the seat furthest from where I'm standing. He stretches his long legs out and then throws one arm over the back of the metal chair next to him.

He doesn't look in my direction again.

Chapter Ten

"Wicked Game" – Stone Sour

Tyke

As I sit here locked in a room full of people struggling with addictions, I know the point is to listen to their stories and find comfort in the fact that I'm not alone. The problem is, right now, I feel more alone than ever. Frannie's words still ring in my head. I don't know why I thought she was different; that I was special to her. It's my own fault for reading into something that was never really there. She was right. We barely know each other.

I do my best not to look at her as she sits across from me and leads the group therapy session.

Now that I've tasted her, I don't know if I can ever pretend that I haven't. I get that this job means a lot to her, and that she wants to protect it, but doesn't she care about hurting me?

"—and that's when I knew I had a problem. I couldn't get my life back on track when she turned me down for the prom." I fight the urge to roll my eyes at this idiot.

The only thing I know about this Arnold guy is that he's never been able to get over his high school crush turning him down. He's a fucking nut job. Who lingers for years on a woman turning them down? A woman he never had a shot at to begin with.

Next time I see Dr. Shepherd, I'm going to request not to come to any more of these sessions. What will listening to some crazy guy babble on do for me?

I shift my weight in my chair, catching the attention of Josie Sullivan. She smiles at me from the next chair over, biting her lip and motioning to the empty seat I'm resting my arm on. I shrug. Josie takes that as an invitation and slides over next to me. At first I think about moving my arm, not wanting to lead her on because I'm simply not interested, but then I glance across the room and catch Frannie's perplexed expression. I know it's a dick move, but I want to make her jealous. I want to show her that just because she doesn't want me, doesn't mean that someone else won't.

Josie is an attractive woman. Fake, but attractive all the same. I've spoken to her in passing at the Grammys, but she was more interested in hitting on Noel. She's a known fame-whore, and rumor has it she slept her way to her first record deal.

Josie's brown eyes stare up at me, and she flashes her best flirty smile. "Thanks for the seat."

As Arnold continues to prattle on about his most debilitating moments as a teenager, I lean into Josie's ear and whisper, "You're most welcome."

131

My eyes flit in Frannie's direction. I see the pain in her eyes as she focuses all her attention on Josie and me, and that's when I know it's not over between us, giving me all the motivation I need not to give up just yet.

I make it to Frannie's office well before our scheduled appointment time. Last night while I lay awake in my bed, I did nothing but think of her. Making her jealous yesterday was fucked up on my part, but I was hurt and I couldn't help but lash out.

I tried to convince myself to let her go, but I still want her. There's no denying that. But it can't just be me—I want her to want me back just as much. The file she has on me probably gives her the impression that I'm some womanizing man-whore who has no feelings, and I hate that. I don't want her to write me off just because she thinks what we did in the woods meant nothing. I need to make her see that I meant what I said about our connection being strong, and that I feel that, for some reason, we are fated to be together.

I pull out another green guitar pick and write two simple words, *Miss you*, on the back, sticking it between the petals of the red rose I picked from the garden on my way here. I think about laying it on her desk, right in the open, to make sure she sees it, but decide it's better for her to find it after I leave. I place the flower on her chair and then push it under her desk, hiding it from sight.

After I'm satisfied with the flower placement, I take a seat on the couch and wait for Frannie. Moments later she comes waltzing into the room, her dark hair pulled up, showing off her slender neck. The black fitted jacket and skirt she has on gives off an extra edge of professionalism that I know is a message to me. It doesn't make her any less appealing, though.

"You look beautiful," I tell her as she takes the seat across from me.

She crosses her legs and rests her tablet in her lap. "Tyke."

There's a warning in her voice, but that doesn't slow me down. "It's not okay for me to tell you that you look nice now?"

She shakes her head. "No. Professional, remember?"

I hold my hands up in surrender, not wanting to push her anymore. "I'll be good."

She stares at me for a long moment, and then once she's satisfied that I'm telling her the truth, she slides her glasses onto her face. "Did you write anything down in your notebook?"

I open the notebook and stare down at the only song that came to mind last night. Besides humming the tune to "Ball Busting Bitch", I also found myself singing another song. A song where the guy doesn't want to fall in love, but the woman on his mind is the only one in the world who can save him. The pain in the lyrics hit me last night. The game Frannie and I are playing is totally wicked—one that can destroy us both. Desire has made us foolish and we've done something we wouldn't normally do in order to sedate it.

I clear my throat. "I wrote down another song title."

She tilts her head and asks in a voice that's barely above a whisper, "What is it?"

I chew the inside of my cheek. "'Wicked Game.'"

She leans back in her chair. "Can we not make this session about you and me?"

My eyes widen. That wasn't exactly the reaction I was expecting. "You wanted me to write down songs that came to mind, and all I did last night was think of you."

She pulls her glasses off her face. "I'm sorry if you feel like I'm playing games with you. It was never my intention to lead you on. I take full responsibility for what happened, and I apologize to you for that. I promise it won't happen again. I don't want you getting the wrong idea."

"The wrong idea? I know you want me, just like I want you."

Her tough exterior cracks a bit as her eyes drift up to the ceiling. "Tyke, please," she whispers. "Can we just focus on the reason you're here?"

My entire body stiffens. "I'm pretty sure I'm cured. I've haven't had benzodiazepines for nearly a week, and I'm perfectly fine."

She frowns. "There's no curing an addiction. Being here, detoxing away from temptations, is the easy part. Living with it—battling every single day—is where the real work begins, and sometimes—" She cuts herself off and takes a deep breath. "Sometimes you fall off the wagon."

I shake my head. "That's not going to happen to me."

"Don't be so sure," she lectures.

I cross my arms over my chest. "Why do you say that? You can't possibly know that I won't be able to stay away from it. It's not like you know what it's like."

She licks her lips like her mouth has suddenly gone dry. "Actually, I know *exactly* what it's like to fight an addiction."

I raise my eyebrows. "What could you possibly be addicted to? You're perfect."

"There's something you should know about me." Her blue eyes focus on me. "I struggle every day, and since you came into my life..." She pauses and takes a deep breath, letting it out slowly. "I'm a recovering sex addict."

Her admission catches me off guard. "Sex addict?"

My mind spins, trying to get a handle on exactly what she's just said.

Holy—fucking—shit.

"Are you fucking with me right now?" I ask, making sure this isn't some sort of sick joke.

"I wish I was," she whispers.

I scrub my hand down my face as the shock turns to anger. I think about us fucking in the woods yesterday, and how she immediately cut me off afterwards. "Is that's why you blew me off? I'm your *relapse*?"

She shakes her head. "No." She hesitates and then sighs. "Well, yes and no. What happened with us...it was more than just giving in to my baser urges. When you sang that song about me, it touched me, and I couldn't help but give into the physical urge my body craved. I had no intention of beginning a relationship with you."

Things begin to click. "Jesus. You're just like all the other groupies who wanted to screw me."

"No!" she shouts and then quickly covers her mouth and then whispers harshly, "It's not like that."

I want to believe her because God knows she wasn't just some random fuck for me. The thought of what happened between us meaning nothing to her fucking hurts. For some reason, I allowed myself to become emotionally attached to Frannie, and I don't know if it's because she seems to understand me, or because I can't shake the feeling I'm here to save her.

I pick at my leather cuff and wonder out loud, "Then tell me what it *is* like, Frannie. I need to know if I should give up on us or not."

She runs her hand through her hair and looks away, but then turns back toward me with her chin pointed down. "I don't know what you want me to say."

"Tell me how you feel. Tell me if I should fight to make you see that we can work," I urge.

Her brow furrows with confusion. "Why would you still want me after I told you my secret? I'm a mess."

The corner of my mouth pulls up into an understanding smile. "I'm the last person to judge you, don't you think? It's not like I don't have my own sordid past. After all, it wasn't clean living that landed me in rehab."

That earns me a smile. "I suppose so. You are a rock star, after all. I'm sure you've done worse. You've probably been with thousands of women."

I grimace. "I think my dick would've fallen off by now if I'd been with a thousand women."

"I just don't understand why you care so much. We barely know one another."

"That's true," I admit. "But you're the first one to have given more than two shits about me in a long time."

She frowns. "I'm sure that's not true."

"But it is," I defend my statement. "Riff, Noel, and even my own brother have been too busy with their own shit over the past couple of years. I've felt nothing but alone. This last year has been the hardest of my entire life. I've lived on the road with these guys, knowing they're disgusted by me, knowing they really don't want me around. Do you know how shitty that made me feel? To be unwanted? You, Frannie—you make me feel needed, and that's why I'm fighting for you."

She nods. "I've felt that way my entire life. My parents have always been too busy for me or my sister. Annie was the one person in this world I knew would always be there for me, even when no one else would."

Having a twin is unlike any other relationship in the world. Throughout my life, Trip has always been there, even when no one else has been—even now. Even though he was pissed at me, he still cared enough to bring me here to get help.

"I can't imagine losing Trip," I admit.

"Losing Annie was the most difficult thing that's ever happened to me. I know it's no excuse, but that's why I turned to sex. I wanted the closeness. To allow myself the illusion of love, even for a little while, but at the same time keeping everyone at a distance. I don't ever want to feel the pain of losing someone else I love again."

I nod. "So you close yourself off to make it easier? You think that's healthy?"

"I know it's not. That's why I'm determined to turn my life around. I thought by coming here—"

"That you'd be safe from temptations?" I fill in the gap for her. "I'm sorry."

"Don't apologize. It's me who screwed up. I'm the one who should be sorry."

I sigh and stick my hand out toward her, believing that we'll need to start over if we're ever to have a shot at true intimacy. "I'm Tyke Douglas. It's nice to meet you."

She bites her bottom lower lip. "Frannie Mead."

"Friends?" I ask.

She nods. "Friends."

This isn't exactly the relationship I want with Frannie, but I feel bad that I'm the reason that she relapsed, and I don't want to push her to feel more until she's ready. I'll be patient.

I mean, let's face it.

While I'm here, I've got nothing *but* time on my hands.

Chapter Eleven

Frannie

The moment Tyke leaves my office, I sit on my desk and allow my shoulders to sag, guilt washing over me. I wish I didn't have to hurt him. I wish I wasn't like this— that I didn't depend on sex to make me feel better. It's a cycle I desperately want to break. I don't think I can ever have a real relationship with a man until I learn to let people into my heart.

I stand and walk around my desk to work on Tyke's chart, and a gasp leaves my mouth the moment I pull out my desk chair. A single red rose rests on the seat. My heart clenches, knowing that man who gave it to me is someone I can never have.

I pick it up and then sniff its floral scent. It's only then I notice something green poking out from between the petals. Plucking the thin plastic guitar pick from the flower, I smile as I read the words in Tyke's familiar scrawl.

Cutting him off will be one of the hardest things I've ever done, but I need to prove to myself that I'm over this addiction. It's the best thing for both of us. Neither of us are in a good place to begin a relationship.

Arnold adjusts on the couch and then folds his hands in his lap. This is my seventh session with him, and I still feel like I haven't made any headway. The journal idea I'm using on Tyke is failing miserably with Arnold. He never brings it to his sessions with me because he says he doesn't write anything that would be beneficial for me to learn about him.

Every session, he attempts to drag the conversation back to the notorious prom incident. Wayne and I both agree that Arnold needs a little more than addiction counseling. He also wonders why there's no mention of a mental health diagnosis in any of Arnold's medical files because he has obvious psychological issues.

I sigh and ask the one question I've dreaded since Arnold walked into my office for his appointment. "Is there anything else you'd like to discuss?"

"I know you said last time that I couldn't re-tell my story about prom, but I really feel like talking about the situation helps," he explains.

"Arnold, I don't think rehashing the same story over and over is beneficial. We need to focus on your current issues and try to pinpoint where to begin getting you back on track," I explain.

"I know, but..."

I sit and listen to Arnold babble on for twenty minutes about how we need to discuss his prom incident anyway, inadvertently allowing him to get his way by talking about the incident without directly talking about it.

Really, it doesn't matter what he's talking about because my mind is focused on how my next appointment is going to go. It's been two weeks since Tyke and I decided to start over. Two weeks where I've had to pretend that I don't miss his touch. Two weeks since thoughts of him have overtaken my brain.

I'll admit things have been smoother between us with keeping our distance. It's actually been a lot easier to let my guard down around him now that he knows my secret, but it's been difficult to pretend that my body doesn't crave him.

A knock on my door jolts my body alive. "Sounds like my next appointment is here, Arnold. We'll continue this discussion tomorrow."

"Okay, Frannie," he replies as he gets up and heads for the door.

The moment he opens it, Tyke's face comes into view. I take a moment to admire him as he struts into my office. His T-shirt accentuates the definition in his toned chest while his faded blue jeans hug his ass just right.

Stop it! I mentally scold myself. *Stop thinking of him and his insanely sexy body.*

I square my shoulders and do my best to block out the fact that he's getting to me. Tyke sits on the couch with his notebook in hand, tapping a beat out with his thumbs as I take my seat across from him.

"Were you able to think of any new songs?" I ask, just as I've done at the start of every one of our sessions.

He's been pretty reserved and hasn't written anything inside it since the session where he accused me of playing games with him.

He nods. "I did."

This surprises me. I didn't expect him to cooperate, but I'm pleased that he's giving it another shot. "What did you come up with?"

He sighs. "I've been working on a new song. The lyrics aren't quite ready to share, but I did write down another song title."

I catch myself leaning toward him, my chin propped up by my hand. "Will you tell me what it is?"

A selfish part of me hopes that it's another song about me. I know it's wrong to want that, but I like the idea of him still wanting me like I want him.

"It's called "Through the Glass" by Stone Sour."

I quickly flip through the mental listings I have of songs. That particular one doesn't resonate. "I don't think I know that one."

Tyke closes his eyes and begins to sing. The lyrics are haunting and move me to my very soul. It's about a man looking at the person he loves through the glass and how when he gets asked questions, people expect in-depth answers from him.

That line really hits home. Every time I see him, I ask him how he feels, but he always holds back, never giving me the complex truth I know he's hiding behind his smile.

I close my eyes along with him, allowing myself to get lost in the words he's singing. This song may not be about me, but it sure feels like it. More than anything, I wish we could've met under different circumstances—in a time when we both weren't trying to overcome our demons.

But rewinding time isn't possible. There's nothing left but to trudge forward and see what our current situation holds.

When he finishes, I open my eyes to find his green eyes focused directly on me. The right thing to do in this situation would be to drive home the point that, no matter how we both feel, we're still off-limits to one another. But I can't bring myself to do it. The look in his eyes...it's the same one I saw that day out by the fountain. The one that made me ache for him, and lose all resolve once I found out he was thinking of me while he was expressing so much hurt. I feel the same desire to say fuck the rules and allow myself to have him right now, but I take a deep breath and will that feeling away.

"That was beautiful," I tell him. "Sad, but beautiful."

He nods. "Kind of like us together. We're beautiful, but we both have an aching sadness inside."

I smile. "Have you ever thought about becoming a counselor?"

He laughs. "I guess I do sound like one, huh?"

"A little," I tease but then clear my throat, ready to ask questions that I know will be hard for me to hear the answers to. "Do I even want to know what made you choose that song?"

Tyke shrugs. "I'm sure it's not hard to guess that part of it is directed at you. The other part is about my brother."

I raise my eyebrows. "Trip?"

"Yeah," he confirms. "I just feel like it's been forever since he and I really connected. These past few weeks, being here, having a clear head, have allowed me to look back on things I've said or done to him and see how big an asshole I've been. It's hard for me to admit that I hurt him pretty bad. Hell, not just my brother, but Noel and Riff, too. I can't believe I let prescription drugs take me over like that. It makes me never want to touch that shit again."

I reach over and pat his knee. "I'm so happy that you're ready to make big changes in your life. It's epiphanies like this that will give you the drive to stay on the straight and narrow."

He stares at my hand on his knee and then drags his gaze up to my face. "When did you know you were ready to change?"

I pull away from him as I think about one of the darkest moments in my life. I debate whether I should tell him or not, but figure we've already crossed the line of professionalism, so I might as well be open with him.

"The moment I stared at my own reflection in the mirror and was disgusted at what I saw. I'd just had sex with a married man while his pregnant wife was home tending to their other children. I knew he was married before I slept with him, but in the moment, that didn't matter—nothing did. All I cared about was getting my fix and forgetting my life just for a while. I wasn't thinking about how what I was doing could destroy someone else's family. I was selfish and I hated myself for it, so I decided I was going to change. I swore off sleeping with random men—even threw out my birth control to make myself stay clean."

He bites his lip as he processes my story. "I'm sorry I screwed up your sobriety—I truly am—but I can't say I'm sorry for what happened out in the woods. I know you believe that it was just sex, but I care for you, Frannie. You're more than some random lay to me."

Tears begin to threaten my eyes. "I am?"

"Yes." He reaches over and takes my hand, threading his fingers through mine. "Much more. I want to know you."

"What do you want to know?" I whisper.

"Anything. Everything," he replies quickly. "You fascinate me."

I shake my head. "I don't...how...what if someone finds out?"

He shrugs his shoulders. "Let them. There are other jobs out there, Frannie. Don't let a stupid job keep us from discovering if we could be happy together."

"This is a huge risk," I admit.

"Isn't it worth it? Give me a chance to make you happy. All I'm asking for is a chance."

My brain drifts to the thought of what a life with Tyke might be like. There's a fire between us that neither of us can deny, but what happens if that fire goes out? Will we still last then? Will I still be enough? It worries me that if things go south, we might revert to our old ways. But I'll never know what might happen unless I take a risk and follow through with what my heart truly wants.

"Okay," I whisper.

He smiles. "Okay."

He leans over and cradles my face in his hands before pressing his lips to mine. "Thank you."

"For what?" I whisper against his lips.

"For giving me a shot at your heart," he says as he gazes into my eyes.

It's then, at that moment, that I know that my heart's a goner. I've never had someone be so sweet to me, not to mention the romantic little note he left on the pick as well as the heartfelt songs he sang about me. A heart can only take so much thoughtfulness and love being thrown at it before it gives in. I'm not going to rush in, though. My heart still needs to be guarded until I know for sure that he's not going to hurt me.

"All right, everyone line up for a head count," Randall orders.

The clients stand in front of the two vans, waiting for Randall to come through and mark them off on his clipboard. Tyke winks at me the moment Randall passes by him and my cheeks heat up, surely causing a severe blush.

"It's a beautiful day for an art show," Wayne says, causing me to jump.

I place my hand over my heart. "You startled me. I didn't expect to see you here today."

Wayne crosses his hands behind his back in a way that makes his already perfect posture even straighter. "I wasn't planning on attending, but it seems that every client in the facility wanted to join in on this little expedition, so Timothy and I had to come as extra chaperones."

I nod. "Yes, most of them seemed excited when it was announced a couple of weeks ago, so it doesn't surprise me that none of them wanted to stay behind."

There's a long pause of silence between us as we listen to Randall go over the rules with everyone.

"There's no wandering off alone. Everyone must stay paired up."

"I've had nothing but good reports from the clients, Frannie," Wayne says, as soon as Randall's finished.

"Really? Wow. That's great news." Pride fills me, and I'm starting to think that maybe I'm a pretty decent therapist after all. Sometimes it's hard to know if I'm actually helping someone or not.

"Mr. Douglas, especially, has been showering you with compliments. He says you've been working with him about showing more emotion through music. That's very clever, reaching out to the clients through channels they'll relate to best. I think you'll do very well here."

I smile. Leave it to my secret lover to butter up my boss and earn me some brownie points. "Thank you. I really feel like I'm starting to get somewhere with Mr. Douglas."

My grin widens even further knowing that Tyke appreciates the method of therapy we've been using.

Randall opens the doors to the first van. "Dr. Shepherd and Timothy will be in charge of this bus. I'll need the following people on this one: Rosa, Elaine, John..."

"That's my cue," Wayne says before throwing, "Keep up the good work, Frannie," over his shoulder.

Randall turns to the rest of the group and tells them they are in the other van with him and I. Tyke grins as he heads to the van I'm in, while Josie calls shotgun and races toward the front of the van like a little kid.

It takes us about an hour to get to the quaint little town where the art show is being hosted. I've been to several art galas with my parents, but I don't think I've ever been more excited than to go to this particular one, and it has nothing to do with the artists. For the first time since I've met Tyke, we're away from Serenity Hills. It'll be nice to pretend, if only for a little while, what it might be like if we could be in public together.

Although walking through the halls of the art gallery as a huge group kills the illusion that we're alone, Tyke stays next to me throughout the entire tour.

Standing next to him is the hardest thing in the world. All I want to do is reach out ever so slightly and touch him to let him know that he's on my mind, but I can't. Not here. Not now.

Tyke tilts his head, studying the painting before him intently, scrutinizing what it could be conveying. The other clients stand in front of us, blocking us from the direct sight of Wayne, who is lecturing the clients on what he thinks the painting of two little children could mean.

The group moves on to the next exhibit, and it's of a photo of a couple lost in the throes of passion. My pulse increases and my chest heaves as it evokes the memory of Tyke and I together.

The photo must have sparked the same memory for Tyke because he hooks his pinky around mine. My heart thunders in my chest at the feel of our skin connecting. This is completely inappropriate, but I don't care. This small touch is already sending my body into overdrive.

This small touch is so comforting, knowing that he's thinking about me, too.

As quickly as the moment comes, it fades away when Wayne leads the group onto the next painting, and Tyke releases me.

The rest of the tour goes on much the same—simple touches when we're sure no one is looking. I'll admit there's a certain adventure in our little game, dangerous yet thrilling, but it's making me all the more anxious to have Tyke again. By the end of the exhibit, I'm so turned on it's hard for me to see straight.

Tyke must feel the same way because he leans in and whispers, "I have to have you."

My knees nearly buckle as the urge to drag him into the nearest secluded corner and allow him to have his way with me hits.

"Can you meet me by the fountain?" he asks and I nod.

The entire trip back to Serenity, my body is ablaze with anticipation. Knowing I'm going to have Tyke again is making me embarrassingly wet. We sit next to each other but have to refrain from doing anything that would give us away. Josie could turn around any moment, or Randall could glance up in the rearview mirror at the wrong time, and we'd be so busted. Not to mention the fact that I have Arnold squished next to me, on the other side.

"What was your favorite exhibit?" Randal asks openly to anyone who wants to answer.

"The picture of the people fucking," one of the male clients shouts from the back. "That shit was hot."

Tyke and I look at one another and burst out laughing, knowing that was the very painting that got us turned on.

Finally, we make it back to the facility, all piling out and saying our goodbyes as everyone heads to their rooms to rest up before dinner. Tyke and I walk far enough apart so as not to draw suspicion, but each of us knows what lies in wait for us.

I make it back to the cottage and practically run into my bathroom to freshen up. I shove my hair into a cap and jump into the shower, quickly scrubbing every inch of me down before running a razor over my legs and nether regions.

After I'm dressed in a sundress, I head to the fountain, the crisp evening air caressing my freshly washed skin and jolting every nerve in me awake as I sit down on a bench and wait for Tyke.

I casually flip through the book I brought with me to look busy as I wait. It doesn't take long before I see Tyke making his way down the path.

He grins the moment he spots me, but looks around cautiously before rushing down and scooping me up in his arms. "God. You don't know how hard today was, not being able to hold you."

I wrap my arms over his shoulders and toy with the hair on the nape of his neck. "I think I have a pretty good idea."

He crushes his lips to mine and then sets me down. "Come on. I made sure I wasn't followed, but we won't have much time."

He begins to pull me into the woods, but the idea of being out in the open again scares me. We got lucky last time. I think it's better if we don't push our luck.

I pull back on his arm and he turns to me, a perplexed expression on his face. "What's wrong?"

I tip my head toward the cottage. "This one's mine. I think it would be much more private."

He glances around and then smiles. "Lead the way."

Quickly, I sneak him inside. Once the door is shut, he shoves me up against it and attacks my mouth with his. As much as I would love to take our time and savor every moment of our passion, we both know time isn't on our side.

I wrap my arms around his neck, and he pushes my sundress up around my waist before picking me up, my legs wrapping around him, as he presses his thick erection against me. I writhe against it, hungry for him to be inside me.

When he walks us over to the bed, he lays me down and slowly slides my dress up my body while kissing a path up my torso. Once he gets to my breasts, he pulls back and removes my dress completely.

"No bra or panties this time?" he teases.

"I figured they would only get in the way." I grin at him and then my eyes trail down his body. "You're still completely dressed. I don't think that's fair."

He laughs and grabs the back of his shirt, yanking it over his head in that sexy way that guys do, completely ruffling his hair up in the process.

My eyes travel down his toned body and take a moment to appreciate all the artwork etched into his skin. Tyke Douglas is most definitely a tasty treat.

Tyke drops his gray shirt on the floor and raises one eyebrow while he grins at me wickedly. "Better?"

I lick my lips and scoot to the end of the bed. "Much."

I quickly unbutton and unzip his jeans, shoving them, along with his boxer briefs down around his narrow hips. His cock springs free and I take a moment to trail my tongue down one side of his "V" before continuing my path down his shaft.

I wrap my lips around the tip of him, and he groans. "Holy fuck."

Dirty talk from Tyke is encouraging. It pushes me to keep going because I'm obviously pleasing him.

I wrap my fingers around his shaft and tug in rhythm while I work him deeper into my mouth. His breathing becomes ragged, and he tangles his fingers in my thick hair. I've never claimed to be an expert at giving head, but I feel pretty damn proud at how much he's enjoying this.

Pre-come drips onto my tongue, and I taste the saltiness of his excitement, so I begin to slow my movements. I pull away and stare up at him. His green eyes are lust filled as he strokes the side of my face with his thumb.

I grab his arm and tug him onto the bed with me. Tyke kicks his clothes the rest of the way off and I straddle him, his erect cock, still slick with my saliva, glides against my folds as my hips grind into him, the tip of his cock hitting my clit as I work. I close my eyes and lean back, cupping my own breasts as I get lost seeking my own pleasure.

My arousal coats him, and I quicken my pace. Tyke's gaze never leaves me as the familiar tingle of bliss tears through my body and Tyke squeezes my hips as he watches me come apart on top of him.

"Jesus, I nearly came just watching that," he says as he leans up and presses his lips to mine. "You are too fucking sexy for your own good."

Before I have a chance to respond, he flips me onto my back and covers my body with his own. He trails a path of kisses across my jaw and then whispers in my ear, "I can't wait to be inside you again."

I wrap my legs around his waist and his cock presses against my entrance. "I want you there."

With one swift thrust, he's inside me. He stays still for a moment and allows my body to stretch around him, but then begins to move at a deliciously slow pace.

"Heaven. Even better than I remembered," he says with a raspy tone in his voice.

Each time he pulls out and pushes back inside, his pelvis makes contact with my clit. I spread my legs wider and grab his ass, attempting to control his rhythm.

"You like that?" he murmurs as my fingers dig into his backside.

"Ohhh, yeah," I whimper.

I should be embarrassed. I'm sure I sounded like some cheap porn star just then, but the truth is, I'm enjoying what he's doing and I don't want him to stop.

"You want it harder?" he asks and then gives me one hard thrust. "Huh?"

"Oh, God." I pant as every nerve ending in my body ignites.

"That's it, baby. Come for me again."

With that vocal cue, I lose all control. My body jerks as I come for the second time, and my vision goes dark from the intensity.

The moment I come back to my senses, I freeze. "Hold on."

I reach into my nightstand and unearth the emergency stash of condoms I bought when I made a run to the store last week. After the randomness of the woods, I wanted to be prepared if there was ever a next time with Tyke, even as much as I was trying to fight it.

He simply stares at me, and I shrug. "I got them just in case we ever happened again."

He nods. "Smart thinking, considering I can't leave this place to get them."

The foil crinkles in my hands as I tear the package open. Tyke leans back, pulling himself out of me so I can roll the condom onto him.

Once it's on, Tyke settles back on his forearms and his cock slides back into me with ease. Now that we know we're protected, he begins pounding into me at full speed, sweat slicking his back as his muscles work to find their own release.

It doesn't take long before his movements become more rigid and a deep moan rips out of his throat as he comes hard. I stare in amazement as this beautiful man gets off on the pleasure of my body.

Small tremors shake through his body before he sighs and then opens his eyes to gaze upon my face.

"Fucking beautiful," Tyke says, leaning down and crushing his lips to mine. "You're never more breathtaking then when you completely let go."

I smile up at him lazily as I reach up and push his hair back from his face. "You're the one who's beautiful—inside and out."

This time, it's Tyke who blushes, leaning in and kissing me again. "How did I ever get so lucky as to find you?"

I toy with his hair. "I don't think luck had anything to do with it. A string of bad choices brought us to rock bottom, and then finally getting our shit straight brought us to one another."

He smiles. "Like fate?"

I bite my lip and think about how I've always laughed of the idea of fate being real, but in this instance, it seems very fitting. "Like fate," I agree.

After we cuddle for a few more moments, we quickly work on cleaning ourselves up before we have to go face everyone at dinner. Tyke leaves the cottage first as soon as he's sure no one is around, and then about fifteen minutes later, I make my way toward the main house.

"Hey, Frannie," Kimmy calls from behind me, making me jump.

I rub the back of my neck. "Oh hey, Kimmy. I didn't see you there."

She laughs next to me. "No, I'm guessing your mind is elsewhere after having Tyke Douglas in your cottage."

The blood instantly drains from my face and my heart pauses for a beat.

Oh shit!

Kimmy nudges me and laughs. "Girl, don't worry. Your secret is safe with me. I won't say a word to anyone."

"Kimmy...I..." I scrub my hand across my forehead, completely lost for words.

"Relax, Frannie. If it were me in your position, I'd pounce on him, too. He's so sexy." She grins. "So tell me, is it just sex between you two, or what?"

I bite my lip. "I'm not sure. I don't think so. When we're together it feels right, and that scares me."

Her brow furrows. "Why?"

I pull my lips into a tight line. "I've never been in a real relationship before, and I have no clue what in the hell I'm doing."

She laughs. "First of all, you've got to be doing something right. I've seen the way he looks at you when he thinks no one is watching. He's crazy about you. And secondly, just be yourself. The best relationships are the natural ones."

I give her a small smile. "How'd you get so wise?"

She shrugs. "I've got five siblings, and I'm the oldest. They all come to me for advice."

"If the design thing doesn't work out, you should think about going into counseling," I tell her.

When we make it to the main house, I tell Kimmy that I'll see her later, needing space to freak out about the fact that our secret isn't so secret anymore. I make my way into my office and sit at my desk before firing up my laptop. I quickly type my passwords in and log into my email, needing to focus on something else before I have a complete anxiety attack.

The first few are spam emails but then one catches my attention. The subject line reads: *I have something you'll want to see.* It's from an anonymous sender, which is even more puzzling.

I debate leaving it alone, worried that it's one of those crazy virus emails with a link inside that will crash your computer, but then decide to at least open it.

Dr. Mead,

I have something you'll want to see. Tell me if this is you and a certain rocker in this video. If you don't want this to go viral, you'll email me back asking for my demands.

Sincerely,
A Concerned Citizen

My eyes widen as I make it through the email and then I quickly reread the text before my eyes see the thumbnail of the attachment.

Oh—my—fucking—God.

No.

NO!

This cannot be happening to me.

I click play on the video as my heart races and turn down the volume on my computer. The shaky camera focuses on Tyke and I in the woods, catching the moment when I practically beg Tyke to fuck me.

The camera stays on us as he thrusts into me and I beg him to fuck me harder. I watch in horror as I writhe against the rock as I come, and then it shows where he shoots part of his load inside me and then pulls out.

The video stops and the breath I've been holding whooshes out of me. What in the hell am I going to do?

One thing is for sure, I'll do whatever it takes to keep that video from going out to the world.

I square my shoulders and fire back a reply.

What do you want?

And now I wait.

Chapter Twelve

"No Matter What" – Papa Roach

Tyke

Frannie is unusually quiet at dinner. I try, subtly, to catch her eye when no one is looking to make sure she's okay, but she won't even look in my direction.

I lean back in my chair, perplexed about the entire situation. I thought we finally had things worked out—that we were going to give "us" a shot—why won't she look at me?

"Since we've all had a long day, I think it would be nice to have an evening off. Group therapy is cancelled for this evening, but I highly encourage you to use the time for personal refection," Dr. Shepherd informs the group after we finish dinner.

The room begins to buzz as everyone considers having time on their own. Most of them discuss getting a card game together in the recreation room. Another client asks me to join, but I politely refuse because the only thing on my mind is finding out what's bothering Frannie.

The moment she gets up from the table, I follow her. "Dr. Mead? Can I have a moment of your time?"

I'm careful to address her properly in front of everyone as to not raise suspicions. No one pays much mind when she instructs me to follow her to her office.

Once we're alone she closes the door and then turns to me, tears streaming down her face. I quickly cross the room and wrap my arms around her in an attempt to comfort her.

"What's wrong?" I ask.

She sniffs. "People know about us, Tyke."

My breath catches as I pull back from her so I can see her face. "Who?"

"Kimmy saw us go into my cottage together earlier today, but she swore she wouldn't tell anyone."

I furrow my brow. "Do you trust her?"

Frannie shrugs. "I don't know. I think so. Gah! I'm not sure because when I checked my email today I got this."

She walks over to her laptop and shows me the email she received.

My eyes hone in on the video and my hands begin to shake as anger washes through me. "Is that what I think it is?"

She nods. "It's us in the woods. Someone filmed us, Tyke. What are we going to do? If this gets out not only will I lose my job, but the press will know all about you coming to rehab."

159

I scrub my hand down my face. "I couldn't give two shits about my reputation, Frannie. It's you I'm worried about. I know how much this job means to you."

I sigh. She'll be so screwed if this gets back to Dr. Shepherd. As much as I want to run out there and threaten bodily hard to each and every person here to make them confess, I know I can't do that. I have to keep my cool and figure out whatever this sick fuck wants.

"Did you reply to this?" I ask.

"Yes. I haven't heard back though."

I thread my fingers behind my head and stare up at the ceiling in attempt to keep my cool. "I want to kill them. I want to beat the shit out of whoever did this. They've got some fucking balls."

Frannie grabs the hem of my T-shirt. "I know exactly how you feel. I'm beyond pissed—and scared—but we can't lose our heads. We have to be smart about this. They can ruin everything with a few clicks of a button."

She's right. Another media scene portraying Black Falcon in a negative light would probably push Riff over the edge. He's pissed at me enough already.

Even though I couldn't give a fuck if people saw another sex tape of me, knowing the world was able to see that private moment shared between Frannie and me makes me sick to my very core. I want that look in her eyes when she comes to only be mine. I don't want to share that part of her with the rest of the world.

I take a deep breath and try to relax my shoulders. "Can you forward me this email? If they respond, send it to me immediately so we can figure this out together. Okay?"

She stares up at me with tears in her blue eyes. "Okay."

I lean over her desk and write my email address on a Post-it note. I hand her the paper. "I mean it. We're in this together. I'm not going to let anything bad happen to you."

I pull her to my chest and hold her in my arms. I know she feels lost without her twin, but I want her to know that she doesn't have to feel so lonely anymore because she has me. I'll be there for her.

Chapter Thirteen

"I Write Sins Not Tragedies" – Panic At the Disco

Frannie

It's been five days since I replied to my blackmailer and still haven't received any word back. Every day that I sit here in this place, I grow more and more paranoid. I'm driving myself batty analyzing every single thing that every single person does here. Any one of them could have sent that email, and I'm determined to find out who in the hell is fucking with me.

Tyke leans his head back against the couch in my office and sighs. "Do you think it's Arnold? The guy's not right upstairs and could've been stalking you."

I sag my shoulders. "I don't know, Tyke. It's possible, I guess. I just don't know what he'd gain from doing this to us."

"You don't know what the asshole wants because they haven't replied with their demands, and yet the video still hasn't gone viral. I've got Trip keeping tabs on the tabloids for us, too."

I squeeze my eyes shut. "You told your brother?"

Tyke shrugs. "Don't get your panties in a bunch. He won't say anything. Besides, he's cool with it."

I raise my eyebrows in surprise. "He is? He doesn't care that you're screwing your therapist?"

He pulls me into his lap. "First off, this is more than just sex. We've already established that. Secondly, my brother's happy when I'm happy, and you, Frannie Mead, make me happy."

I melt into him as he kisses my temple.

He pushes my hair away from my neck and nuzzles into me. "I can't wait until we can be together without all this secrecy."

"You really think there's a future for us outside this place?"

"Of course I do," he states confidently. "Don't you?"

"I dream about it, but I don't know how it will all work if we don't see each other very often."

He sighs. "It's true I'm away a lot, but that won't stop me from flying out to you every spare chance I get, and you can fly out to wherever I'm at on the road."

I stiffen in his arms. "I don't fly."

"At all?" he questions.

"Like *ever*."

"Can I ask why?"

Since we seem to be at a point where we are truthful with one another, I begin to tell him exactly why I won't step foot on a plane again. "My sister...her plane went down in the Atlantic Ocean. None of the passengers survived, and all that was ever found of the plane was a partial piece of wing. Ever since then, I've been deathly afraid. It's been four years, and yet I can't seem to get over it."

"That's understandable," he says as he rubs my back. "I think that reaction is perfectly normal."

"Well, my family doesn't think so. My mother thinks it's ridiculous that I can't get past my fear and pretend like they aren't evil killing machines."

"Maybe someday you'll feel differently but until then, no one should push you."

"Thank you." I wrap my arms around him, loving that he seems to understand my feelings about the situation.

I sigh as we stay locked in our embrace. "What are we going to do about this email? Do you think we need more time apart to throw people off our scent?"

"What good would that do? They've already caught us on tape. There's not much we can say to dispute that," he answers.

"I don't know." I pull back so I can look him in the eyes. "We can always deny it. The video doesn't zoom in on our faces too much."

He shakes his head. "Believe me; your face was pretty clear. They'll know it's you."

I toy with his hair, thinking of a new plan. "Well, what if you appear interested in someone else here? Do you think that would lead people away?"

"No. That's a terrible idea. And I won't do that to you." The tone in his voice is adamant.

"Come on, Tyke. We'll both know it's just for show, and I'm not asking you to sleep around—just be extra nice to other women." I take a deep breath. "I know it's a crazy, irrational plan, but will you just try until we can figure out who is behind all this?"

He huffs. "I don't like it."

"For me?" I bat my eyes at him. "Once it's over and you're out of here, we can come clean. By then it won't matter as much if the world finds out we're together."

His body shifts below me, uncomfortable. "Okay, I'll do it, but you have to promise that you won't get all jealous because this is your idea. If you start acting like a psycho stalker, I'm done with the fucking game."

"Fair enough. But I promise to keep my inner crazy on lockdown."

For the next week, after our little plan of diversion is set in motion, Tyke does exactly as he promised. He's overly nice to every female within five feet of him, but I can honestly say it doesn't bother me in the slightest because the moments when no one is looking and he winks at me, I know that I'm the only one on his mind. That he's being overly flirtatious to protect me. Because I asked him to.

It's a completely weird and screwed-up situation, but one I feel is completely necessary until we find out who in this place has dirt on us.

While most of the women respond to his innocent come-ons with blushes, smiles, and giggles, there's only one person who seems to be taking it a little too seriously.

Josie Sullivan.

It's no secret Josie demands to be the center of attention, but she's completely eating up every ounce of what Tyke throws at her. I know it shouldn't bother me that's she's reading too much into what's going on between them, but I can't help it. Her body is amazing, and she's a celebrity. Any woman who tells you that type of competition doesn't worry them is a liar. I wish he would focus on someone else more, but Josie seems to be putting herself in close proximity to him all the time now.

I turn my attention back to the products in front of me. While Kimmy is on the other side of the store buying cleaning supplies for the facility, I'm being sneaky and checking out pregnancy tests in the pharmacy aisle.

It's been three weeks since Tyke and I first had sex, which by my calendar makes my period a week late. I know it's probably just the stress of everything going on causing the delay, but it doesn't hurt to know for sure.

Once I find the test that most doctors seem to recommend, I quickly pay for it and shove it into my purse before I go and search for Kimmy.

The entire ride back to Serenity, I listen quietly as Kimmy drives and babbles on about her design school courses. It's totally rude of me to just pretend that she has my full attention, but I can't help being distracted by the fifteen-dollar test that has the potential to be a gamer changer.

"Frannie, are you okay?" Kimmy asks. "You seem distracted. Is it Tyke?"

I shake my head. Even though Kimmy knows that Tyke and I've fooled around, I don't feel the need to divulge any additional information about our relationship, especially until I find out who is behind the video.

It could be anyone, so I'm on high alert with all my secrets.

"No. That was a one-time thing. He hasn't crossed my mind really since then," I lie.

She frowns. "I've noticed him being overly flirtatious with everyone but you lately. Do I need to nut punch him for being a dick?"

I burst out laughing. For some reason, the thought of petite Kimmy punching Tyke is comical. "No. But thank you for the offer."

She smiles. "What are friends for?"

It's a nice thought—being friends—but I can't allow myself to give in to the idea, no matter how genuine she seems. She has stuck to her word about keeping my secret, though, or at least I think so. Wayne hasn't let on that he knows anything if she has blabbed to him.

After I say my goodbyes to Kimmy, I make my way down to the little cottage that's been my home for the last month and quickly lock myself inside. The plastic sack crinkles in my hands as I pull the pregnancy test out of it and read the directions. It says it's best to use the first morning's urine, but I can't hold out until tomorrow.

After peeing on the cotton tip of the white stick as instructed, I place the cap on and place it on a piece of toilet paper on my sink. I stare anxiously as I watch the saturated cotton inside the test begin to change the lines on the test. When not one, but two pink lines pop up in the window, my breath catches.

No.

No. No.

No. No. NO!

This is the completely wrong time for this to be happening. I knew it was a possibility, but never did I think it was going to actually happen. Tyke doesn't want a baby. He told me that himself. And while I've just came around to the idea of trying to let my guard down

167

and become something more than a friend who fucks from him from time to time, I know we're not ready for this.

Neither of us.

Chapter Fourteen

"It Goes Like This" – Thomas Rhett

Tyke

The ringtone on my phone wakes me from a deep sleep. I roll over and grab it off the nightstand and answer when I see Trip's name pop up.

"No rest for the wicked or what?" I ask.

He chuckles. "I've been up working, smartass. The track has a huge event coming up, so we're running around like crazy trying to get things ready."

"Damn, another event? You're making money hand over fist now with that place."

"I don't know about all that, but it's definitely doing a lot better financially than when I first got there. My girl has done some amazing things to promote our business."

My brother's happy. Probably the happiest I've ever seen him. I'm glad he's found someone. I didn't understand his infatuation with Holly before, but now that I've met Frannie, I'm starting to understand wanting to spend all your time with one woman.

"That's great, Trip," I tell him. "But what does all that have to do with calling me before the rooster even fucking crows?"

"Sorry, bro, it was the only time I'd have time to call you today. I wanted to let you know that Noel spoke with the label yesterday. They want the new album done within two months. Do you have any songs for it yet?"

I sigh. "No, not yet, but I'll get cracking, and as soon as I get out of here, hopefully I'll have some decent lyrics and melodies together so we can go straight into the studio."

"Awesome. I knew we could count on you. We'd never be able to make the new record without your crazy ass. You're a lyrical genius. Hold on, Tyke." The rustling sound of him putting his hand over the receiver while he speaks to someone else pours through my phone. "Sorry, man, gotta go. I'll call you soon."

"All right. Later," I reply before we disconnect.

As I lay there, Frannie's face is the first thing that pops into my mind as I think about leaving to reunite with my band.

This idea Frannie has about me hitting on other women to draw attention away from us messing around is the stupidest fucking thing I've ever heard. I tried to convince her that it was a terrible idea, but she was convinced it wasn't. She can be very persuasive because all I want to do is make her smile.

I hum a rhythm that's been working its way into my brain over the last few days. For some reason, the urge to get back to writing music has hit me hard. I'm not sure if it's the small piece of happiness I've found recently with having Frannie in my life, or the fact that I want to finish this album and get not only the band back on track, but myself as well.

I pull out my phone to type down the lyrics that hit me as I think of the melody.

You . . . you don't see how much you mean to me.

How you make me work hard to be the man I'm supposed to be.

Frannie's face is all I see as I type out the words. It's true she probably doesn't see how I really feel about her. I mean, hell, why the fuck would she believe that a recovering drug addict like me, stuck in this place, would actually have feelings for her? I'm sure she still thinks this is a relationship of convenience.

I mumble a few more sentences but nothing seems fitting so I close the app and check my email. It's then I see the email that Frannie forwarded to me of the video of us fucking in the woods.

I can't resist. I open the video and turn the sound down low. My eyes drift down to Frannie's face and the expression she wears is absolutely the sexiest fucking thing I've ever seen. She wants me. She needs me.

My cock begins to throb and swell as I remember what it feels like to be buried deep inside her. Absently, my hand drifts down into my boxers and I grab my shaft. The only way I'm going to get rid of this boner now is to rub one out.

I pause the video, needing something to help me with the job at hand. I reach into my shower bag and grab a bottle of lotion before pulling my shirt off and lying down. My boxer briefs quickly get shoved down my hips, before I squeeze a small amount of lotion into my hand. The sensation of my fingers around my stiff cock, stroking, is nowhere as pleasurable as Frannie's pussy, but it'll have to do.

I restart the video, the moans coming from Frannie, coupled with watching me fuck her on film quickly causes every nerve in my body to tingle. My pace quickens and the moment I see Frannie come, I lose it. I close my eyes and try to fool my brain into thinking I'm balls deep in her, sliding against her slick flesh while giving into my own pleasure.

I shoot my load all over my stomach and lower chest as I stifle back a moan. I rub my thumb over my head and wipe the rest of the dripping come off my tip.

Holy fuck. This woman is going to be the death of me if I don't start banging her more than twice a month. After cleaning up, I'm finally relaxed, and drift off to sleep with thoughts of Frannie on my mind.

The next morning I make it down to breakfast before Timothy even has time to make it up the stairs and get me. Ever since jerking off to that video of Frannie I've been horny as fuck. I can't wait until all this treatment bullshit is over and I can get back to a normal life—one that includes fucking Frannie whenever I want.

Most of the other patients—or *clients* as all the staff call us—are already in their seats ready for breakfast. Frannie isn't here yet, so I sit next to an empty chair to save it for her.

"Hey, hot stuff," Josie purrs as she plops down in Frannie's seat. "You're looking good enough to eat this morning."

Her come-ons make me want to roll my eyes so fucking bad. This girl is so not my type—not that I even had a type, looking back on all the random groupies I've fucked around with over the last year. And Gabby Rodriguez, I don't even want to think about that screwed-up mess. Trip had been right about her. She was absolutely no good for me.

Josie's still staring at me, waiting on me to flirt back with her like I've been doing lately. I'm really not in the mood to put up with this little game today, but I don't want to piss off Frannie, so I play along.

I lean back and casually throw my around the back of Josie's chair and give her my most devilish smirk. "Well, why don't you come take a bite?"

She giggles and twirls her bottle-blond hair around her index finger as she slides her tongue along her top teeth. "Maybe I just might."

I'm still pretending to be loving this wicked banter between Josie and I as I turn my head and notice Frannie staring at me with a pained expression.

Fuck.

I told her this wasn't a good idea.

She's pissed. How I'm ever going to drive it home to her that I am not some fucking douchebag, out to hurt her?

That's it. This little fucking game is over. Either way, Frannie is going to be pissed at me, but I'd much rather it be for me doing the right thing and not flirting with people in front of her face.

The rest of the meal, Frannie doesn't even look at me. Josie, on the other hand, won't leave me the fuck alone.

For the third time in the last ten minutes, I shove Josie's hand off my thigh. I furrow my eyebrows at her and tell her to stop each time, but this bitch is persistent as fuck.

I finish my meal in record time, because the second Frannie leaves this table, I'm going after her.

My gaze never moves from Frannie. Her plate has hardly been touched and yet she continues to sit there and pick at it. I need her to at least look at me.

Getting desperate for some sort of communication with her, I think of the only excuse I can to engage her in front of all these people. "Dr. Mead, is my appointment still right before lunch?"

She shakes her head but doesn't look in my direction. "No, it's after."

I knew that. It's been the same time every other day since I started here. I just needed to ask her something, *anything* that would make her speak to me.

Frannie pushes back from the table. "If you will excuse me, I have some work I need to get finished."

I go after her, careful to not seem too passionate in my chase in front of the others, but she speeds up when she notices me hot on her heels, rushing through the office door before trying to shut it in my face.

I wedge my boot against the jamb, and she narrows her eyes at me. "Go away, Tyke."

"No," I tell her firmly and push on the door. "Let me in and tell me what the fuck is going on."

She rolls her eyes but steps back reluctantly, allowing me to enter. The moment we're alone, I question, "What the hell was that back there? You promised you wouldn't get pissed. This was your idea, remember?"

She wraps her arms around her torso. "This isn't going to work, Tyke."

"Your idea? Yeah, I already told you it wouldn't."

"No, I meant you and me. We're no good for each other."

I look at her confused. "Why would you say that? I've already told you how I feel about you. If you think I'm just going to throw that away—"

"You say that now," she cuts me off. "But soon you'll be leaving. I'll be just another woman you spent a couple months with, and that will be that. There's no real tie between us—nothing forcing us to stay together when you're on the road and I'm still here."

I need to make her see how ridiculous she's being. She wants to push me away because of the fear she has that I'm just going to hurt her and leave her.

Without permission, I take her into my arms. She stills like a statue, but that doesn't stop me from grabbing the back of her neck and grazing my thumb along her delicate skin. "I know what you're doing, but I'm telling you right now that it isn't going to work. You're stuck with me, Frannie, so you might as well stop trying to push me away."

Tears pool in her blue eyes, and I can tell my words are affecting her. She relaxes in my arms and stares up at me. "I wish that were true."

"Believe it, Frannie. Believe in me. Believe in *us*. We can make this work; you just have to stop pushing me away. Trust me. I'm not going to leave you. You don't have to fear being left behind by me."

A soft sob comes out of her as she lays her head against my chest and finally returns my embrace. Pain radiates off her and I can feel it sinking into my bones. Frannie has been hurting for so long over her twin's death. I'm not sure if I'm the best qualified person for the job, but I'm going to do my damnedest to heal her broken heart.

After I leave her office, I still know deep down there are so many things left unsaid between the two of us. I'm doing my very best to open up to her and tell her exactly how I feel about her, and yet it seems like she's still keeping me at arm's length.

I take a seat out by the fountain and prop my guitar on my thigh. Every time I come out here, I think of Frannie. This has become our place.

I pop the cap off the ink pen I brought out with me and open the notebook that Frannie gave me. The melody that was running through my head last night is still screaming at me. I need to get it down on paper.

The only lyrics I can think of all have to do with how I've been feeling lately about Frannie. All this pushing and pulling has my head spinning. One minute, I'm sure everything is going to work out, and the next moment, I don't know what the fuck is happening between us. It drives me crazy, but being with her is worth it. I want to protect her from her pain. She makes me want to be better—not just for her, but for the band and myself.

As I strum the strings, words flow from me.

Push and Pull
Your skin makes me wanna touch you
Be a part of your world
So I push you, but I won't let you fall
But you're a hard girl to get through to
All I want is to hold you and tell you it'll be all right . .

When I push you . . .
You pull me back

ROCK MY BODY

There's nothing like, a love like that
A love like that
Let me ask you
When's the last time you've felt like that
Bet it was with me
Bet it was with me

I'm falling for you
It's easy to see
Without you girl, I just ain't me
There's no future without you
Give it a chance girl, give into the pull

When I push you . . .
You pull me back
There's nothing like, a love like that
A love like that
Let me ask you
When's the last time you've felt like that
Bet it was with me
Bet it was with me

I stare down at the unfinished song, and it hits me. There's definitely more than just a physical connection going on between Frannie and me. It's entirely too early to say this, but I think I might just be falling in love with her.

Chapter Fifteen

"Try" – Pink

Frannie

The guilt is really starting to get to me. Every time I give Tyke an out to walk away from me, he doesn't take it. As a matter of fact, it only makes him fight harder to stay and convince me that he's not going to hurt me.

Since Annie died, I haven't been close to anyone. Not really. My father never mentions Annie and has very little time for me. Mother is, well . . . Mother—only concerned with herself. I never really had any other girlfriends who I was close to. They were more like acquaintances because Annie was my closest friend and the men in my past were just random passersby.

But Tyke . . . he's different. Even though I'm here to help him overcome his addiction, he's helped me in more ways than I can count. He's the first person to be genuinely concerned for me, the first person who seemed upset when I cried. But not only has he helped me personally, but professionally, he's my greatest success. The one client I seem to really be getting through to.

I know I've kept my being pregnant a secret from him because I've convinced myself that he'll throw me away the first chance he gets, but maybe that isn't a fair assessment of his level of commitment. He's been nothing but accepting, and completely there for me when I've needed him over the past couple of weeks. Maybe he can handle the news of a baby.

I sigh deeply and stare down at his chart as I wait for him to come into my office for his scheduled therapy session. My mind is made up. I'll tell him what I've been keeping from him so he'll understand why I've been so upset lately.

The moment Tyke steps into my office, I frown as I take in the beaten-down expression on his face. This takes me aback because yesterday he seemed perfectly fine. It makes me wonder what happened between then and now.

I stand up and walk over to him as he shuts the door behind him. "Something wrong?"

He rubs the back of his neck. "I've been working on some songs for the new album. Trip called yesterday and we went over some of the things the label has demanded, and it worries me that we won't be able to produce enough songs in time. I've only written one so far. I'm pretty proud of it, but the rest are total shit."

I poke my bottom lip out and wrap him into a hug. Tyke sighs into my hair as he returns my embrace. "It'll come together. I believe you can do it. You're amazing."

"It wouldn't worry me if I had more time, but they want us in the studio in two weeks to record new material, and we're not ready. It's times like these, when I'm stressed, that I . . . "

He trails off, reluctant to finish his sentence, but I think I have a pretty good idea of what he's eluding to.

I pull back and stare up at him. "Do you feel like you need to use?"

Shame washes over his face at my question, telling me the answer without him even speaking. It's then I switch into therapist mode, using the techniques that I've been trained in.

"This is where you need to find the will inside to steer clear of the substances that you used for comfort when you feel stressed and anxious. You need to find other ways of calming those feelings, beside drugs."

Tears pool in his eyes. "I really am a fucking junkie, aren't I? I didn't want to believe it. Going through detox was a huge fucking wake-up that I was fooling myself, but now . . . the craving is fucking *eating* at me." He pauses. "I don't want to be this way. I don't want to feel this way every time I get news that's too hard to handle. What kind of man does that make me?"

I grab the hem of his shirt as the desperation rolls off him. I need to make him see how far he's come already, and that he's well on his way to overcoming the demons that plague him. "Listen to me, Tyke. You are a strong man. You can beat this. You have to find the will. You have to find something that's worth fighting for."

A tear slips down his cheek, and my heart breaks. The moment he reaches up to swipe it away, I grab his wrist and wipe it away for him with my free hand. "Don't be afraid to cry with me. God knows you've seen me do it enough. Let me be the person who's there for you, like you've been there for me."

"I don't want to be weak, because if I am, how am I ever going to be strong enough for you? I want to be the rock you lean on," he whispers.

I stare into his eyes as I stroke his face. "We'll be each other's rock."

With that, I kiss his lips, quieting his fear that he's not man enough for me. His mouth works in time with mine as his body begins to relax against me. This is helping take his mind off the anxiety he's feeling, but I can tell we've got a long way to go before he has a firm handle on his addiction. Being able to divert his need to use will be huge for him—once he figures out healthy ways to deal with issues that stress him.

For the time being, I know telling him that I'm pregnant won't be good for him. He's got enough stress, worrying about the band's new album, without me springing the news on him that I'm having his baby. I'll tell him, when the time is right.

When I'm sure that he can handle the news without relapsing.

The cell on my desk rings just as I'm finishing up my notes from Arnold's session. Mother's name flashes across the screen, and I sigh while I answer. "Hello, Mother."

"Francine, darling. It's so good to hear your voice," she replies and I stiffen, recognizing this tone as the one she uses when she's trying to butter me up.

"What is it now, Mother?" I ask, snapping the laptop closed.

"Is it a crime for a mother to simply call her daughter and be nice?"

I roll my eyes, because for her, yes, it is. "I know there's something you want or else you wouldn't be calling."

"Oh, all right," she huffs. "There is something I want, but I would also like to see you. I miss you, darling."

I raise my eyebrows. That's the first time she's wanted to spend time with me in a long while.

"I'm going out of town next weekend, and I'm asking you to please watch Spencer and Ruby for me. Last time I had to leave them with Nickolas, and the poor dears were shaking little messes when I returned. I don't want to inflict any additional trauma on them. Will you please do this for me?"

Poor Nickolas, my parents' private chef, hates those two damn dogs almost as much as I do. I bet he was fuming that he got stuck being their caregiver when I refused my mother's request last time. Mother's lucky that Ruby and Spencer weren't poisoned by the time she returned.

"Oh please, Frannie." My mother's plea sounds genuine, and while I'm not completely thrilled about the idea of dog sitting the two little mongrels, I do like that she's actually sounding sincere this time.

Besides, a little distance between Tyke and me might be a good thing. A little time for me to get away from this place and reflect on my situation, and how I'm going to break the news to him, might be beneficial.

"I'll do it," I tell her. "I'll take the train first thing Friday morning and be there by dinner."

"Oh, thank you." The relief in her voice comes through crystal clear. "I can't wait to see you, dear. It's been too long since I've seen my girl."

Her last sentence chokes me up. I remember a time when she would have ended that same line in the plural because she would be referring to both Annie and I. It was nice back then. When we felt almost like a family, versus this discombobulated mess we are now.

"I'll see you soon," I tell her before I end our call.

I stare down at my hand, resting protectively over my stomach, and wonder if it will be as easy for me to pretend this baby didn't exist when I give it away to some family who is ready for a child. Handling the loss of my sister has been devastating, and I just don't know how I'm going to handle carrying a child that I'm eventually going to give away.

I wrap my arms around my torso and inhale deeply. Tyke's scent lingers on my skin and clothes. It was harder than expected to tell him goodbye this morning, but it's something I'm going to have to deal with very soon.

The train pulls into the station, and I quickly gather my bag. That's the thing about quick trips back home—packing is very light.

I make my way to the front of the station, smiling when I find our driver, Ricardo, wearing his signature black suit and white gloves as he waits by my family's black Lincoln Town Car. "Ricardo, it's so nice to see you. How are the little ones?"

He takes my bag from me and opens the back door. "They're excellent, Ms. Mead. The little one just had his fourth birthday last weekend."

"Four?" I say as I climb into the backseat. "I can't believe he's that old already."

"Time flies when it comes to children. My oldest will be fourteen this year," he says with a proud smile that accentuates his white teeth against his dark complexion. "Having children is the most rewarding thing in the world."

"I bet," I reply before he shuts me inside, and I place a protective hand over my stomach.

One day, when I'm settled and with a man who's ready for a family, I'd love to experience the same joy that Ricardo does. I think having a child will be an amazing experience, and I'm looking forward to that someday, but just not right now.

Once he deposits my bag in the trunk, we head toward my family home, and it doesn't take long before we reach Lincoln Park. The moment Ricardo pulls onto Burling Street my palms begin to sweat. It's not that I'm scared of my parents or anything, but it's just so hard for me to be here without Annie. Everything in this place has a memory of her attached to it.

He pulls up to the largest house on the street, and I stare up at the immaculate gray home with all its breathtaking architectural features. It wasn't until I grew up and started mingling with people outside our family's social circles that I realized how lavishly we actually lived. Before losing my sister, my world was all about proper social standings and finding the right CEO husband who would enable me to continue in that manner. I didn't know that the rest of America didn't have the same upbringing I did.

After losing Annie, and getting lost in the wild life of college crowds, I learned that engaging in meaningless sex took my mind off my pretentious world, and made me forget what it would be like to endure it without my confidant.

Ricardo opens the car door and I step out, beginning my ascent toward the house. The moment I enter the house, Ruby and Spencer come sprinting down the staircases, barking as loud as they possibly can. I kneel down and pet them as they wag their tails and lick my hands, causing me to smile.

Damn those cute little pests for making me love them even though I don't want to.

"Francine? Is that you?" Mother glides into the room wearing a pressed skirt and blouse.

Her dark hair is pulled into a tight French twist, and her makeup is perfect. To most women, this would be office attire, but for my mother, it's her outfit for just another day around the house.

I stand to greet her. "Hello, Mother."

She stretches her arms out and embraces me in a firm hug before pulling back and kissing both of my cheeks. "Let me take a look at you."

Her eyes inspect me carefully as she pulls away, and she pulls my arms out to my side. "You look different. Have you met a man?"

My mouth gapes open. How in the hell could she possibly know that?

I'm at a loss for words for a moment, stunned by her perceptiveness, but I do know that I'm not ready to tell her about Tyke just yet. "Why would you assume there's a man?"

She smiles slyly and arches a perfectly manicured brow. "Because, Dear, you're practically glowing . . . which means there's a man."

I laugh and roll my eyes. "You and your assumptions. No, there's no one."

"Well, good." She takes my arm and wraps it in the crook of hers as she leads me off to the parlor, where she just came from. "I've got someone I want you to meet."

Oh, boy. Here she goes—matchmaking again. When is she ever going to learn that these stuffy suit types don't do a thing for me? Wishful thinking on her part, I guess.

We enter the room and my father and a couple of men in suits are standing around, puffing on cigars and drinking brandy from expensive crystal glasses. My father is fifteen years my mother's senior, pushing well into his sixties. His hair is a little more silver than the last time I saw him six months ago and his fitted gray suit hugs his thin body.

The moment Father spots me, he smiles and pulls the cigar from his mouth. "Gentlemen, I'd like you all to meet my daughter, Francine, who is home for the weekend."

I walk over and hug him and kiss his cheek, knowing that while I'm here I have to play the part of doting daughter. "Hello, Daddy."

The men take turns greeting me, each taking the time to shake my hand and introduce themselves to me. It's not until I get to the last man when I understand that this is the one Mother intended for me to meet.

He's tall, broad-shouldered, and extremely handsome. The definition in his chest is obvious, even through the tailored jacket and dress shirt he's wearing. The dark hair on his head is styled neatly, complementing the black-rimmed glasses perched on his nose, and the hint of a smile playing along his lips tells me that he's checking me out as well.

"Hello, Francine. I'm Jacob Myers, CEO of Mead Enterprises." He gives me a firm handshake that lasts just a little too long as I process what he's just said.

I see exactly where Mother was hoping this would go, but I hate to break it to her that I'm simply not interested in any man who isn't Tyke Douglas right now.

I smile politely. "It was so nice to have met all of you, but if you'll excuse me, I just arrived and need to get settled in."

A collective "It was nice to meet you" response echoes around the room, and my mother's lips pull into a tight line as I pass by her. Clearly, she's disappointed that I'm not all over my father's new hunky CEO, but she's just going to have to get over that.

I toss my purse onto the bed and then flop down next to it. I don't know why I'm so exhausted. It's not like riding on the train is hard work or anything, but all I feel like doing is napping.

My phone vibrates inside my purse, and I dig around to retrieve it. Ever since that stupid video email came in, I've been obsessive about checking any and all messages the moment I receive them. It's nerve-racking waiting on a response from the blackmailer.

My email app shows one new message so I quickly open it, and my heart begins to race when I see that it's from the same anonymous address.

This subject line simply says: *You're Not Special.*
I swallow hard as I read on.

Thought you'd want to know what he does behind your back. Imagine all the fun he'll have on the road.

Sincerely,
A Concerned Citizen

When I scroll down further, I find a photo attachment. I click on it and gasp the moment the picture appears on my screen. Tears burn my eyes before they spill out because there, clear as day, are Tyke and Josie . . .
Kissing.

Chapter Sixteen

"Change" – Deftones

Tyke

The strings beneath my calloused fingers vibrate with the rhythm of the new song I'm working on. It's a grungy, up-tempo beat that could definitely be considered single material. I hum the bar as I pause and jot down a few notes into my notebook.

I can't wait to get into the studio and lay down some tracks to a few of the songs I've written over the past couple of days. Ever since Frannie and I opened up to one another, I feel like a weight has been lifted, allowing the creativity to radiate from me. It's been a long time since I felt so focused.

"Hey, Tyke," Josie's voice cuts through my concentration and grates on my nerves.

This chick is fucking relentless.

"Hey."

I answer without glancing in her direction, hoping she'll take the hint that I'm busy and go away. Unfortunately, that doesn't work, and instead, she plops down next to me on the bench in front of the fountain and sighs. "I've never been out here before. It's nice. A little too quiet for my taste, but nice."

"Well maybe you should go back inside, then," I snap, giving her a more direct hint that she's not wanted out here.

It doesn't faze her because she shrugs. "I'd rather not if you're out here."

I shake my head. "Look, Josie, you and me . . . it's not going to happen." She opens her mouth to protest but I quickly cut her off. "*Ever.*"

Her lips twist and her head snaps back. "You can't turn me down. Men don't do that to me. Not when I offer then what I'm about to give you."

I scrub my hand down my face and count to ten in my head so I don't fucking lose it with this pushy bitch. "Read my fucking lips: I'm—not—interested. Go away."

She flinches, but then grins before reaching over and grabbing my face and smashing her lips to mine. This takes me by surprise, and I quickly shove her off me. I wipe my mouth with the back of my hand as I stand. "Don't ever touch me again."

The grin on her face falls when she takes in the contempt in my expression.

I don't give her a chance to say anything else before I grab my shit and get the fuck out of there. Flirting with these unstable women was a horrible fucking idea. I'm so glad Frannie finally came to her senses because I don't know how much longer I could have put up with Josie's psychotic, pushy ass.

When I get back to my room, I pull out my phone and text Frannie. She only left this morning, but I miss her already. This place isn't the same without her.

I fire a text off to let her know that I'm thinking of her.

Tyke: I miss you.

I lay my phone down on the nightstand and then drift off to sleep as I wait on her response.

The next morning, I shove my legs over the side of the bed and sit up. I scrub the sleep out of my eyes and then reach for my cell.

No response from Frannie. A frown creeps over my lips. I'm severely disappointed. I think our relationship is at a point where I warrant a reply, especially considering it only takes a couple seconds to respond back to a text.

I finish getting ready, deciding not to let it get me down too much because it's possible she was really busy, or her phone could have been dead after traveling. As soon as I make it to the dining room, I find myself face-to-face with Josie, who doesn't look too pleased to see me this morning. Her glare tells me that if she could shoot me and get away with it, I'd already be a dead man.

I think the bitch finally got the hint. All it took was for me to be a major dick to make her understand that she and I weren't going to fucking happen.

Throughout breakfast, I obsessively check my phone like a crushing schoolgirl, waiting for Frannie to message me back. I've sent her three more texts but won't allow myself to send any more because it would just make me look even more desperate.

It's not until it's nearly dinnertime that I begin to worry, choosing to wander around outside because I'm too antsy to stay in the main house.

Mine and Frannie's relationship is still pretty fresh, and we've got a lot to learn about each other as we continue to grow together, so I'm not sure if this lack of communication is an indication that she's pissed at me for something that I'm unaware that I've done, or if she's just busy. I need to let her know that if I've done something, I'm sorry.

I set out toward her cottage, completely unsure if I can even get in, but that's the best place to leave a note without it being discovered.

One of the things I've learned during this treatment program is to tell people exactly how I feel, instead of bottling my emotions up. Doing that was one of the things that pushed me deeper into my downward spiral. I hope Frannie, of all people, will understand that I need communication.

When her cottage comes into view, I quicken my pace and rush to the front door. I turn the knob, but it's locked tight.

"Damn," I mutter to myself, before heading around to the side of the building.

The first window I try is locked, too, but the second opens with ease the moment I push up on the glass. I glance around, and when I'm sure that nobody's watching, I shove the window completely open and hoist myself inside.

It looks exactly the same as the last time I was in here—the last day I was buried deep inside her.

I know it's a touch creepy, but I pick up a pillow off her bed and bring it up to my face. Her flowery scent invades my senses as I inhale deeply.

It makes me miss her even more.

After I put the pillow down, I make my way to the small desk across the room and pull a pick from my pocket and write "Miss You" on the back of it. I place it on the desk, along with a piece of notebook paper with a single song title on it: ""What If I Was Nothing" —All That Remains."

My hope is that, no matter what she's pissed at me about, she'll forgive me and understand that I'm not going anywhere.

I'm humming the song, thinking of how accurate the lyrics are in describing how I feel toward Frannie, when I glance down into the small wicker bin beside her desk. A small pink box with the word *pregnancy* catches my eye. I suck in a quick breath.

"What the fuck?" I question out loud, bending down and pulling the box out of the trash.

The words *pregnancy test* make my eyes widen and my heart does a double thump in my chest. I recall our little incident in the woods, knowing the fact that I came inside her, if Frannie *is* pregnant, that baby belongs to me.

I swallow hard and lick my suddenly dry lips. I told her I wasn't ready to be a father. If she's pregnant, no wonder she's not speaking to me. I probably seem like a complete fucking asshole right now.

The urgent need to find out if she is pregnant rushes through me. I could try calling her, but seeing as how she's not even returning my texts, she's probably even less likely to take a call from me.

I flip the wicker basket upside down, dumping all of the contents on her floor. Nothing but paper and other pieces of trash litter the ground.

No test.

I jam my fingers into my hair, gripping handfuls of it in my hands as I rush into the bathroom and find another trashcan. I flip that one over as well, thinking it's empty, too, until a ball of toilet paper makes a small *thud* as it drops onto the wood floor.

My hands shake and I reach down to unroll the paper, revealing a small plastic stick. I let out a slow breath through pursed lips as I flip the stick over in my hands, exposing the little results window. Two pink lines appear, clear as day.

I rush back into the main room, and rummage around in the mess I've made on the floor before I find the box. My eyes quickly scan the back panel until they find confirmation that two pink lines mean that Frannie's pregnant.

Pregnant.

HOLY FUCKING SHIT!

I brace myself against the desk, and I clamp my eyes shut.

Fuck.

Shit.

Dammit.

I pinch the bridge of my nose as my anxiety levels hit a new all-time high and every muscle in my body shakes. It was situations like these that drove me to prescription drugs in the first place—the feeling of being lost in a situation that I can't change.

The need to use something to help me relax crawls through my skin, turning on its seductive promise to make me feel better. The thought of giving in hits me hard. I could turn away and leave this place: go find something that will settle my nerves and make me forget.

As soon as that last thought rolls through my brain, I realize what will happen if I walk out of here. Not only will I be walking away from sobriety, I'll be walking away from Frannie, basically confirming that she was right not to trust me. That I'm a selfish bastard who runs from things, who hides in a world where things stay foggy just so I don't have to deal with my problems. It would kill me if she thought of me that way.

I meant what I told her the other day: I *want* to be a stronger man for her.

Standing in that little cottage, the need to stay clearheaded hits me like a ton of fucking bricks. I don't want to pretend. I want to deal with the situation. I want Frannie to let me in and allow me to help her get through this.

Together.

Chapter Seventeen

"Say It" – Blue October

Frannie

All weekend long, I ignore every message Tyke sends me. One thing my blackmailer had correct is that I'm nothing special to him, because if I really mean something to him, he wouldn't be lip-locking with Josie Sullivan the moment I'm out of sight. If I were special, kissing her wouldn't have crossed his mind.

I turn my phone on and swipe my finger over the screen as the train approaches the Cincinnati terminal. A new message catches my eye, and I click on the little envelope. The anonymous emailer has gotten a little braver. They haven't allowed so much time to elapse between contacts this time. The subject line of this email simply reads: *It's Time.*

By now you know that I'm capable of digging up dirt. You should know that I've done my research on you as well. Don't think I don't know exactly who your father is, and how much money he's worth. Between Tyke Douglas and yourself, you should be able to come up with enough money to allow me to live a pretty comfortable lifestyle. So here is my demand. I want two million dollars, in cash, brought to me by the end of this week. That should be ample time to pool your funds. On Friday I will email you again with instructions on where to leave the money. If you're thinking of blowing off my request, Dr. Mead, I'd think again. I'm sure a nice woman like you has plenty of skeletons in her closet if someone chose to dig around enough.

Sincerely,
A Concerned Citizen

I scroll down and find an old picture of me with my top off at a college frat party attached to the email. This was taken a couple years ago when I was in the height of my random sexual Olympics. I don't even remember the name of the guy whose lap I'm straddling in the photo. One thing's for sure: I won't give whoever this is sending me these emails any additional incentive to go digging around in my past. No good will come of it.

After I collect my bag, I exit the train and make it out to passenger pick up, fully expecting Wayne to be waiting for me like the last time I arrived, but I'm surprised when I spot Kimmy leaning against her beat-up red Honda, a huge smile on her face.

"Surprise! I volunteered to pick you up," she says as she greets me with a hug.

I stiffen in her arms, not expecting the warm greeting. "Thank you."

She pulls back and then heads toward her trunk. "It was no problem. Besides, I figured it would be a good time for us to talk."

While I highly doubt the blackmailer is Kimmy, I don't like the way she said that. It's like she knows some juicy secret that she can't wait to spill, and it puts me on edge.

Traveling down the highway toward Serenity, I glance over at Kimmy, silently willing her to spill whatever beans she's holding.

Finally, she takes a breath and asks, "What's going on with you and Tyke?"

I shove my hair back from my face. I know she knows about us, but I'd like to keep exactly what she knows to a minimum. "Nothing more than what you already know."

She shakes her head. "Oh, I don't think so. There's got to be more. You should've seen him this weekend."

The picture of him kissing Josie floods my brain, and I can honestly say I didn't miss him at all after seeing that. As a matter of fact, just thinking about him doing that pisses me off.

I sit quietly, trying to pretend that I don't want to hear what exactly Tyke did this weekend, but my damn curious brain wins out and I ask, "What should I have seen?"

"Ha!" Kimmy laughs and smacks the steering wheel. "I knew there was more than just sex going on with the two of you. If I tell you what I saw, will you tell me about what's going on?"

I should say no, but it would be nice to get some of these feelings off my chest. It might be stupid and naive for me to confide in her, but I haven't had anyone to talk to about what's going on with me. Talking to Kimmy would be nice.

"Deal."

"Awesome." She grins even wider. "Okay, so while you were away, it was like he was lost. Tyke moped around, checking his phone every five minutes. It was totally cute. Of course, no one else but me seemed to notice how sad he was because he keeps pretty much to himself most of the time, with the exception of his random flirtiness last week, but that's beside the point. That guy has it bad for you."

Warmth grows inside my chest at the thought of Tyke missing me, but the fuzzy feeling is instantly ripped away when I think about that picture I was sent. "I don't know, Kimmy."

"Wait. Hold up. You think he doesn't? Have you *seen* the way the man looks at you?" she asks, flabbergasted.

I stare straight ahead as I think about the possibility that the blackmailer may have just been at the right place to catch a picture that would make Tyke appear to not give a shit about me. It's possible, I suppose, that I have the situation all wrong, but a picture speaks a thousand fucking words.

"Now, I've told you a little something. You going to tell me how serious the two of you are?" Kimmy's question pulls me away from deep thought.

I sigh. A promise is a promise.

"We're pretty serious, I guess," I tell her honestly. "We barely know each other, and yet when we're

199

together, it always feels so intense. I don't think we're going to work out, though."

"I'm sorry. That sucks." She frowns. "He seems deep, like he's always got something on his mind, and a hard person to get to know."

She's quiet for a moment and then she smiles. "When you say intense . . . does that carry over into the bedroom?"

I blush fiercely, and decide it can't hurt to be a little candid about our sex life.

"It does."

I glance over at her, and we both burst out in a fit of giggles. It feels good to laugh. It's been far too long since I've done that.

The moment we park at Serenity, I make my way to the cottage to drop off my bag before I set off to find Tyke. I need answers. After unlocking the door, I set my bag just inside the entry without going all the way in and then quickly relock the door.

I pull my cell out of my pocket and send a quick text to Tyke.

Frannie: I'm back. Want to see you. Where are you?

I keep my phone in my hand as I make my way to the main house, hoping that even though I've ignored his texts, he'll answer mine. I check the time on my phone and see that it's almost time for dinner to be over, so I make my way toward the dining hall in hopes of finding him. Before I get there, my phone chimes with a new message.

Tyke: By the fountain in five.

It's time we get everything out in the open. If he means what he says about wanting to be with me, then now is the time for him to prove it. He can also tell me why in the hell he was kissing Josie Sullivan.

When I come to the top of the hill, I allow my eyes to travel down the path and find Tyke, sitting on a bench, facing the fountain. He's too far away for me to be able to read his expression, but he's staring straight ahead, like he's lost in deep thought.

The moment I step into his line of sight he stiffens, which takes me aback because I don't think he knows that I know he kissed Josie.

"Hey," I say as I approach him.

He leans forward and rests his elbows on his thighs as he rubs his palms together. "Why didn't you text me back this weekend, Frannie?"

I bite my lip to keep from lashing out. I don't want to be the cause of a relapse. So instead of saying anything, I stand there and allow the silence to wrap around us.

Tyke stares at me for a long moment, gauging my reaction. When I don't reply, he closes his eyes and takes a deep breath. "Were you ever going to tell me, or were you hoping I would go away and never find out?"

My mouth gapes open, but I quickly shut it. "I don't know what you're talking about."

"You don't, huh?" Tyke stands and reaches into his back pocket and pulls out a slender piece of plastic. "Then tell me what the fuck this positive pregnancy test was doing in your trash."

The breath whooshes out of me, and I clutch my chest as the guilt sets in. "You broke into my cottage?"

"Don't try to change the fucking subject." When I still don't answer, he raises his voice. "Tell me!"

I knew I should've told him, but I had my reasons for keeping quiet. "Why would I? You don't want a baby, remember?"

"Don't give me a bunch of bullshit, Frannie. It was wrong of you not to tell me, and you know it. I told you if something happened, we'd deal with it together. If you ever expect a relationship between us to work—"

A sarcastic laugh bubbles out of my throat. "What makes you think I want anything to do with you now?"

"You don't mean that." Pain flickers over his face.

It's a low blow, but he needs to know that he hurt me and that I can never trust him again.

I square my shoulders as I fight back tears. "Why wouldn't I? It's obvious you don't care about me, so why would I want a relationship with you?"

Two long strides and he's in front of me, gripping my shoulders as I try to turn away, but he pinches my chin between his thumb and forefinger and forces me to look at him. "I don't know what's gotten into you, but I care more about you than anything else in this world right now. Frannie . . ." He swallows hard and places his hand on my stomach. "I need you. Don't break my heart. Give me a chance to be a good man to you—to *both* of you."

I close my eyes and let the tears stream down my face. It takes a moment before I have the courage to look at him again and remain strong. "Then why would the blackmailer send me a picture of you kissing Josie?"

I fully expect him to break into a string of excuses on why his lips were locked on another woman, but he doesn't do that. Matter of fact, he does something that startles me.

He laughs.

I stare up at him with a perplexed expression because I'm positive he's lost his ever-lovin' mind. "Why are you laughing? It's not funny."

He wraps his arms around me and pulls me into his chest. "Oh, Frannie. Is that why you're mad at me?"

I push my hands against his chest, attempting to shove him back a bit, but without much luck. "Yes. That's exactly why I'm upset. Explain yourself."

His shoulders relax a bit. "She kissed me out of nowhere. I shoved her off and told the bitch to take a fucking hike. Whoever is snapping pictures and videos of us was obviously spying again and caught that."

He wipes a tear off my cheek with his thumb. "I'd never hurt you like that. When I told you that you were special to me, I meant it. I'm sorry I didn't tell you right away about that kiss."

I wrap my arms around his neck and inhale his scent. "I'm sorry I didn't tell you right away that I was pregnant. It was wrong of me."

He hugs me back and whispers in my ear, "No more secrets, okay? From now on, we handle everything together."

"Speaking of everything, I finally got a response from the blackmailer."

Tyke pulls back. "Did they send demands?"

I nod. "They want two million dollars, in cash, by Friday."

"Fuck," he says. "That's a lot of fucking money to keep a goddamn video from hitting the web."

"Tell me about it."

He sighs. "Looks like you'll be hitting the road with me after the video goes viral."

I furrow my brow. "What do you mean?"

"I'm not giving anyone that much money to keep the fact that I'm with you a secret. I don't give a fuck if the world knows that I'm in love with you. I suppose you'll be jobless when Dr. Shepherd sees it, so you'll have plenty of time to come with me on the road."

My eyes widen at his admission. "You . . . you *love* me?"

He leans in and presses a soft kiss to my lips. "Yes. You and this baby are my world now. I won't let anyone hurt you. Trust me to do right by you. We'll take out this asshole together."

My heart does a double thump in my chest. Tyke Douglas just told me he loves me. Tears streak down my face as I envision a life without darkness—one filled with light. I can picture him holding me in his arms as we stand over a crib and watch our baby sleep. God, it seems so farfetched, but damn if I don't want it to be true. This could be my shot at happiness.

I trace my fingertips over the stubble on his cheek and stare into his green eyes—eyes that reflect nothing but love as he stares back at me. He's told me exactly how he feels. There's no guessing because he shows it in his actions, too, and I wonder if I can ever love him back the same way.

As soon as I allow myself to think about it, the answer swells in my chest. Yes. Yes, I can love him back because he's been nothing but kind and loving to me since we met. How can I not admit that I feel the same way about him?

I smile just before I whisper, "I love you, too."

He picks me up in his arms, and he spins us around before he sets me back on my feet and cradles my face in his hands. "I'm going to make you happy, Frannie. I swear it."

It's then that I realize my mistake. All this time I never understood that in order to find love again, all I had to do was open up my heart to the possibility of it.

Chapter Eighteen

"Nobody Knows" – The Tony Rich Project

Tyke

It's been a long time since I've felt like my life had true direction—even longer since I was in a situation that made me happy, without it having anything to do with Black Falcon.

It's hard to admit, but it took me finding Frannie and going through some majorly fucked-up shit before I could relate to what the rest of my band mates were experiencing. I finally understand why Black Falcon sometimes took a backseat to the things going on in their personal lives.

The time has finally come where I'm ready to reconnect with the guys. To sit down and have a heart-to-heart about everything that's been going on. I'm ready to sit down and open up about my feelings and tell them exactly what pushed me over the edge.

It's time they knew exactly how bad my anxiety is.

Trip answers his phone on the second ring. "Brother! How are things in the big house? Bubba make you his bitch yet?"

I roll my eyes. My brother is an absolute idiot. "Fuck you, dude. It's rehab, not prison."

Asshole.

He snickers into the phone. "Oh right, my bad." Trip pauses for a long moment before he asks, "You clean and sober yet?"

I adjust the phone against my ear. "I haven't been this clearheaded in a long time. I've confronted a lot of issues here, but we still need to talk—*really* talk. I think I'm finally ready to have a sit-down with you and the guys. I'm ready to listen to whatever you guys have to say. To show you guys that I'm back and ready to be a part of this band."

"It's about fucking time!" Trip exclaims. "I need the mad scientist back in the lab with me. This new album is going to be sick with you laying down the melodies and lyrics."

I smile, glad that we're almost back to the way we used to be. No bickering or finger pointing—

just being brothers and talking music.

We sit in silence for a moment and a thought rushes to mind. "Do you think the guys would be willing to come here?"

"So we can all sit down and talk? Yeah, man. I think they'd do anything to help you get better. Riff and Noel love you, too. They might not tell you like I do, but we all care about you, Tyke."

I rub the back of my neck as a single tear falls from my eye. "You know, you can be an all right bastard sometimes."

Trip chuckles into the phone. "I have my moments. Speaking of moments, what's going on with you and your hot doctor lady?"

I sigh and lean back in my chair. "I'm in love, man."

"In love? Shut the fuck up! No shit? Wow." Even I can hear the wonder in his voice. "It's about fucking time. You aren't getting any younger over there."

I laugh. "Fuck you, dude. Twenty-seven isn't old. I'm in my fucking prime. Speaking of prime . . . there's something else I need to tell you."

"Shit? What?" His tone suddenly growing serious. "I don't like when you say shit like that because it's usually followed by bad fucking news."

"Well, it's not bad, exactly, just . . . unexpected," I tell him.

"Hot doctor lady is knocked-up, isn't she?" he asks, but the inflection of his voice makes it seem like he already knew.

"She is," I answer honestly. "And it's mine."

"Wow. Goes to rehab to get straightened up and comes back with a woman and kid. Weren't you pissed at Noel and Riff for this very thing?"

I run my fingers through my shaggy blond hair. "I guess I didn't fucking get it before—the whole wife and kids thing. I didn't understand how anything could ever be more important than the music, you know. It's taken me getting into the same situation to see just how things change when you fall in love. I owe Noel and Riff both a huge-ass apology—you, too. I'm sorry, Trip. I'm sorry for giving you shit over Holly. I'm truly happy that you've got her."

Trip sniffs on the other end of the line. "Shit, man. Now you've gone and made me turn on the fucking waterworks like a pussy. Thank you. You don't know how fucking nice it is to hear you say that. It's good to have you back, brother."

I smile. "It's good to be back."

If I keep pacing back and forth like this, I'm going to wear off the gray paint on the porch floor. It's hard to recall a time when I've felt this nervous. Trip and the guys were already in Kentucky when I talked to my brother yesterday, so they were all game for driving out to Serenity today. Now is my time to prove to the band that I'm clearheaded and worthy of their trust again. I hope they can see that I've changed in the weeks that I've been here and welcome me back into the fold, without the crazy tension we had before.

The hum of an approaching engine catches my ear and my body stills as I stare intently at the winding driveway. A blue minivan pulls into view, and I laugh. Never in all my years did I ever expect Riff to be the guy who cruises around in one of those soccer mom mobiles.

My palms begin to sweat as the van parks, and I know it's time to face the guys. Noel hops out of the passenger seat first, Trip following a close second through the sliding side door in the back. Riff exits last.

Riff's extra tall Mohawk, tattoos, and lip ring makes the whole minivan situation even more comical. It so doesn't fit the tough guy persona he'd always portrayed to the world until he married Aubrey.

I make my way off the porch so I can get a better look at Riff's vehicle.

"Nice ride," I tell him, a smirk on my face as I clasp my hand with his and give him a quick chest bump, and then do the same with Noel and my brother.

Riff's lips twist like he's doing his best to fight back a smile. "Shut it, fucker. It's practical."

I roll my eyes. "Now you sound like Aubrey. Man, does she have you whipped."

"Ha!" A sarcastic laugh bubbles out of his throat. "You just wait. Your time's coming."

I rub the back of my neck and stay quiet, knowing that my brother has probably told them about my situation with Frannie.

"Yeah, that's right. No more smart-ass jokes now I've brought up the hot doctor lady," Riff teases. "We know all about that shit, but don't worry, we won't let it slip. Trip already told us it's a secret because she works here."

I nod my head as heat floods my cheeks.

"Pretty soon you'll be driving one of these bad boys." Riff jerks his thumb over his shoulder in the direction of his vehicle, and then points his gaze in my brother's direction. "Both of you."

Trip throws his hands in the air, palms up, in protest. "Whoa. Whoa. Whoa. There's no way in hell I'll ever be driving a fucking mom mobile. That shit's lame."

"It's going to be funny to see them both eat those words when they have kids." Noel laughs as he teams up with Riff. "They have no idea what they're in for."

Riff folds his tattooed arms over his chest. "Oh yeah."

Trip shakes his head. "Nuh-uh. Not this guy. Even when Holly and I start making babies, I'll still have a sweet-ass ride. My girl is a Mustang fanatic. There's no way she'll be caught dead driving one of those."

Noel and Riff exchange a knowing glance before both of them chuckle.

"Keep telling yourself that, dude." Noel smiles and then his gaze flits over to me for a brief moment before returning to my twin. "Your brother is about to be Team Dad soon, and he'll tell you the same thing, so you might as well get prepared because it's going to happen."

Before we have a chance to say anything else, the screen door shuts behind us and we all turn and face the porch. Frannie stands there, watching us, and she's never looked more beautiful. Her dark hair falls in long waves over her shoulders and the black skirt and blue top she wears only bring out the blue in her eyes even more. She smiles warmly, and I can't pull my gaze away from the absolute perfection before me.

"Damn," Trip says next to me. "*That's* the hot doctor lady? She's fine."

I jam my elbow into his ribs, and he grunts. I turn to Noel and Riff. "Guys, this is Dr. Francine Mead. She's my addiction therapist."

Frannie walks down the steps carefully in her heels. "Hello, gentlemen."

I walk over and take her hand, helping her off the last step. My fingers linger against her skin a little too long, but it's hard not to touch her. Keeping how I feel about her secret is so—fucking—difficult. I wish I could

211

shout it from the rooftops, but I know doing that will cause problems for her, so I force all my feelings to stay locked up inside.

I quickly introduce her to all the guys, each of them nothing but respectful as they shake her hand. A few years ago, they would've competed to catch her eye and steal her away from me, but now that they've all settled down, they only have eyes for their respective woman.

"I'm so glad you could all make it out. When Tyke told me he'd invited all of you to sit down and talk, I couldn't have been happier. He's made some real progress with his addiction, and I think it's very important that he be very open with all of you so that you can support him through his recovery. He's going to need your support, as this will be an ongoing struggle to stay clean for the rest of his life," Frannie tells them.

If I were the old me, I would've denied everything that she's saying, but I know now that I *do* have an addiction and that it's impossible to deal with things alone. I'll need the guys' support if I'm going to succeed in taking control of my life.

"I know you all have crazy schedules, so if you gentlemen will follow me, we'll get our group session started," Frannie instructs the guys, before turning and heading back toward the main house.

When the guys enter into the place that's been my home for the better part of the last two months, Trip lets out a low whistle. "Damn, the brochures on this place weren't fucking kidding. This is a palace."

"It hasn't been too bad staying here," I say as I stand beside my brother.

Trip's head turns in my direction, and there's a smart-ass grin all over his face. "I bet."

He doesn't elaborate, but I know exactly how my twin thinks. In his mind, I've been fucking the hot doctor lady all over this fancy place, but what he doesn't know is how god-awful the days I spent detoxing were. That was the worst experience I've ever lived through, and the biggest wake-up call I've ever received. Not only did this place give me the woman that I'm in love with, but a fucking eye-opener, too—showing me just how fucked up I was, and that I need to change.

Frannie leads us to her office and pushes the door open. Two folding chairs have been brought into the space across from the couch.

"Have a seat, gentlemen. Tyke," she turns to me, "you might want to grab your guitar. Playing a song may help you break the ice."

I nod. "That's a great idea. I'll be right back." I lean in to kiss her cheek, but she presses a hand against my chest, and I suddenly remember that I'm not allowed. "Sorry."

She smiles. "Soon, we won't have to worry about all that. We'll leave here together, and you can kiss me any time you want."

"You've finally decided to give us a real go?" I waggle my eyebrows. "That'll be nice."

"Indeed," she purrs. "I've decided that I can't give you up." She shrugs. "I'm addicted to you now."

I smile. "I'll be your vice any time, babe."

Frannie laughs. "Hurry back. I'll get the guys all settled in."

After rushing up to my room and grabbing my baby from the corner, I hurry back to Frannie's office.

Around the corner, I can hear Riff's voice drift into the hallway. "Do you think it's too soon for Tyke to come back on tour with us? Is he ready?"

"Tyke has done a one-eighty since he's been here. He's clearheaded and seems focused. One of his biggest priorities has been working on new songs for the next album. He's worked very hard to prove not only to all of you, but to himself, that he's ready. I think as long as he maintains that drive to succeed and stays away from any outside factors that may tempt him to use again, he'll do very well," Frannie tells the guys.

Hearing what she thinks of me without her knowing I'm listening makes me smile. I love that she believes in me.

"I think Tyke's biggest challenge will be himself. He lets everything get in his head and convinces himself that bad shit's going to happen. He's been that way since we were kids," Trip chimes in.

"He's well aware of that problem, too, and he's working hard to find other outlets for his anxiety—music being one of them," Frannie says.

"And let's not forget Gabby. We have a few more shows left with Sex Arsenal on this tour. Once he's back, she'll be trying to get her hooks into him again," Noel adds.

"I don't think that chick will be an issue anymore. He's got hot doctor lady now," Trip counters.

"Mr. Douglas, please call me Frannie," my girl corrects my brother, and it makes me smile.

"No way. Hot doctor lady fits you so much better." He laughs.

Noel clears his throat. "I think you better call her Frannie. Holly will chop off your nuts if you keep calling another woman hot."

All the guys laugh.

"Holly loves my nuts too much to hurt them," Trip jokes. "Besides, she's going to want kids someday and keep up with all you assholes popping 'em out left, right, and center. I have to tell you, though, I'm excited to be an uncle. I'm going to have fun spoiling that kid."

"That's so sweet of you, Mr. Douglas."

"Frannie, please just call me Trip. We're family now, right?"

"Okay," she replies.

It hits me. I can really picture this happening—a future with Frannie. I can see her interacting with Trip and the guys, and I know she'll get along with Lanie, Aubrey, and Holly. Frannie fits into my world perfectly.

I take a deep breath and push open the door. All eyes are on me, and it's suddenly very quiet in the room. Pressure crushes down on me as I take a seat on the couch next to the chair Frannie's sitting in, just like when we're in a session. I need to explain to these guys how I feel, and like Frannie says, the best way to do that is through music.

I adjust the guitar on my knee. "Since I've been in therapy with Frannie, she's helped me open up about my feelings though song. She's had me write down songs that express the way I feel at different points through my journey here. When I was going through my playlists, I found an old The Tony Rich Project song that really resonated with me. It's called 'Nobody Knows,' and it talks about a guy who feels so much pain inside but keeps it completely to himself, shutting everyone else out. That's exactly what I've done for the last year. I pushed you all away. I let the worry about Black Falcon falling apart eat at me so much that I had to find a way to keep myself from going crazy. I turned to prescription drugs, and when that was no longer enough, I used whatever I could get my hands on to go with it."

I strum the opening chords of the song and start to sing the lyrics. It's hard to admit so openly just how lonely I felt, so I close my eyes as I let the emotion pour out of me through the words.

When I'm finished, I take a deep breath and open my eyes to meet all of their gazes. I want them to see me— to know I'm clearheaded and one-hundred-percent dedicated to this band again.

"I convinced myself that the band no longer matter to you guys. All I saw was you had wives and girlfriends now and your priorities changed. Black Falcon was no longer the number one thing in your life like it was mine. I didn't understand what you guys were going through but now, I completely get it. Since meeting Frannie, she's made me understand that you can love two things: music and your woman. I'm sorry."

"I'm sorry too, Tyke," Noel says. "I'm sorry that we made you feel that way. Next time come talk to us before going off the deep end."

"Yeah, man, we'll understand. We won't know you're feeling left out or anxious if you don't tell us how you feel," Riff adds. "That's what we're here for, to help each other in rough times."

I nod while relief washes through me that we're finally getting everything out on the table. "I swear there will be no more drama from me. I fucked up. I know that now, and all I can do is say that I'm sorry, and that I *will* work hard, every day, to stay clean and focused."

"We know you will, man, and we're all here to support you—and kick your ass if you start to fuck up again." Trip holds his fist out for me to bump. "We're brothers." He glances at Riff and Noel, who nod in agreement. "All of us. We've got each other's backs. Always. That's what makes us the greatest fucking rock band on this planet."

I pound my knuckles into his and wipe away the tears that have fallen down my face. "I love all of you guys."

I sniff and try to regain my composure as I turn in Frannie's direction and place my hand on her knee. "I especially love this lady right here. I'll never be able to thank her enough for showing me how to open up, and letting me see that sharing my feelings is okay."

She places her small, warm hand on mine, and she smiles. "I love you, too."

Finally, after struggling for the last few years, I feel at peace, and the nagging thoughts of doom are the furthest thing from my mind because, surely, nothing this good is bound to fall through. Everything in my life seems to be falling into place.

Chapter Nineteen

"Creep" – Radiohead

Frannie

Tomorrow is the day the blackmailer will be expecting their two-million-dollar payment. Tyke and I have both come to the conclusion that we aren't paying the money, so it's inevitable that we will be outed.

Deciding to go on the road with Tyke is a huge deal. I'll essentially be leaving everything I've worked so hard for behind, but I've decided I would like to try my hand at helping the less fortunate with their addictions. I think helping people who have absolutely nothing will be a better way of dedicating my time. I'd even love to find a place where I could simply volunteer my time.

I'm focusing on the letter of resignation I've been working on for the past twenty minutes on my laptop when a knock on my office door startles me. "Come in."

Wayne strolls in, looking impeccable as ever in his pressed suit and matching graying hair. "I don't mean to disturb you, but Timothy is about to start doing random room inspections while Randall is leading a group activity outside, and I would like you to assist him so it can go faster."

I close the lid of my laptop and smile. "Sure. I'd be happy to help."

"Great, thank you. Timothy is already on the second level," Wayne informs me and exits the office just as quickly as he came in.

When I find Timothy upstairs, he has a clipboard in hand, making notes. His towering frame was intimidating when I first arrived here, but I've come to know him as a big teddy bear, one who's strictly by the book. I don't know him personally; I just know that he takes his job very seriously.

"Hi," I greet him as I step next to him. "Wayne asked me to help you toss the rooms. Are we looking for contraband? I've never searched someone's things before."

Timothy nods and pulls his gaze away from the paperwork in front of him. "We sweep everything. Addicts, especially ones who have been here before, are very good at hiding anything they don't want to be caught with. The ones sent here through court orders are the ones who are the most likely to hide things. The ones who elect to seek treatment themselves tend to be the clients who really do try to abstain from whatever they're addicted to. Don't take those assumptions as gospel, though—go through every nook and cranny. Here," he hands me a pair of rubber gloves, "You'll want to wear these."

"Got it," I say, understanding exactly what I'm to do. "What room would you like me to do first?"

He checks his clipboard again. "I just came from Tyke's room—he's clean. Arnold is next on my list, so you can take him, and I'll take the next one on the list. If you find anything, come get me and we'll inventory it together."

"Will do." I step over to the room next to Tyke's and point at the door. "This one is Arnold's?"

After I get confirmation that it is the right room, I twist the knob and head in. My hands grow clammy in the rubber gloves as I begin poking around in Arnold's drawers. Everything in here appears to be typical—socks, underwear and a never-ending collection of sweaters, which I still find fucking weird considering the temperature outside.

Next, I move on to the closet, where I find all of Arnold's khaki pants hung neatly in a row.

"Doesn't this guy ever get tired of wearing the same shit," I mumble to myself.

After I have swept every drawer and the closet, the last place I'm supposed to look, according to all the movies about prison I've ever seen, is underneath the mattress.

I pull back the cover and sheets on Arnold's neat bed and pull the pillow from its case, finding nothing. Finally, I lift the mattress, and my eyes land on the notebook I gave him a few weeks ago. I pick it up and turn it over in my hands. This doesn't look like it contains any paraphernalia, but I'm curious as to what this thing might contain since Arnold refuses to allow me to see it.

It's an invasion of privacy, but I open it up and flipped through it. There are a lot of weird scribbles—drawings of flowers and prom dresses—and it seems to have several journal entries. That doesn't surprise me at all. I shouldn't have expected it to be filled with anything other than the one incident that I know he's obsessed with.

Just as I'm about to close it, a name catches my eye, and I quickly flick the page back to make sure I really just saw what I thought I did. There, amongst the intelligible scribbles, is a heart with the words Arnie plus Annie scratched across the middle of it.

It could be a coincidence. I mean, how is it possible that one of my clients, other than Tyke, would even know about my sister. Annie is a common name, right?

I go back to the first page and begin scanning the pages with a more careful eye. Sentence after sentence, line after line, the same name appears. Annie . . . Annie . . . Annie.

"When Annie turned me down for Junior Prom at Walter Payton . . ."

"I watched Annie from afar, but she didn't know. She didn't suspect. One day, I wanted to make her love me. Annie should've been mine."

I gasp and cover my mouth with my hand. Goose bumps erupt all over my body and a chill runs down my spine as I stare at the thoughts of a clearly unwell man, but what shocks me even more and confirms my worst fear is that he lists the high school that Annie and I attended.

"Oh, my God." I remember him. Arnold is Arnie, from our high school. I remember when he asked my sister to prom, and I laughed at him while my sweet sister let him down easy. It was cruel of me to do that, but we were seventeen and I couldn't believe a four-eyed geek like Arnie thought he had a snowball's chance in hell with Annie.

I race through the book where each page chronicles Arnie following my sister to college and then on to adult life.

"I was supposed to be on that flight with her, but the idiot cab driver made me late by taking a route that lead to a traffic jam. I'll never forgive myself for not dying with her. We were meant to be together forever, dead in eternal bliss. The feelings I had toward Annie didn't go away. I had to find a way to continue my obsession. Lucky for me she had an identical twin sister. It felt too good to watch Frannie the way I did Annie. I could pretend she was my Annie. If I couldn't have Annie, I would have her substitute."

I swallow hard as things begin to click and fall into place. If Arnie went from following my sister to following me, he could've been lurking around that frat party and taken that picture of me that the blackmailer sent. That was shortly after Annie died, so it would fit with the timeline.

"My parents found out about my obsession. They found my scrapbook where I created pictures of mine and Frannie's wedding. I thought it was beautiful. My mother thought it was disgusting. They wanted to send me away—lock me up where I couldn't follow Frannie anymore, but I couldn't have that. My parents cut me off—took my trust away, but that won't stop me. I'll find ways to get money. No one will take my Frannie away from me. No one. I'll kill anyone who tries. So, I ran away. Changed my name and followed her to the rehab

center I knew she got a job at. This is the perfect place for me to get close to her."

My heart thunders in my chest. If this hadn't been discovered, how far would Arnie have gone? Would he have hurt me? Would he have hurt Tyke?

"You okay in here?" Timothy's deep voice causes me to jump.

I place my hand over my chest as I turn around to face him. "I . . . I don't know."

"You look like you've seen a ghost," he says, stepping farther into the room. "Did you find something?"

I nod and hold out the notebook to Timothy with a shaky hand. "You could say that."

Timothy's brow creases as he takes the book and tucks the clipboard under his arm. His eyes scan through the last entry that I read and his head snaps back up to meet my stare. "Has he hurt you?"

I shake my head. "No, but . . ."

I hesitate. If I tell Timothy about the things Arnold has been emailing me then I'll be fired before I have the chance to quit. Timothy is too straitlaced to keep this secret for me.

"But what?" he probes.

I might as well lay it all out. It's better coming from me than from Arnold. God knows what he's capable of, or what he'll do when he discovers that I know exactly who he is and what he's been up to.

"I believe Arnold has been emailing me—blackmailing me with pictures and videos." I pull my phone out of my back pocket and pull up the picture of me with Tyke. "He sent me this after catching us in the woods."

Timothy squints as studies the thumbnail on the screen. "Are you saying you've been having an inappropriate relationship with a client?"

I pull the phone back and stuff it into my pocket. "It's wrong—unethical and completely against the Hippocratic Oath, I know, which is why I was just in the middle of writing my letter of resignation. I knew this was going to come out because someone filmed us, but I was hoping by quitting it would all go away. I tried to stop it from happening."

He sighs. "You know I have to report this, don't you?"

"I know," I whisper. "I'm so sorry."

Timothy takes a moment to scan my face and his lips turn down into a frown. "I can see that, and for what it's worth, I'm sorry that I have to say something. If it didn't go against everything I believe, I would keep it to myself." He lays Arnie's journal on his clipboard. "I'm going to go explain everything to Dr. Shepherd. He'll take over from here."

I nod. "Okay."

While I'm in my cabin packing, a knock on my door causes my heart to sink. I'm sure this is Wayne coming to fire me.

I open the door and surprise washes over me when I discover Tyke standing before me, looking absolutely edible in his jeans and T-shirt.

"Tyke? What are you doing here?" I question.

He pushes his blond hair back from his face and then shoves his hands deep in his front pockets. "Dr. Shepherd and I just had a talk in his office."

I bite my bottom lip. "What did he say to you?"

"He knows everything about us, and he mainly questioned how I felt about the situation. He wanted—" A grin crosses his face as he pauses for a brief second. "He wanted to know if you had taken advantage of me in my vulnerable state, because you crossed the line with me since I was your client."

I run my fingers through my hair. "And?"

Tyke laughs. "I told him you raped me."

I smack his arm. "That's not funny. This shit is serious."

He grips my hips and tugs me closer to him. "I know. That was a poor choice of joke. I told him that I'm in love with you, and that I pursued you until you finally gave in. I explained how you fought against the inevitable really hard, telling me how wrong it was, but I made it impossible for you to not fall in love with me."

I put my arms around his neck. "You did make it tough on me to hold out."

"I'm glad you find me irresistible." He kisses my lips. "I love you, Frannie. No matter what happens. I want you and me and this baby to be a family. I want the real deal with you."

"I love you, too." The tears burn as they pool in my eyes. To hear him say he wants that with me stirs something deep within me—a longing for someone else in my life to love wholeheartedly and completely. It never occurred to me, until this beautiful man walked into my life, just how much I want a family of my own. Now, I can't see myself being without him.

He wipes the tears from my cheeks as they stream down my face. "I hope these are happy tears?"

I nod and sniff. "They are. I can't see myself without you now. You mean more to me than you'll ever know."

"I think I have a pretty good idea how you feel," he whispers before crushing his lips to mine.

He pulls away. "Come on. Dr. Shepherd sent me to get you. He wants to talk with us together."

Tyke leads us back to the main house, hand in hand. I guess there's no point in hiding what's going on between us now that the secret's out. The moment we enter the main house through the back door, we come face to face with Sue, who is busy at the island in the kitchen, preparing dinner.

"Frannie." Sue arches an eyebrow at me.

I know she probably didn't expect this from me after I was so adamant that this very thing would never happen, but what can I say—I'm in love. So I simply shrug as I pass her by, and she shakes her head and smiles.

We get the same reaction from the rest of the clients. They all seem to be shocked that we're together, which at least means we hid our affair well.

Josie crosses her arms as we pass by her, her eyes examining me from head to toe while she wears a nasty scowl on her face. Obviously, she thinks the better woman has not won in this situation, but to hell with her—to hell with all of them who are judging me right now. I love this man.

When we make it to Wayne's office, Tyke and I continue to hold hands as we take the seats facing the desk.

Wayne steeples his fingers and touches them to his lips as he takes in our show of solidarity. "So I see everything that Timothy and Tyke have filled me in on is true, Frannie?"

I sit a little straighter in my seat. "Yes. We are together."

Wayne nods. "Clearly. And the Arnold situation . . . well, I would like you to know that he has been dealt with. Arnold was transferred to an inpatient psychiatric facility where he will be examined and held there until the physician on staff feels that he is no longer a threat to you or anyone else in society. We also confiscated his phone and deleted all 1,457 pictures and videos he had stored—most of them of you, by the way, so he should no longer be a problem."

I relax a little in my chair, glad not to have to worry about a video of me having sex with Tyke being leaked all over the internet. "Thank you. I appreciate that."

"While I can't promise you that he won't be released at some point in the future, knowing to be on the lookout can at least be of some comfort. But I wouldn't fret too much if I were you. Arnold has lost touch with reality, and I think he'll be locked up for quite a while."

"Again, thank you, Wayne. That makes me feel a lot safer," I tell him.

"Good, good. Well, the next order of business is the two of you," Wayne says. "Since Mr. Douglas was a willing participant in the affair, I see no reason to involve the authorities, or anyone else for that matter. Because this occurred here, at my facility, typically I would be forced to let you go, but since Timothy has informed me that you had actually already prepared your letter of resignation, I will accept that and consider the matter at hand closed. This is a little unorthodox, but if you need a letter of recommendation, I would be happy to do that for you."

My eyes widen. I didn't expect this to be so easy. "That's very generous of you. Why would you do that for me?"

"You really did some superb work here with the clients, Frannie. You took the time to get to know each of them as individuals, and giving them journals to help them express themselves was very impressive. I believe what occurred between you and Mr. Douglas was a one-time situation, and I trust that, in the future, you will be more careful when it comes to being intimate with a client."

I put my hand up. "I promise you, this will never happen again."

"It better not," Tyke chimes in, and Wayne laughs.

Wayne stands and extends his hand out to me. "I wish you the best, Frannie. Tyke," he turns and shakes Tykes hand, "take care, and remember you can always come back if you need to."

Tyke shakes his head while he wraps his arm around my shoulder and pulls me into his side. "No need, Doc. I've got my own personal counselor now."

Standing on the porch with Tyke, while we wait for our ride to pick us up, drives home the fact that I'll never see this place again. The pure beauty of this place will never leave my mind. I've never been in a surrounding as peaceful as this. Serenity Hills is definitely a fitting name for this facility.

The screen door slaps closed behind me and Kimmy comes bouncing out in a bright orange skirt with an off-white top. Her blond hair is pulled into a high ponytail that swings as she makes her way toward me. "I wish you didn't have to go, Frannie. We were just starting to be good friends."

I poke my bottom lip out. "I know. It makes me sad that I won't see you anymore. There's always emailing and video chatting?"

She laughs. "In this place—doubtful. You know the signal is crappy here, but emailing is a definite must. You still have my address from when I wrote it down earlier, right?"

I nod. "I do."

The moment the purr of a motor creeping up the drive catches our attention, Kimmy embraces me in a tight hug. "Take care, Frannie."

"You too, Kimmy. Keep at the design school thing. You've got a real eye for that stuff," I tell her.

"Frannie?" Tyke's voice causes me to turn my gaze in his direction. "I'll wait for you by the car."

Tyke kisses my cheek and then grabs my bag off the porch and carries it out to his brother's car.

"Have fun with the sexy man meat." Kimmy gives me a wink before heading back into the house, leaving me alone on the porch.

I turn and gaze up at the tall columns of the porch, taking one last look before I turn and head toward Tyke, who is waiting for me with open arms.

Chapter Twenty

"Slow Ride" – Foghat

Tyke

It feels fucking amazing to be back, staring out at a sold-out arena while the four of us play our hearts out for the fans is like being home again. It was a long, hard road to get back to this place, but I feel like all that we've been through in the past few years has made us stronger as a unit. We really are a family.

I glance over at Riff who smiles at me as he plays the rhythm of "Ball Busting Bitch" while Noel bends at the waist and belts out the chorus. My bass matches the steady beat of Trip's crazy-ass drum playing, taking the song to another level.

Black Falcon is back, and we aren't going anywhere any time soon.

Contentment fills every inch of me, and I glance over at Frannie who's waiting at the side of the stage with

Lanie and Holly. What almost felt like the end of one of the world's greatest rock bands was just the beginning to one of the most infamous love stories: mine and Frannie's.

Frannie smiles one of those breathtaking smiles at me, and I can't help but to fall in love with her all over again. My woman has a heart of gold. Not only does she challenge herself with nonprofit work as an addiction counselor, but she also puts up with my crazy ass. She couldn't be any more perfect for me if she tried.

We play the last few notes in unison while Noel thanks the crowd. The fans jump, push, and pull one another trying to capture one of the tiny picks I fling to them. Being a rock star is insane.

I follow the guys off stage and immediately find myself in Frannie's waiting arms. "I missed you."

She giggles as I press my lips to hers. "I didn't go anywhere. I've been right here watching you play the entire time."

I continue to assault her with kisses. "You were too far away. Next time, I'm just going to have to bring you out on stage with me."

She shakes her head. "You're ridiculous."

As I'm about to kiss her again, a familiar voice halts me in my tracks.

"Did you find one for us to play with, Tyke? It's been a while, but I'm game," Gabby says as she licks her lips while checking out Frannie.

I try to push Frannie behind me, not liking the idea that Gabby would even think that my girl is some random groupie. I open my mouth to tell her to piss off, but Frannie beats me to it.

"Gabby, is it?" Frannie asks in a smooth tone.

Gabby lifts her chin. "Yeah, what of it?"

Frannie steps around me. I reach out to stop her, but her determined blue eyes cause me to freeze. She clearly wants to handle this.

Frannie extends her hand to Gabby. "I'm Frannie."

Gabby glares at her but finally shakes Frannie's hand. "So?"

"I just wanted you to meet the woman who owns Tyke Douglas' heart. This is your one and only warning to stay away."

"And if I don't?" Gabby fires back.

A wicked grin slides over Frannie's face as she steps into Gabby's personal space, making her seem very intimidating in a crazy way. "I'll make you wish you had."

Gabby swallows hard and her eyes flick from Frannie to me before she steps back. "Fuck this. He's not worth it."

Frannie stands there with her glare fixated on Gabby as she hurries out of sight.

I come up behind her and pull her back into my chest. "I didn't know you were such a badass, babe."

She laughs. "I'll do anything to protect you, including fighting off crazy ex's."

I kiss the top of her head. "The feeling's mutual. I'd maul a bear for you."

She turns to face me. "A bear? Really?"

I nod. "Yeah, I'd make that fucker wish he'd never been born if he messes with my babies." I reach down and place my hand on her stomach. "I love you, Frannie."

My fingers fly over the strings of my bass as I bust out the last few licks of the song. Things have really come together since we found our way back into the studio as a cohesive unit. The day Frannie and I left Serenity Hills, I took her back to the place I own with my brother Trip. It's in the hills of Kentucky, not that far from Noel and Riff. Since Noel and Riff have the kids running around their respective places, we did most of our songwriting sessions at our house.

These tracks that we've come up are unlike anything we've ever done before, and we blew through the songwriting process. I wrote like a man possessed. Everything just flowed out of me. The melodies, the beats—*everything.* We have a mixture of dark, dirty beats that I'm sure the fans will go crazy for, as well as some soft ballads, most of which I wrote with one woman on my mind.

"That sounded amazing, Tyke," Jimmy, the producer says into my headphones as soon as I'm done with the song.

I open my eyes and adjust the headphones on my head. "Thanks, man."

"Why don't we lay down a vocal track for "Push and Pull"? You up for it?"

I nod and my eyes flit over to Frannie, who stands behind the glass in the booth, watching me intently as I work. She hasn't heard this song yet. It's the one I've held back to surprise her with. Staring into her eyes, knowing she's growing rounder every day with my child, makes me smile. I know it's the perfect time for her to hear me sing the words I have written just for her. I never get sick of telling her that she's always on my mind, and how much I love her.

I place my bass back on the stand and say, "Let's do it."

I step up to the mic as the melody we previously recorded begins to play. I remain focused on Frannie's blue eyes as I open my mouth and begin to sing.

"Your skin makes me wanna touch you
Be a part of your world
So I push you, but I won't let you fall
But you're a hard girl to get through to
All I want is to hold you and tell you it'll be all right . .

When I push you . . .
You pull me back
There's nothing like, a love like that
A love like that
Let me ask you
When's the last time you've felt like that
Bet it was with me
Bet it was with me

I'm falling for you
It's easy to see
Without you girl, I just ain't me
There's no future without you
Give it a chance girl, give into the pull

When I push you . . .
You pull me back
There's nothing like, a love like that
A love like that
Let me ask you
When's the last time you've felt like that

Bet it was with me
Bet it was with me."

When I'm finished with the first take, I fully expect Jimmy to tell me to get ready to do it again, but instead I hear his voice cut through my thoughts with an entirely different message. "Hot damn, man, I think that was the one. It's like a new fucking record. We got the entire song on the first take. Everything was perfect—the pitch, the emotion. Wow. I'm impressed. If I'd known you had that in you, we would've let you take the lead on a few songs before."

I laugh. "I don't know if I'd have been able to do that before. That woman in there beside you has blessed me with a new lease on life."

I wink at Frannie and smile when she mouths the words, "I love you."

It's in that booth, staring at the people I love through the glass—Frannie, Trip, Noel, and Riff—that I finally find peace with myself. Those people in there are my family, and I would do anything in this world for them, and I vow never to return to the dark hell of my addiction ever again. I will be stronger. I will always be a man that Frannie and my child will be proud of. I'm going to make sure that the rest of our forever is fucking perfect.

Epilogue

"Marry You" – Bruno Mars

One Year Later

Frannie readjusts the veil on the top of her head as she stares at herself in the mirror. After a few moments, she begins to spot some of her twin's features in herself. It makes it feel as if in some small way she's standing by her side on this special day.

As she stares in her own eyes and pretends they're Annie's, she smiles. "There you are. You don't know how much I wish you could be here with me. I miss you— every day, but I'm in a good place now. Tyke makes me so happy, Annie. He loves me so passionately and completely that he doesn't give me a chance to ever feel lonely or unwanted. You'd really like him."

A knock on the door startles her as she pulls her attention away from the reflection and says, "Come in."

The door opens and in walks Tyke with a baby in each arm. Frannie's heart instantly warms at the sight of her soon-to-be husband holding their twin boys, sleeping in his arms.

Tyke's crooked smile greets her before his words. "Hey, Mom. Are you ready for our big day?"

She leans over and softly presses her lips to his, scolding him quietly. "It's bad luck for you to see me, you know."

Tyke smirks. "I don't believe in luck—only fate, and baby, you're mine. Nothing will ever change that."

One of the boys begin squirming in Tyke's strong arms and then lets out a wail loud enough to wake his brother who also begins to cry.

Both babies crying at the same time would probably make most first time parents frazzled, but not Tyke and Frannie. Instead, they smile at one another, knowing that the powerful connection their twin boys feel toward one another has already begun. When one's in pain, the other will know.

Another knock on the door occurs before it opens and Frannie's soon-to-be sister-in-law, Holly, comes rushing in with Aubrey and Lanie at her side.

Aubrey immediately stretches her arms out to Tyke. "Need a little help in here?"

Frannie smiles as Aubrey and Lanie each take one of her boys into their arms. "I think they're hungry."

"No problem," Aubrey says. "We'll get them all taken care of so they can sit with us and watch their parents make it official."

"Don't forget their Uncle Trip and Aunt Holly," Lanie adds before turning to Holly with a huge smile. "I can't believe you're finally making Trip an honest man."

Tyke laughs. "My brother has been waiting on this day for the last three years."

Holly blushes. "I know he has, but waiting was the best thing for us. We've grown so much closer, and the track is doing the best it's ever done. We're finally ready."

"I'm glad he has you, Holly. You make him happy," Tyke tells her.

The wedding coordinator rushes into the room red-faced. "There you all are. It's time."

Frannie nods, and then turns her attention back to her babies. "Let me kiss them before they go."

Aubrey and Lanie bring both the little boys swaddled in blue blankets to Frannie so she can lean down and kiss each one's pink cheeks. "You boys take care of each other."

"We'll see you out there," Lanie tells Frannie before she and Aubrey leave the room holding the babies.

Frannie turns toward her future husband who takes both of her hands into his large ones, and threads his fingers through hers. "I can't wait to marry you. You make me so happy."

Tyke releases one of her hands and cups her cheek, stroking his thumb over her delicate skin. "You're my definition of happiness, babe. We're always and forever."

She melts into him as he leans in and kisses her passionately, knowing that this is just the start of their happily ever after.

Holly Pearson stands behind the double wooden doors that separate the sanctuary of the church from the rest of the building. Through those doors is the beginning of her new life as a married woman, and she couldn't be more ready to start it.

The blond wedding coordinator stoops down in front of Noel's son and Riff's daughter and straightens their clothes before it's their turn to walk down the aisle. "Okay, James and Hailey, remember to stand nice and tall and take your time walking. Hailey, don't forget to toss the petals as you go, and James hold the pillow nice and tight."

Holly smiles warmly down at the children before bending down and kissing them both of the cheek. "You two are adorable."

"Yuck!" James exclaims as he wipes away Holly's kiss, causing the soon-to-be bride to chuckle. "Girl germs."

"Girls don't have germs," Hailey scolds him instantly, shaking her blond curls in the process. "Boys do."

"Nu-huh!" James shouts back, his blue eyes narrowed at Hailey.

"Shhhh! Children," the wedding coordinator says, trying to diffuse the situation.

The moment the woman moves away from the kids, James sticks his tongue out at Hailey, and she smacks his arm.

"Ow! Brat!" he whispers harshly.

"Poo-poo head!" Hailey fires back.

James scrunches his brow. "I don't like you."

Hailey curls her pink lip up. "Well, I don't like you either."

"Children!" The wedding coordinator warns them again. "I'm about to open the doors. Let's be quiet and smile. Ready? One...two...three."

On three, the heavy wooden doors open and the children march side by side down the aisle. A collective awe fills the room when the crowd spots how absolutely adorable James and Hailey are. James is wearing his all black tux with his Chucks, and Hailey wearing a beautiful tulle dress and pink Chucks both put out a mini rock star vibe.

Through the crowd, Holly's eyes meet Trip's bright green ones. The traditional tuxedo he purchased has been dressed up in true Trip fashion with a black dress shirt and vest, the only pop of color is a pink tie that matches the rest of the wedding party. The thick, black hair on the top of his head has been slicked back for the special occasion.

Holly smiles as the wedding march begins to play and her father, Bill, holds his elbow out to her. "Ready, honey?"

"Yes. I've never been more ready for something in all my life," she answers and then hooks her arm through the crook of her father's.

Their steps match in time as they glide to the altar. Each movement brings her closer to Trip. As Holly floats past the guests in the pews, it warms her to see people she's really gotten to know over the past few years sitting there. Aubrey and Lanie have become like sisters to her, and the woman walking behind her, Frannie, has been nothing but lovely to her and made her an aunt to two of the cutest babies on the face of the earth. Someday, when they're ready, she knows that she and Trip will be great parents and will have nothing but support around them when the time comes.

Max, her best friend, stands proudly beside Trip with a huge smile on his face. He winks at her and mouths, 'love you' just before the pastor asks, "Who gives this woman to this man?"

Bill squares his shoulders and replies, "I do."

Her father turns to her and lifts her veil, kissing her cheek before putting the sheer material back over her face and placing her hand in Trip's.

Trip takes both of her hands in his and rubs his thumbs over her knuckles. His green eyes fix on her face, and his plump lips pull up on one side, revealing the devilish grin that she initially fell for. "You're beautiful."

This only makes Holly's smile grow wider as she can't believe how unbelievably lucky she is to have found the one man on the planet who loves her unconditionally. This rugged tattooed badass before her has the heart of pure gold, and his love was something she would cherish for the rest of her life.

The pastor then turns his attention to Frannie as her father gives her to Tyke.

A double wedding isn't anything new, but this one is special. The Douglas men are finally settling down and Holly can't help loving the fact that one of the world's most eligible bachelors only has eyes for her.

She stares lovingly into Trip's eyes as their vows are exchanged. The weight of all of their family and friends witnessing this profession of love overwhelms her, and this typically tough girl breaks down and the tears stream down her face. This is the happiest day of her life, and she can't wait to share every moment she has left on this earth as Mrs. Trip Douglas.

As Aubrey holds one of Tyke and Frannie's newborn son in her arms, she glances lovingly over to her husband, Riff, who has their newest edition in his arms.

Their second daughter, Libby, was born not long after their oldest daughter, Hailey, was able to walk. The last three years with Riff have been a whirlwind, but she wouldn't have it any other way.

Riff smiles as he notices her watching him while their toddler sleeps in his arms during the wedding ceremony. Oh, how she loves that man. She didn't think it was possible to love him more than she did when she first met him, but she finds that every day their love for one another grows stronger.

Riff leans in to whisper in her ear. "You want another?"

Aubrey bites her lip as she stares down at the little bundle cradled in her arms and then refocuses her gaze back onto her husband, nodding. "The more the merrier."

He leans in and kisses the soft flesh below her ear before he says, "We'll work on that tonight."

She giggles and then covers her mouth, trying her best to keep quiet as their friends get married before them. Suddenly, she can't wait for tonight, because making babies with Riff is one of her most favorite things to do.

Noel spins Lane around on the dance floor at the reception. Only being three years into their own marriage, they still feel like newlyweds, and are always on the lookout for reasons to touch one another.

Lane giggles as Noel dips her and then brings her back up to place a soft kiss on her lips. "Can you believe that every single member of Black Falcon is married?"

A cocky grin breaks out over Noel's face. "I can. I read about that every day—all the hearts broken all over the world because the sexiest men on the planet are taken."

She stares up at her sexy husband and raises an eyebrow. "Where are you reading this?"

He shrugs. "Everywhere. It's been all over the web."

Lane rolls her eyes. "You are so full of your self."

A hearty laugh rumbles though Noel's chest. "You've only known me your whole life, and you're just now figuring that out? You like me cocky. You know you do."

She bites her lip as she debates on denying it, but knows he'll just see right through it like he always does. "You are too much."

Just when the song ends, a new one begins. The DJ begins playing a song that's very dear to Lane's heart. It's the song Noel sang to her the night she saw him in concert, and they fell even more madly in love than they've always been.

"Did you have him play 'Faithfully'?" Lane asks, thinking that it's surely not a coincidence.

"Maybe," he answers and then presses his lips to hers. "It is one of my most favorite songs."

"Mine, too," she whispers.

The lyrics to the song wrap around them as they continue to sway to the beat and stare into each other's eyes. No greater love ever existed between a man and a woman.

Their love is faithful and will last forever.

...And they all lived happily ever after...

**Turn the page for the first four chapters of
Phenomenal X by Michelle A. Valentine**

Phenomenal X

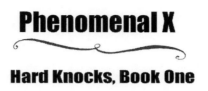

Hard Knocks, Book One

Michelle A. Valentine

Chapter
ONE

"Blessed are the meek, for they shall inherit the earth"—
Matthew 5:5

There's no better way to ruin a perfectly peaceful flight than sitting between two complete strangers. I always request an aisle or window seat if I can, but this flight was booked solid and the unhelpful lady at the check-in desk told me there was absolutely no wiggle room to change seats.

The older gentleman on my left keeps turning toward me and smiling, probably hoping I'll strike up polite conversation with him, but I'm just not in the mood to be nice. I'm leaving Portland, leaving behind the only life I've ever known, and the only thing I feel like doing is keeping quiet and praying that I'm making the right decision.

This morning my father went into one of his lecture-filled rages, telling me what a horrible person I was when I sprung it on him that I would be on the ten o' clock flight to Detroit to go live with Aunt Dee, his eccentric sister. My parents, especially my father, have always been great at controlling my life. Which is exactly why I'm leaving now.

I've followed his plan for the last twenty-one years, and it's brought nothing but heartache. I'm ready to make my own decisions about what's best for me.

While the other passengers settle in around me, I quickly flick through my text messages. The anger in Father's messages is crystal clear. The same thing said a million different ways: for me to stop this nonsense of starting my own life, and come back home where I belong. Where I'm safe.

I shake my head and shut my phone off before slipping it into the seat-back pocket in front of me. "No can do, Father," I mumble to myself.

A mother and her twin sons fill the three empty seats in the row ahead of me. They are sitting in the first row, directly behind the wall that separates the first class patrons from the rest of us lowly coach passengers. If I had to guess, I'd say the twins are about twelve or so. Their brown hair pokes out from underneath the matching baseball caps they have firmly pulled onto their heads. The hats match their red shirts with some wrestling guy on it. I can tell it's wrestling from the logos. I remember sneaking around to watch the televised show with my younger brother when he went through a phase of loving that sort of thing.

Just then I notice an extremely tall, broad-shouldered man wearing jeans and a blue button-down shirt, with his sleeves rolled up to his elbows, board the plane. Even with his shirt on I can tell he's all muscle underneath it. The definition in his chest and arms is undeniable as the fabric strains against his pecs and biceps. Intricate tattoos cover every inch of exposed flesh on his arms, and I immediately know he's the kind of guy my mother always warned me about—which does nothing to decrease his appeal.

I bite my lip as my eyes scan further up and take in the dark hair on his head. It's got a little bit of length to it and is styled to messy perfection. His strong jawline has some light stubble, like he forgot to shave this morning, and the fact that his nose isn't perfectly straight—indicating it's been broken a time or two—only adds to his rugged good looks. The way he carries himself, chin up with a daring expression, exudes confidence. Everything about him says he doesn't take crap from anyone, which is a highly attractive feature in a man. And that body...*yowza*! It's absolutely delicious and belongs on the cover of a magazine. It's designed for masses of women to enjoy devouring with their eyes because in the flesh, that's exactly what I'm doing.

And I'm loving every minute of it.

My heart pauses for a beat the moment this man locks eyes with me. When I don't immediately turn away, a slight hint of a smile plays at the corner of his full lips. Briefly, I'm mesmerized, and then realize I'm still thinking about his body, and I'm biting my lip.

He winks at me like he knows exactly what's on my mind before he slides into an empty row of seats in first class. A short, thin man with a mullet and a beard takes the aisle seat next to him.

I lean my head back against the seat and sigh, feeling the heat in my cheeks. That man is dangerously sexy and way out of my league.

The two boys in front of me begin waving their arms above their head. "X! X! Back here! Can we get your autograph?"

The letter X is all I hear them chant over and over as the small man who boarded the plane last turns around and says, "Not now, boys. Phenomenal X is trying to rest." The hot guy beside him must be this "Phenomenal X" person because after the little man says that to the kids, he immediately leans over and says something to him. Mullet Man nods before turning back around to address the two boys. "Send something up, and X will sign one thing for each of you."

"All right!" exclaims one of the boys as they give each other a high-five.

The rest of the plane begins to buzz as the knowledge that a celebrity is on board the flight spreads. While I find the man extremely attractive, I have no clue who he is and I can't bring myself to get excited about it. I have too much on my plate to be interested in some guy who would never give someone like me the time of day.

Soon an assembly line forms as people begin to pass things up the aisle into first class. I almost feel sorry for him as it continues through taxiing, take-off, and while we are up in the air. The poor guy will probably develop writer's cramp before the flight is over.

After I turn down the stewardess' offer of an in-flight beverage, allowing her to assist the old man beside me who orders a tomato juice, I lean my head back and close my eyes. I try not to think about the one hundred texts Father is probably sending me right now, each repeating to me, over and over, that I'm running out on my problems back home. It isn't something I want to keep rehashing with him.

My eyes jerk open the moment something cold and wet covers my legs. My mouth drops open as I stare down at my tomato juice-covered lap.

This is *so* not happening to me.

The juice drips onto the floor, and I glance down at my shoes and the bag stuffed under the seat in front of me—everything is covered. I press the call light to request assistance from the flight attendant with cleaning up, taking care to hold my hands out away from my body.

The elderly man next to me frowns as he pushes up his glasses to survey the damage. "I'm sorry, young lady. These old eyes don't see like they used to. I didn't mean to knock that cup into your lap."

I can see the sincerity on his face and offer up a small smile because I don't want him to feel any worse. "Accidents happen. No worries."

The flight attendant approaches our row and leans over to turn the call light off before glancing down at me. "Oh, dear, looks like we've had a bit of a spill here."

I stare up at her and wonder how she can be so calm in this situation, but I can tell this is the type of woman who doesn't get worked up easily. There's not one strand of blond hair out of place in her updo, and her blue eyes sparkle with kindness.

I glance down at my soiled clothes. "Can I have a towel or something? I checked all my clothing, so I don't have anything extra to change into."

"Come on up front with me and we'll see if we can get you cleaned up," she replies.

I nod, grateful for her offer. "Thank you." Anything is better than smelling like rotten tomatoes for the remaining three hours of my flight. I glance over at the older man beside me. "Do you mind letting me out?"

He begins to move out of the way. "Of course not, young lady."

I follow the flight attendant through the first class section into the front galley of the plane. She reaches into a stash of canned club sodas and hands me one, along with a handful of plain white washcloths.

She frowns at me. "Sorry, it's not much, but try blotting it out the best you can. Taking out the smell will make your flight more comfortable. I would offer you a first class seat since I'm sure your seat is a mess, but unfortunately, it's all full."

"She can sit here," a deep, rumbling voice says.

When I look up, my gaze locks onto a pair of the lightest blue eyes I think I've ever seen. They're practically see-through. If I thought he was attractive from a distance that is nothing compared to the sight of him up close. The intensity causes my stomach to flip and my knees grow a little weak. I swallow hard. Considering every seat is filled, I find myself confused as to where exactly *here* is. As inviting as sitting on his lap for the next few hours may be, I don't want to open that naughty can of worms. He seems like way too much man for me. I don't think I can handle someone so...*intense.*

"You're willing to give up your seat for her, Mr. Cold?" the attendant asks.

He shakes his head. "No, but my manager will give her his seat."

Mullet Man's head jerks toward him. "I *will?*"

Mr. Cold rolls his neck and glares down at him with a stare so intense, it's almost frightening. "You have a problem with that?"

"N—no, of course not, X," he stutters, clearly intimidated by the beast of a man beside him. "She can totally have my seat."

Mr. Cold jerks his chin toward the back. "Then beat it."

Mullet Man quickly gathers his things and heads back to my tomato-stained seat in coach without another word. I glance over at the flight attendant but she simply shrugs and walks back down the aisle to continue passing out drinks.

I glance at the empty seat next to possibly the most attractive, yet scary, man I've ever come in contact with and my heart does a double thump. I can only imagine what sitting next to him for the next three hours is going to do to my cardiovascular system. My heart will never survive. It will explode from all the extra beats.

I pour the club soda onto the rag and begin blotting my jeans. I press and rub until practically every inch of my pants and shirt are soaked. Not exactly the greatest first impression to make on a celebrity, but this is the cleanest I'm going to get considering I'm thirty-five thousand feet in the air.

I sigh and then lay the now orange cloth on the drink cart in the galley and head toward Mr. Cold. I sit in the oversized gray leather seat, surprised at how much more room there is up here versus back in coach. I've always been curious as to what riding in first class would be like.

The weight of Mr. Cold's stare presses on me like a ton of bricks. I know I can't sit next to him for the next few hours and not say anything, so I might as well get it over with and thank him.

"Thank you for the seat. That was really kind of you."

His eyes drift down my body, and then back up to my face. "Don't mention it. You looked like you could use a little help, so I helped."

I roll my bottom lip between my teeth as he continues to gaze at me. His eyes are the kind people write songs and poems about. They're light blue and crystal clear. I've never seen someone with such intoxicating eyes. It nearly steals my breath every time I look into them.

Before either of us can say another word, someone passes a blank sheet of paper over my shoulder. "Give this to X. It's for a kid in the back."

I take the paper and slide it onto Mr. Cold's tray. "My, aren't you popular."

He nods and begins scratching his name across the sheet. "How about you?"

I furrow my brow. "How about me, what?"

He glances over at me and smirks. "Would you like me to sign something for you? A piece of clothing...bare skin, perhaps?"

I grimace because I don't exactly know what he's famous for. If I had to guess, factoring in the kids' reactions, I would say he's a pro athlete of some type. Still doesn't mean I need, or even *want*, his autograph— especially not on my bare skin.

"I'm good, but thank you."

He lifts his eyebrows in surprise. "That's a first."

Suddenly I feel bad for sort of insulting him. He was nice enough—if you call ordering a worker around nice—to give me a seat in first class. I should at least try and be gracious.

"I'm sorry, that was rude of me. If you would like to sign something for me...that would be great."

Mr. Cold chuckles as he hands me back the paper with his signature just in time for another autograph request to come from the back. "Don't ask out of obligation. I hate that shit. Do what you want, not what you think people want you to do."

His words hit me and remind me that's exactly what moving to Detroit is all about. Like a good little girl, I've always done what's expected of me. I went to a Christian college to please my father, and dated boys from our family's church so the guy would fit my family's ideal mold of what a good boyfriend should represent—all to please Father. None of it made *me* happy. Every time I wanted to explore the world, or taste some of the different fruits life had to offer, I was always reminded that some fruit is forbidden for a reason. Frankly, I was sick of always being told what to do and how to feel. I take a deep breath. It's time to start living my life on my own terms.

"You know what? You're right. I don't want your signature. I don't even know who you are."

His gaze snaps to me and my newfound toughness wavers a bit under the intensity of his stare. Panicking slightly, I feel the need to backpedal. "Don't get me wrong, I'm grateful for the seat, but I don't want an autograph."

He smiles and a tingle erupts in my belly before spreading through the rest of my body. He's got a great smile, and paired with those gorgeous eyes of his, it's a deadly combination of sexiness. I imagine many women have lost their ever-lovin' minds because of that smile.

"What's your name, beautiful?"

My heart does a double thud as I swallow hard and try to remember what my own name is. That smile is causing me to go a little batty myself. Not that anyone could blame me. After all, this stunning man just called *me* "beautiful."

"Anna Cortez."

His eyes dance with amusement.

"Cortez," he repeats.

The way my name rolls off his tongue sounds so sensual and naughty. It's almost as if he's trying to turn me on and make me squirm on purpose for turning down his stupid autograph. "Is that Spanish?"

"It is," I answer simply. "It means 'courteous.'"

"Ah, sassy and smart, I see," Mr. Cold teases. Or at least...I think he's joking. It doesn't seem like he's pissed or anything because he's still grinning. "It's nice to meet you, Anna Cortez."

"Likewise, Mr..."

Oh damn. Do I call him Mr. X? Or do I refer to him as Mr. Cold like the flight attendant did? I hate being stuck in these awkward social situations. I've never claimed to be a big people person.

Luckily for me, he fills in the gap. "You can call me Xavier."

Things begin to click for me. "Is that where the X comes from?"

"It is."

I lick my lips before I wonder out loud, "How about the 'Phenomenal' part?"

His eyes flick down to my lips and then back up again. "I could tell you, but I think it'd be a whole lot more fun if I showed you where that portion of my name comes from."

Why do I have the distinct feeling that this man has just propositioned me after sitting next to me for less than ten minutes? No one, other than me, gets into these jeans that fast. "I think I'm good without that too."

"You're a good girl, aren't you, Anna?" Xavier asks, trying to feel me out.

"I'd like to think so, but if you asked my father that question right now he might tell you I'm the spawn of Satan," I respond easily, and then immediately wish I could take the last part back. I tend to ramble when I get nervous, thus exposing all my secrets and this guy is the last person who needs to know my life history. Besides, it's not like he really cares anyhow. He's obviously one of *those kinds* of guys Father always warns me about. The kind who only wants one thing.

Xavier shakes his head. "I've met some actual demons from hell and trust me, beautiful, you're the furthest thing from evil I've been around in a long, long time. Your father needs a wakeup call. I could tell the second our eyes met that you were a sweet one."

"You...you noticed me...before?" I question, blown away that the little eye lock we shared when he got on the plane had made an impression on him too.

He goes back to signing his name and shrugs. "I always take in every inch of my surroundings, and any man would be a fucking fool if he didn't notice you."

I feel the blush creep into my cheeks from the full-on flattery. I've never had a man talk to me so...so...*bluntly* before. All the guys I've ever dated have been good guys. Polite, with proper manners. Xavier makes my toes curl with a simple look and a few dirty words.

Yep. I'm so out of my league.

It's difficult, but I jerk my attention away from this dangerous man next to me and study my nails, doing my best to keep my eyes from wandering back to my left. I can't help being intrigued by him. If I were the kind of girl who did naughty things with random hotties, I would be all over his offer to find out just how phenomenal he is—in a heartbeat. But as things stand, I'm still a good girl. I know I am, even if my father challenges that fact. All because I ran away from a man I'd promised to marry.

"You're quiet over there. Did I piss you off?" Xavier asks with what I assume is a tender tone but still has a touch of a natural growl to it.

I chew on the corner of my lip. "No. You didn't. I was just thinking."

"About…" he prods, and he glances down at my arm and zeroes on the spot where Father's too tight hold left some marks.

My hand instantly covers the small bruises, not wanting him to ask about them. Explaining how things got a little out of hand when I told my father I was leaving isn't exactly something I want to discuss with a man who I don't know.

I fold my arms over my chest, careful to keep the spot hidden, and stare down at my stained outfit, wishing I hadn't checked all my clothes. "Nothing you would want to hear about, I'm sure. No one likes to listen to a perfect stranger's drama. Besides, I'm positive my life is boring compared to yours—there's no autographs in my normalcy." I add a little teasing at the end to lighten the mood.

Xavier slides his index finger under my chin and then softly pinches it with his thumb, forcing me to look at him. "You're frowning. Why?"

His immediate concern for my happiness takes me aback, and I raise my eyebrows. I can't very well spill my entire tragic life story to this man, even though the sincerity of his intentions shine in his gaze. I didn't expect this type of reaction from him, so I'm thrown off balance for a moment, unsure of how to respond. "I, uh…"

His eyes never leave mine as he says, "A frown doesn't belong on a face like yours, beautiful. Ever. I'm just curious who put it there."

"No one put it there," I whisper, trying to block out that fact that this slight touch from him is sending my body into overdrive.

"Did your boyfriend upset you?"

I should say I don't have a boyfriend because I'm positive once Jorge discovers I left town with no intention of ever returning, he won't want to see me again anyway. Technically I'm single, and I have the feeling this is exactly what Xavier wants to hear from me. Spending the next few hours in such close proximity to him, I'll never be able to fend off his direct advances without eventually agreeing to have sex with him as soon as we land. If he knows I'm unattached, he's the type who'll never give up. No need to dangle a steak in front of a hungry lion.

"He isn't the problem. I'm fine, see." I give him a small smile, hoping he stops prying before I get caught up in my own lie about being taken.

"Not sure I'm buying that weak-ass smile."

His lips pull into a tight line, and I fully expect him to release me, but he doesn't. Xavier's fingers stay in place, burning into my skin. "It's fine if you don't want to say what's on your mind. I get that. But no more frowning for the rest of this trip, or I might be forced to find other ways to make you smile just to piss your boyfriend the fuck off."

His finger traces down my neck and across my collarbone, leaving a trail of fire in its wake.

My mouth drops open and I can't stop myself from asking, "What kind of ways?"

Damn my stupid curious brain. That just set him up for all kinds of dirty talk.

He tries to fight back a smile, but it doesn't work. It comes at me in full, glorious force. "More ways than that sweet brain of yours could ever imagine."

He leans into me, and I can't do anything more than tense because his hand slides up the side of my neck in a very intimate gesture. He's close enough that, if I pushed forward a couple of inches, our lips would meet in what I imagine would be an earth-altering kiss.

"I could do things to your body that most women only dream about while reading their dirty romance novels, and I promise you'd fucking enjoy it."

I stare up at him speechless. Wow.

Just...*wow*.

I can't believe he just said that to me.

Xavier licks his plump lips. "No strings attached, and your boyfriend would never have to know." He leans in and whispers in my ear, "I just want a little taste."

My breath hitches and I close my eyes. The thought of allowing this man to have his way with me is very tempting. So tempting in fact that, for a moment, I seriously consider agreeing. The opportunity to possibly have the best sex of your entire life doesn't come along every day, and I can tell just by looking at Xavier Cold that his skill in the bedroom likely knows no bounds.

He would be the perfect act of rebellion. Going against everything my life currently represents—a representation I'm desperate to break away from.

I want to say yes to him, I really do, but no matter how hard I fight to break away from the good girl persona, I know random sex with a stranger will never be my kind of thing.

I open my eyes and they instantly lock on his cool blue ones. I take a deep breath and whisper, "No."

His brows shoot up, like he can't believe he's just been turned down.

"*No?*"

My chest begins to heave. For some strange reason, turning him down is hard. It's like my body is defying my brain and becoming aroused, even though my head is screaming for me to run as far away as I can.

Xavier sucks in his bottom lip and slowly pulls it between his teeth. "You don't seem so sure about that *no*, beautiful. You want to change your answer? I'll be gentle with you, I swear. You don't have to be afraid of me."

"I, uh…"

I, uh…what? There's nothing to even consider here. I don't know why I'm having such a hard time giving him a firm no—one that sounds like I mean business. Even *I* realize I'm throwing him mixed signals by allowing him to touch me and whisper dirty promises in my ear.

Desperate to get myself out of the intense mess I've allowed to go on too long, I push him back a bit and turn to the middle-aged, brunette lady sitting across the aisle from me. "Do you have any blank paper, please?"

She nods and reaches under the seat in front of her to retrieve a bag. After digging around for a moment, she finds a small notebook and rips out a page. "This is all I have."

I return her smile with one of my own. "Thank you. It's perfect."

I turn and redirect my attention to Xavier, who watches me with a mixture of amusement and curiosity. "The only thing I would like from you is your autograph. *Nothing* more."

I lay the paper on his tray, but he doesn't take his eyes off me. "That's all, huh?"

"That's all," I confirm.

He adjusts the paper on his tray and then glances back up at me. "We'll see."

This little game with him is exhausting. If we keep this up, by the end of the flight I'll either want to kill him or screw his brains out, and neither of those things are on my scheduled to-do list on the path to starting my new life.

I lean my head back and shut my eyes, and pray I can sleep my way through the rest of the flight. Ignoring the dangerously sexy man sitting only inches away from me is the only way I'll stop my body from taking him up on his offer.

Anna

A gentle nudge on my forearm startles me, and I'm quickly jerked back to reality. I've just fallen asleep while sitting next to a ridiculously delicious man. Quickly running my fingers around the corners of my mouth, I make sure I haven't drooled all over my face.

God, this is so embarrassing. I just pray I wasn't snoring. I got very little sleep last night while I lay awake in my bed, dreading the thought of facing my father. The possible scenarios of what he would say when I told him I was leaving Portland to move across the country had played on a continuous loop through my mind, all of them ending with my father not supporting my choice and trying to stop me—which is exactly what happened. I'm just glad I knew enough ahead of time to make arrangements for my neighbor, Kayla, to wait outside my house with the motor running so I could make a quick getaway. Father had no intentions of allowing me to follow through with my plans, which is exactly why he left me no choice but to sneak out of my house and into Kayla's car the moment he turned his back.

Leaving home was the hardest thing I've ever done, but I had to go. I couldn't take being smothered any more.

"The pilot just announced that we'll be landing in approximately thirty minutes, so I thought you would like to know," Xavier says. "You fell asleep so quickly I figured you were exhausted, so I didn't bother you. I have to say, you're different from most women I've met, Anna."

Curiosity gnaws at me as to what exactly he means by that, and I can't help asking, "Different how? Because I refuse to sleep with random men who proposition me?"

He shrugs. "No, not that. I just don't recall that I've ever bored a woman to sleep before. You didn't even seem the slightest bit fazed with me sitting next to you when you zonked-out. Matter of fact, you seem indifferent toward me, which is refreshing...in an odd way."

I laugh. "You *prefer* when people deny your requests?"

The corner of his mouth turns up, revealing what I'm sure is his best panty-soaking smile. "No, but I admire how you stick to your principles and don't back down. Most women aren't like that."

I smile. "I do believe that's a compliment, Xavier."

His grin gets even bigger. He's clearly pleased with himself. I bet in that sex-crazed brain of his, he thinks he's getting somewhere with me.

"So, what's in Detroit?"

My mind stumbles, not ready for such a simple question. I was fully prepared for more sexy banter.

"A fresh start."

His expression turns quizzical, so I explain. "I need to start over, I have family there. My cousin Quinn and Aunt Dee have offered to help me out."

Xavier glances back to coach, where his manager occupies my old seat. "I know the old man you were next to isn't your boyfriend, and the woman on the other side of your assigned seat isn't your girlfriend, so I'm thinking your boyfriend isn't on this flight with you. He's not a part of this fresh start?"

I take a deep breath. Since we're off this plane in a few minutes, and I'll never see this man again, I may as well come clean. A little truth can't hurt.

"No, he's not. No one I know from Portland is."

He raises his eyebrows. "The boyfriend isn't going to come after you?"

I shake my head. "I sort of ended things with him."

"Is that why you're running away from Portland? Can't face breaking some poor schmuck's heart?" he asks with a playful tone.

I fold my arms across my chest. "I assure you that I didn't break Jorge's heart."

He smirks. "You don't honestly believe that, do you?"

"Why wouldn't I? Jorge and I were never really in love. Our families are close, and us being together was expected." If arranged marriages were still legal, that's exactly what would've happened with Jorge and me. We were more like siblings than anything else. I loved him, but not in the way that made me know deep down he was "*The One.*"

Recognition flashes across Xavier's face. "So you're escaping an overbearing family that tries to control your life. Aren't you afraid that your aunt will try to push more things on you that you don't want?"

He's good. He's practically figured out my entire life story with just that little bit of information. I should shut my big mouth right now and not indulge him further, but it's actually nice to talk to someone about this—especially since it seems like he understands how my family tries to push their beliefs on me. It's like he can connect with me on some level.

"Aunt Dee isn't like that. She's really cool. The exact the opposite of my father."

He nods. "I grew up like that myself—in an overly religious household. It's rough living with people who are passionate over certain...beliefs."

Xavier pauses for a beat before he asks, "So how pissed is your dad that you took off without his consent?"

My mouth drops open a little. "How did you know that?"

He shrugs. "You're a good girl who has a controlling father, it's not hard to figure out. You want freedom. I can sense it on you from a mile away. I understand why you're leaving."

"You do?" Surprise rings in my voice. No one other than Quinn and Aunt Dee have empathized with me before. Most people from back home will freak out and call me a fool once they figure out I left. People don't understand that sometimes ideas of perfection in a family get carried a little too far. It's nice that he seems to get it.

"I do. Being trapped in a life that you didn't choose is no fucking picnic, no matter how good it may appear to people outside of the situation. I've been there myself. So, yeah, I get it, and I don't blame you. No one should be forced to live their life in any way other than how they choose."

I stare at him, amazed he knew exactly what I was thinking. He's been where I'm at, and he doesn't look down on me for running away from my life. For a moment it's easy to forget he's a sexy celebrity and not just a regular man—one I would like to get to know better.

"It's nice to hear someone agree with me for a change. I don't like defying my father but I felt like if I didn't get away, I was going to drown in a world full of ideas and beliefs that I don't necessarily agree with."

"When you say beliefs, I'm going to assume you mean religion."

I sigh. "Yes. Not that I'm a non-believer, I just don't like having it shoved down my throat all the time."

His blue eyes search my face. "You really are a sweet girl." Before I can reply to that statement he continues. "I'm glad that you refused me. I'm no good for you."

With our gazes locked, I suddenly forget why I was so put off by his advances in the first place. Maybe my assumptions about him were wrong. He would make an excellent friend—if I weren't so insanely attracted to him.

"You don't seem so bad to me. You're easy to talk to."

He swallows hard. "That's because you don't know me. Believe me, beautiful, I'm bad fucking news. A nice girl like you should run away from me as quick as you can."

My chest heaves while the intensity radiates off him and wraps itself around me. Something about him pulls me in, and I can't explain why I suddenly feel like we are kindred spirits, both running from something. I know he's not good for me—he even said so himself—but I can't stop my stupid body from being attracted to him.

My eyes drift down to his lips, and the thought of what they would feel like on mine washes over me. I imagine they're demanding yet gentle, all at the same time. Thinking like this is dangerous and will lead me down a road I'm not sure I'm ready for, but I can't help doing it.

"You can't keep looking at me like that. I want you. If you give in to me, there's no going back, and you're not ready for someone like me. I don't have the best self-control, and I'm a very selfish man." His voice is tight, like he's struggling between what he *should* do and what he *wants* to do.

Just like I am.

He leans in closer and runs his nose down the length of my jaw, pausing for a brief second to kiss the soft skin beneath my ear. My breath catches and I clench my thighs together to calm the ache he's just created between my legs. It gives me some relief, but my damn naïve curiosity won't let his last words go.

"How am I looking at you?" I whisper.

He tugs my earlobe lightly with his teeth. "Like you're begging for my touch." He inhales deeply through his nose and then growls, "I haven't even kissed you yet, and I'm already fucking hard. Spend the night with me. Let me show you just how good I can make you feel."

I close my eyes. Even though his dark promises of passion are tempting, I can't give in to him. I don't willingly give my body over to complete strangers.

"No," I say again, so faintly that I barely hear it myself.

His tongue teases the bare flesh on my neck. "I don't typically beg, beautiful, but if begging gets me access between those creamy thighs, I will. Just give in to your desires."

He's right.

And, damn it, I hate that he's right. I do want him, more than anything I've ever wanted in my entire life. He pulls back and stares into my eyes, searching my face for permission to pleasure me.

Electricity zings between us, and every nerve ending in my body comes alive. My willpower falters a bit. How many times can I turn down something I really want? If I'm being honest, right now, my body craves nothing more than to experience sex with this powerful man, even though my logical mind knows it's wrong, and I've always been more of a "follow your head, not your heart" kind of girl. I stare into his eyes, willing the word "no" to tumble from my lips again, but no sound comes out.

The landing gear unlocking from the underside of the plane causes my pulse to race under my skin. I need to make a decision because I know the moment I step off this plane I'll never see Xavier again.

The plane jolts, and the tires screech against the runway, but Xavier's eyes never stray from mine as he awaits my answer. While we wait to exit the plane our eyes remain locked, and a thousand scenarios run through my head. I don't even realize that we haven't said a word to one another for several moments. No words are needed to know what we are both thinking.

It's impossible for me not to sit here and stare at him, and not imagine his mouth on mine.

The flight crew opens the door, and all the passengers around us stand and begin exiting the aircraft. I swallow hard as his eyes drop down to my lips and then back up to my eyes.

"What'll it be, Anna Cortez? Are you in, or are you out?"

My heart bangs in my chest, but as much as I would like to experience what he's offering, I have to stick to my guns.

"I'm out."

I stand and turn to exit, but freeze when Xavier grabs my wrist, my skin igniting from his mere touch. My eyes snap down to my hand as he stuffs a paper into it. I flick my gaze back up to his and a grin plays along his lips. "Let me know when you change your mind."

He releases me and immediately my skin craves his warmth again. I consider tossing his autograph back down at him, but for some reason a part of me wants to keep it so I can be sure this time spent with him wasn't just a dream. It'll be a nice memory to hang on to. That Phenomenal X is real and, at one time, was very attracted to me. I tighten my fingers around the paper and take a deep breath.

"Goodbye, Xavier."

Before he has an opportunity to make any more sexy promises, I turn and flee the plane, stuffing the paper into my back pocket. My heart still beats a million miles a minute. I need to find a place I can calm down and regain my composure.

Once I'm safely in the terminal, I dash into the first ladies' room I find. The urge to splash cold water on my face surges through me. I definitely need to cool off, but I don't want to totally ruin my makeup, so I resist. I pull my long brown hair back and then pull it to one side as I rest my hands against the counter and stare at myself in the mirror.

I'm searching hard to find what someone like Xavier would find so appealing about me. My button nose and dark hair don't exactly stand out against my tan skin. My green eyes are only thing I've always been complimented on. The light color against everything else dark really seems to *pop*.

I sigh and reach into my back pocket for my phone. I need to call Aunt Dee, and I need to get out of this place and as far away from Xavier as possible. A growl escapes my lips as I frantically begin patting the empty pockets of my jeans. "Shit," I mutter to myself.

The last time I had my phone was on the plane when I shut it off after checking my father's messages. I didn't bother grabbing it from the seat-back pocket when I moved. My shoulders sag when I realize I didn't grab my bag from under the seat either. I'm going to have to go back and hope I can sneak on the plane and get it.

I make my way down through the terminal back to the gate I just came from. It's completely empty and I'm afraid to try and get back on the plane. The last thing I need is TSA all over me. I lay my head on the gate counter, trying to not lose my mind, but my stomach clenches and I'm about two seconds from having a nervous breakdown.

It's gone. My phone is gone.

Deflated, I flop down on the nearest seat. Great. Just great. I move out to a new city and before I even set foot onto its soil, I lose my belongings. Numbers for everyone back home are programmed into that phone.

I shake my head in disgust. I'll never hear the end of it when Father finds out about this. I rub my forehead and fight back the building tears.

"Excuse me, miss? Can I be of some assistance?" a somewhat familiar voice questions. I glance up as the same flight attendant who helped me when I had tomato juice incident approach me from the gate. She offers up the same sweet smile she gave me when she spoke with me before. "Are you all right?"

I sniff, fighting back the tears. "I'm missing my phone and my bag. The last place I had them was on the plane—before I changed seats."

She nods in agreement. "Mr. Cold asked me to let you know that he has your belongings."

My eyes widen. "He does?"

Relief washes through me, only to be flushed away when I realize I have no way of getting in touch with him again. "I have no way of reaching him."

She tilts her head and I hear the questioning tone in her voice when she says, "He said you have his number?"

I knit my eyebrows in confusion. *I have his number? What's he talking about? The only thing he gave me was...*

Wait a minute.

I reach in my back pocket and pull out the paper containing his autograph, or at least I thought it was his autograph. I unfold it slowly and take in the thick, manly scroll.

Anna Cortez,

Call me when you
change that no.
I'll be waiting.

Xavier

I swallow hard as I stare at the number listed below his signature. Even in a simple note, his commanding tone makes my insides jitter.

A war rages within me. The exhilarated half of me is excited that I'll likely see Xavier again, but the rational half knows that means I'm in for trouble. Trouble I'm not sure that I can resist.

However, one thing *is* clear, if I want my phone and other personal belongings back, I have no choice but to call him.

Heaven help where it may lead.

Anna

I head out into the warm Detroit summer and spot my family the moment I'm outside. Aunt Dee and my cousin Quinn wait in the loading zone for me as I wheel two large suitcases packed with all my clothes and shoes. I kept my eyes peeled at baggage claim, hoping to see Xavier and reclaim my items so I could be done with him for good, but there was no sign of him anywhere. The fact that I'm going to have to call that sexy beast of a man looms over me.

Aunt Dee greets me with a warm smile as I approach. "Anna, sweetheart, how are you? You look beautiful, darling, absolutely stunning, except for that hideous stain all over you. Looks like someone doused you with their drink."

"It's great to see you, Aunt Dee."

I giggle at her words, laced with a thick Spanish accent, as I take in the multicolored bandana tied around her head in a chic, yet fashionable way that blends into her hairstyle. Like I said, Aunt Dee is a little eccentric. She's an artist—a painter and a sculptor—and her creativity typically carries over into her wardrobe. Much like the tie-dyed maxi-dress she has on. "I hope this stain comes out. I didn't bring a lot of clothes."

"I know just the trick to get it out once we get home." She pulls back and inspects me from head to toe. "You look so much like your mother. Doesn't she, Quinn?"

I glance over at my cousin who is wearing a pair of cut-off shorts and a black tank top. Quinn has always been whom I would consider the most beautiful person in our family. We're exactly the same age, but it's hard to compete with her gorgeous brown hair and legs that go on for days. She's drop-dead gorgeous, and every man around always notices her. She's not stuck on herself though, which makes me love her even more. She's about the most down-to-earth person I know.

Quinn smiles at me before wrapping me up in a hug. "I'm so glad you're here, Anna. We are going to have so much fun this summer."

"Aye, girls...but not too much fun," Aunt Dee warns. "Your father would have my head on a stick. He is the last person on earth I want on my back."

Quinn pulls back. "How did this morning go?"

Allowing my eyes to flit back and forth between my aunt and cousin, I frown. They know how bad it was for me back home. We talk all the time, and Quinn is like a sister to me. If it weren't for their support, I wouldn't have had the guts to walk away like I did. "It was bad. I'm sure he's still blowing up my phone telling me that I'm making a huge mistake."

Aunt Dee shakes her head. "That's where your father and I differ in opinion, Anna. Marrying a man you don't love to please your family is a much larger mistake. He should want happiness for you, not sorrow."

I nod. "I can never thank you enough for giving me a place to escape to."

She cups my face. "It's no problem, sweet girl. I wouldn't want my Quinn to be forced into something like that and, someday, I hope your father will change his mind and see that what he was trying to do was wrong."

Emotions build inside my chest, making me nearly burst as I fight against them. I don't want to have a breakdown right here on the curb at the airport. I swallow hard.

"Me too," is all I can whisper.

My aunt's face twists with pity. "Awww, come on. Let's get you home, yeah?"

A single tear slips from my eye. It's not until this very moment that I realize how serious all this is. For the first time in my life the unknown is staring me in the face and I'm scared shitless, yet exhilarated at the same time. I've never felt this free—this alive.

Quinn takes one of my suitcases and loads it into the trunk of her mom's Prius. "I can't believe you fit all your stuff in two bags. It would've taken at least ten for my shoes alone."

I shake my head and smile. "You and your shoes. I've never known anyone more obsessed with them."

She grins, and it lights up her gorgeous features. "I'd like to think only Imelda Marcos could rival me. I would love to peek in that lady's closet."

I roll my eyes as we shut the trunk. "I could think of so many better things to do with my time than explore an eighty-year-old woman's shoe collection."

Quinn's eyes widen like I've just cursed her out. "Are you *kidding* me? The woman is famous for having over three thousand pairs of shoes. Aren't you the least bit curious to see that?"

I laugh as I get in the backseat and Quinn slides in up front next to her mother. "Honestly, I find it a little disgusting and wasteful to have so much excess."

She shakes her head as she fastens her seatbelt. "Always the realist, aren't you, Anna? One of these days something is going to break you out of that conservative shell of yours."

"You know I've been this way since birth, Quinn. It'd take a real miracle to change my views after twenty-one years," I answer, a hint of amusement in my voice.

"No. Not a miracle, Anna—a man," she teases. "We're going out tonight to find you a hot piece of male ass to loosen you up."

My mouth drops open, completely mortified that Quinn is talking to me like that with her mother around. It would be one thing for her to say that to me when we were alone, but it's absolutely mortifying in front of an audience. My father would've given me a stern lecture and forbidden me to ever see Quinn again, even if she was flesh and blood. He wouldn't care. Someone like Quinn doesn't fit his mold.

When I don't reply, Quinn glances back over her shoulder, gauging my reaction. "Come on, Anna. Mom is completely cool. She's a single woman too. She gets it. Don't ya, Ma?" Quinn nudges Aunt Dee's elbow with her own.

Aunt Dee nods. "I do, but dear, you have to remember how Anna was raised. She isn't used to people being so open and free."

Quinn sighs. "Uncle Simon is too hardcore. I can't even imagine living with him. It must've been torture."

I adjust in the seat. It's hard to hear someone else confirm that your life has been a living hell. I mean, I've known for a while now that I haven't grown up like most people, but it's been the only life I've ever known. Even though Aunt Dee and Quinn promised to help get me on my feet, it still wasn't easy leaving.

There are so many things that are uncertain now, but I'm ready to face whatever comes at me, head on.

"Oh, and I talked to my boss about you yesterday. Andy says he can use another waitress since the one he just hired quit, so the jobs yours if you want it. All you have to do is fill out an application and you can start right away," Quinn informs me.

I smile and place my hand on her shoulder. "I'll never be able to thank you enough. I'm truly grateful"—I put my other hand on Aunt Dee's shoulder—"to both of you."

Aunt Dee pats my hand. "You're more than welcome, dear."

I lean back in my seat. No matter how many times I thank them, it's never going to be enough. It's like they have given me a chance to live life my way for once. I'll always be grateful.

"Anna, I know you probably don't want to think about this right now, but I think you need to give your father a call and let him know you're safe. My big brother will worry himself to death if he doesn't at least know you're with me. He's probably worn a path in the marble floor and driven your poor mother crazy by now," Aunt Dee says as she merges onto the freeway.

I sigh. "I can't. I lost my phone on the plane."

"Oh, shit," Quinn says. "Do you have the insurance plan so you can get a new one?"

I shrug. "No idea. Father pays the bill. But it should be okay because I know who has it and I have his number, so I can get it back. All I have to do is call him and make arrangements to get it...and my purse."

Quinn jerks around in her seat, concern written all over her face. "Anna, I know this being on your own thing is new to you, but you cannot make friends on airplanes. You never know what kind of whack-job you're sitting next to. How did a stranger end up with your things anyhow?"

I glance down at my soiled clothing and replay the moment I met Xavier in my head while I explain what happened on the flight.

Quinn furrows her brow. "So some rich guy has your stuff and wants you to call him."

"I guess, if you want to look at it that way."

"Looks like he took a special interest in making sure he'd get to see you again." She smiles. "Girl, sounds like you've got more game than I gave you credit for. That must've been some conversation on that flight because he could've easily turned it into the flight crew."

I roll my eyes and feel my face heat up, revealing a blush. There's no way I want to repeat the things Xavier said to me. I shouldn't have allowed him to speak that way to me. I should've stopped him, but I'd be lying if I said I hadn't liked it. "You're ridiculous."

Quinn gasps, making a big show of being shocked before nudging Aunt Dee's arm again. "He's hot, isn't he? I know that look."

I raise my eyebrows. "What *look*?"

She smirks. "The one that says I-just-met-a-really-hot-rich-man-that-totally-wants-to-jump-my-bones-and-I-just-might-let-him. Trust me, Anna, I've had that look a few times myself." She laughs. "So tell me all about him."

"Quinn, I don't really know him," I say.

"You spent four hours next to the man chatting. That's longer than most first dates, so spill, sister."

I laugh at her forwardness. "I hate to disappoint you, but I slept most of the way."

She twists her lips. "You must be one hell of a sleeper to get a man that sprung without much conversation. Come on, Anna. At least tell me his name."

I lick my lips as his face pops into my mind. "Xavier."

"Oh, *rawr*. That's a definite hot guy name. Tell me more. What's he look like? Details, girl. De-tails."

I chew on my bottom lip. "He's really tall, has really broad shoulders, tattoos and he's sort of..."

"Oh my God, what? The suspense is killing me," Quinn whines.

"He's famous," I blurt out.

Quinn's eyes widen. "Who is he? If you say Xavier is Ryan Reynolds' real name I will wrestle you for his phone number."

I chuckle. "No, it's not Ryan Reynolds. I would've probably freaked if I sat by a celebrity I actually recognized."

She frowns. "So he's not super famous, just a little famous?"

I shake my head. "Oh no, he's popular. I'm just not sure what for. He signed autographs the entire flight."

She tilts her head to the side and her eyes drift up toward the ceiling. "Hmm. I don't know anyone famous by the name Xavier and I study the tabloids proficiently, so he must be known by something else."

"Does Phenomenal X ring a bell?"

"Ring it? It fucking smashes it! I can't believe you didn't know who he was! He's only *the* hottest man in wrestling, and the newest playboy to grace the cover of all the magazines." She tsks. "You really are the most sheltered human on the planet. This needs to be rectified immediately."

"And how do you plan on making me worldlier?" I tease.

"Easy." She grins and the wicked twinkle in her eye scares me a bit. "You're going to start by sleeping with a known bad-boy."

I shake my head. "Oh, no. No way, Quinn. I don't do things like that."

"Maybe old Anna didn't, but new Anna will. You came out here to live a little and be free. What better way to experience true rebellion than messing around with a guy who's the exact opposite of everything you're used to. Plus, as a bonus, Uncle Simon will hate it. It's a total win-win for you." The confidence in her tone tells me she believes what she's saying down to her soul.

"I don't know, Quinn. That's a huge step for me. I'm not sure I can sleep with some guy I barely know. That's crazy." I glance over at Aunt Dee who is shaking her head at Quinn's evil-genius plan.

I sigh. "How about we compromise? I'll call Xavier and ask him to meet us somewhere so I can get my stuff back. I'm not promising to sleep with him though."

"As long as we can meet him in a bar or something, it's a deal. I'll need some liquid courage to speak to that beast of a man." She claps her hands together and then digs through her Coach bag to find her phone. "Get his number out. We're setting this up before you have a chance to talk yourself out of it."

If I didn't desperately need my phone back, I'd never call Xavier. Just the memory of the way he made me feel without really touching me on that plane is enough to make me nearly combust. I'm in way over my head here, but Quinn's right. I need to do the exact opposite of what I would normally do. I hope I know enough to keep me afloat once Quinn shoves me into the shark tank.

The folded paper is still in my back pocket, so I lean forward and retrieve it. "Can I borrow your phone?"

She hands me her phone wrapped in its sparkly diamond case. "Be assertive. Tell him to meet you at Gibby's Bar on Third tonight at nine o'clock. Don't give him a chance to gain the upper hand. With a man like Phenomenal X, you have to take control and show him you aren't the kind of girl who will take his shit. You call the shots and he'll be eating out of the palm of your hand in no time."

A lump builds in my throat as I dial his number. After three rings a distinctly male voice answers the phone. "Speak."

The cold way he answers the phone throws me off guard. I open my mouth to speak, but no words will fall from my lips. All of the witty things I wanted to say to him fly completely out the window.

Quinn nudges my leg, pushing me to say something so I just blurt out the first thing that comes to mind. "I want my phone back."

Xavier chuckles into the phone. "Is that any way to say thank you after I rescued your belongings? Ask me a little nicer and I might just give you what want you want."

"I, um..."

God, what is wrong with me? He has me stuttering like an idiot. This man is infuriating. I wish I wasn't at his mercy, but until I get my things back it looks like I have to play nice with him. "Is there any way you can,"— Quinn nudges me again and again mouths to have him meet us tonight—"meet me at Gibby's on Third tonight and bring my things?"

"That's a really public place, beautiful. I was hoping the next time I saw you, we'd be somewhere a little more secluded, if you know what I mean," he says, amusement lacing his voice.

"No way," I fire back.

"What's wrong, Anna, don't trust yourself to be alone with me? Would it really be so bad if I found my way into those panties of yours?" he teases and the tingle that rippled through me on the plane comes back with full force.

"Please," I say with a chuckle, attempting to make a show that he's not getting to me. "I don't know where you get off believing for one second that you'd be able to get inside my underwear. It's not happening, X."

Quinn's mouth drops open and her eyes widen as she gets the gist of the conversation I'm having with this absurdly sexy man.

"So it's 'X' now, is it? I thought I told you to call me Xavier. X is reserved for people who don't know me." All traces of the playful tone have been erased from his voice.

"I *don't* know you," I answer without any hesitation, because other than the fact he makes my body crazy, I know absolutely nothing about him.

"Not yet." His reply is simple, but confident. "But you will. I'll see you tonight, beautiful."

Before I have a chance to say anything else, the line goes dead. I pull the cell away from my ear and stare down at it.

Shit.

Why do I get the feeling that I'm in for it? I run my hands through my hair as I hand the phone to Quinn. The knowing grin on her face only adds to the gnawing feeling in the pit of my stomach that Xavier Cold is about to be the tornado that flips my world upside down.

Chapter FOUR

Up or down? That's the classic debate most women face when trying to get ready for a night out. I thread my fingers through my brown hair and pull it up off my neck as I stare at myself in the mirror. I twist my head from side to side. Of course I want to look sexy, but I don't want to give Xavier the impression that I'm easy. I'm far from that.

"Oh, my God, Anna. I can't believe you were sitting next to professional wrestling's resident badass. Not to mention one of world's sexiest men alive—according to the last magazine I read. You got to sit next to this tasty treat of a man for nearly four hours…how did you keep from spontaneously combusting right there on the plane?" Quinn wonders out loud as she lies on her belly, scouring the Internet for information on Phenomenal X. "I don't think the guy takes a bad picture, ever. He does the whole 'fuck me' vibe without even trying. Since you're so adamant you aren't into him, you might have to stop *me* from jumping his bones in public."

I allow my hair to fall loosely around my shoulders. Down it is. "Why would someone like him be into someone like me?"

Quinn's eyes snap up in my direction as I spin away from her dresser mirror to face her. "Puh-*leese*, Anna. Please tell me you're not one of those self-loathing chicks who can't see her own beauty. I know you're smarter than that."

I shake my head. "It's not like I just said I was ugly, Quinn. I just meant that he's a celebrity and I'm...well...boring and plain."

She shoves herself up from the bed. "Boring, yeah...I might have to agree with you on that one because if a guy like Phenomenal X showed the slightest bit of interest in me on a plane, we'd be joining the mile high club in a snap—even *if* I had to turn myself into a human pretzel to make it work in that tight as hell bathroom."

She laughs at herself as she makes her way over to me, and spins me back around to face the mirror. "But, Anna, *plain* you most certainly are not. We are Cortez women. We are naturally beautiful. No man can resist our charms when we use them. It's a gift from the deities, designed to help us maneuver this crazy manmade world."

I stare at Quinn through the mirror. "Easy for you to say. You're beautiful."

Her hands slide up on my shoulders. "Not as beautiful as you. I've always been insanely jealous of your nose and green eyes."

My eyes widen at the thought that my drop-dead gorgeous cousin thinks I'm prettier than her. "Really? I can't believe I'm going to admit this out loud, but I would kill for your legs."

She chuckles. "Lots of working out, babe, but don't discount that rockin' bod you've got going on. I'm sure if you allowed yourself to see it, you'd notice that men flock to your beauty." She sighs. "So you see, you have all the tools to be confident—you just need a little experience in how to use them. And you're in luck because I just happen to be an excellent flirting instructor. You can practice tonight on Mr. Sexy."

I frown. "I doubt all the training in the world can help me gain enough courage to flirt with him."

All the overtly sexual comments he made, and the way my body instantly reacted to him, flood my brain. A man like Xavier, who has already shown that he is well versed in how to arouse the opposite sex, is not the ideal candidate to be honing ones flirting skills on. He's the kind of guy a girl like Quinn can handle. But me? I've only had one serious boyfriend my entire life, and as much as I would like to say I attracted Jorge on my own, I can't even take credit for landing him. If it weren't for my father, that relationship wouldn't have happened either.

"Hey." Quinn taps the top of my head. "Whatever's rolling around in there just forget it. Whatever you're thinking about right now, think the opposite. Today is the first day of your new life—out with the old, shy Anna, in with the spunky new one. It's time the rest of the world got to experience some of the fire that I know is hiding inside there. I've seen spunky Anna before and I like her. It's time to explore the world."

That's the second time today someone has encouraged me to be the me who's deep inside—to do what I feel, instead of what I think I should do.

I nod and smile at Quinn. "You're right. That's what coming here was supposed to be about. I need to learn to loosen up and live a little, and a sure thing like

Phenomenal X feels like a good place to begin. I'm so tired of being the good girl, Quinn. The Goody-Two-shoes nobody ever wanted to be real friends with. Did you know I didn't get invited to one single party in high school because kids were afraid I would narc them out?"

Quinn frowns and strokes the back of my head. "Oh, Anna, girl, that's terrible, but I'm sure college was much better, right?"

I shake my head and fight back the tears that threaten to expose the years of sadness that plague me to this day. "Not really. By that time Father had set me up with Jorge who went to another Christian college across the state, and I never accepted any invites to any parties because I was afraid of upsetting Jorge or Father. Even though we're not together a lot, I still feel like you're my closet friend. You're the only person who's ever been really there for me." I wipe a lone tear from my eye and sniff. "Ugh. Admitting that makes it all sound even lamer."

She wraps her thin arms around my shoulders and pulls me in for a tight hug. "Screw all the assholes who can't see how awesome you are. I'll gladly accept the title of your best friend."

I laugh softly and hug her back. "Thank you, Quinn. I feel like you and Aunt Dee rescued me."

She pulls back and smiles. "What are best friends for?"

A couple hours after our heart-to-heart we're seated at a corner booth at Gibby's. Quinn is doing her best to attempt to get me drunk for the first time, and so far it's working.

The fruity drinks she's been supplying me with are delicious, and I can't really taste the alcohol.

I throw back the rest of my drink and Quinn smiles. "Atta girl! Liquid courage, baby. You're gonna need it the moment sexy X gets here."

The moment he walks in the room, it's like the air in the room becomes charged, and I feel a pull toward him. Even in the crowded room, my gaze instantly finds Xavier. My eyes stalk him as he walks across the room to the bar, most of the heads in the place turning as he passes by them.

His presence in a room is one that's hard to miss.

Xavier leans against the bar casually, an elbow resting on the hardwood behind him as he chats with a blond woman and the short, mullet-man I recognize from the plane. Xavier's broad shoulders fill out the black dress shirt he's wearing and like before, he has the sleeves rolled up to his elbows. His gaze drifts away from the company standing before him as he scans the faces in the busy bar.

The instant our eyes lock, all the air whooshes from my lungs. Everything in me screams to look away—that this guy is trouble with a capital T. I should be scared out of my mind that he's staring right at me with those piercing blue eyes—but no matter how much I know I need to fight it, the intense need to find out what his skin feels like sliding against mine pushes me to allow this to happen. I have never lusted after a man like this before and as I realize that I'm undressing him with my eyes, my face flushes and I break our stare.

"Oh, good Lord," Quinn murmurs next to me as she snuggles closer to my side in the booth. "The pictures do not do that man justice. He's sexy as hell, and staring at you like he's ready to eat you alive."

"He's not looking at me like that."

Heat creeps up my neck again, surely deepening my blush. I risk another glance in his direction, and he licks his plump lips before pushing away from the bar, grabbing something off the counter in the process. Quinn's right. He *is* staring at me like I'm the tastiest thing on earth as he slowly approaches me, much like a tiger stalking its prey.

I swallow hard as my heart thunders in my chest. My eyes grow wide as I stare at Quinn.

"What do I do? I'm not ready for this. I can't do this."

Nervous energy spreads through my body and I'm not quite sure how to handle myself. I've never felt this anxious before. The only thing I can think to do is flee from this dangerous man because I already know what's on his mind. The urge to run right out of this bar before a full-on panic attack hits me is at the forefront of my mind as I rapidly become overwhelmed by his presence.

She places her hand on my bouncing thigh and holds it steady. "Calm down, Anna. I know this feels like I'm throwing you to the wolves, but you can do this. Think about what we talked about on the ride over here. You have the tools, remember? Don't let him gain the upper hand at any point. You call the shots. You lead the conversation. Don't let him sweet talk you into anything you aren't ready for, and above all remember that I'm here for you. Just say the word and we'll split."

Her words of comfort help a lot, but they don't change the fact that I'm in a completely new environment. Not only is this my first time at a bar, and the first time I've ever had alcohol, but it's also the first time I've ever allowed myself to think about giving my body over to a man to do as he pleases, just because I want him so much.

Xavier's heady stare bores into me as he approaches our table with a wicked grin. "Anna Cortez." He holds my purse out in front of him with one thick finger. "If I didn't know any better I would say you left this behind on purpose, just to see me again."

I roll my eyes at his cocky tone. "You wish."

His grin widens even more at my snarky comment as I stand and reach for my bag. He quickly wraps his fingers around it and jerks it just out of my grasp, teasing me like one would do to a puppy with a toy. This is pure entertainment for him. I grit my teeth as he holds it out again, only to repeat his silly little game of "keep away." The taunting causes a low growl to escape from between my teeth.

I throw my hands on my hips. "Give me back my stuff, you...you...big *jerk*."

He throws his head back and laughs heartily which only pisses me off more. I'm not trying to be funny. Can't he see I'm being serious?

Those mesmerizing blue eyes twinkle with amusement. "Oh, a temper. I like that. Careful, good girl, you're going to lose that title soon if you get me all riled up with your feisty little attitude. If I get too turned on, I'll have no choice but to take you right here in this bar."

I curl my lip in a mock show of disgust, pretending like I wouldn't love to know just how worked up I'm getting him. I walk around the table to face him, determined to get my things back. "Like I said, *X*, you wish."

The easygoing vibe and boyish charm he exuded only seconds ago disappears as he allows me to wrap my fingers around the strap of my purse that still dangles from his finger. The moment I have a firm grip on it, Xavier grabs me by the waist and pulls me tight against his body—the purse wedged between us is the only thing keeping our chests from colliding. I stare up at his face, fully aware of every point where our bodies touch.

Hands.

Hips.

Knees.

His hand pressing tightly against the small of my back.

The crazy idea of pushing forward a few inches and finding out what those sexy lips of his taste like zings through me, and I bite my lip, causing his crystal-clear blue eyes to drift down to my mouth before slowly moving back up to meet mine. "You're right, beautiful. *I do* wish."

My mouth gapes open. Normally I would have responded with some sort of witty comment telling him he didn't have a chance with me, but I can't deny the way I crave him.

I'm not sure how long we stay there like that, gazing into one another's eyes, waiting for the other to make the next move, or at least say something, but before I'm ready Quinn's voice drags me back to reality. "Anna, do you want to finish your drink? The ice is melting."

Her subtle way of giving me an out if I need one isn't missed by Xavier as we remain locked together. "I should get back to that drink. I can't let it go to waste," I murmur.

Xavier nods, like he understands things are moving a little too quickly for me. "Drinks, like most things, are always the best before time melts away the taste, leaving things bland and watered down. Everything is better when it's fresh which is why I never miss an opportunity when I see something I like. I'm a firm believer in jumping on things right away."

He stays tangled up with me, gauging my reaction to his words—words I don't believe have anything to do with a drink. It's more like the idea of this crazy connection we seem to feel toward each other is just a passing phase, but one we should act on right away.

The waft of cold air hits me hard as he pushes away from me, and I instantly crave the warmth of his body back. I fold my arms around my purse and hug it tight against my chest to keep my fingers from reaching for him. I feel like this is my moment to tell him that I want him—to make some sort of move on him to let him know I'm interested in him. But it's just not me. I'm not that forward.

So instead of telling him that I want him to take me somewhere and prove to me how he got the name "Phenomenal," I stand there like a scared deer caught in the headlights of an oncoming car. I swallow hard and search for anything to say to kill the awkward vibe that's growing between us.

"Thank you for returning my things."

A corner of his mouth lifts up, revealing a tiny smile.

"It was no trouble." His eyes flit between me and Quinn, who is no doubt watching us like a hawk. "I'll let you get back to that drink."

Before I have a chance to say anything else, Xavier turns on his heel and heads back to the people he left at the bar.

My shoulders relax now that I'm no longer pinned under the intensity of his stare. I don't know what it is about him but he makes me feel crazy, which is so not like me.

Quinn grabs my arm and then drags me back down in the booth next to her. "Holy shit that was intense. That guy is so hot for you. Whatever spell you've put him under, you must teach me. I didn't know you had that in you."

"I didn't do anything, Quinn," I answer.

"Exactly!" she exclaims. "A guy like him isn't used to a women not responding to the smallest bone he tosses their way. You've done exactly what I told you to do on the way over here. You've maintained the upper hand."

I really hadn't set out to play some kind of angsty sex game with Xavier, but it seems to be exactly what we're doing. Problem is, I'm not so sure what my next move is supposed to be here.

"Just look at him." Quinn nudges my arm. "He can't keep his eyes off you."

I glance up and find his gaze firmly fixed on me. The blonde who entered the bar with him and Mullet Man affixes herself to him, running her finger slowly up and down his forearm. A twinge of jealously rolls through me, even though I know I don't have any right to be envious. It's not like we're dating or anything.

Xavier glances down at the woman and shakes his head before pushing her fingers off his arm. Her face twists as she crosses her arms over her chest and then plops down next to him like a sulking child who's just been told no.

"Looks like Blondie doesn't handle rejection well," Quinn snickers and I smile.

"I would never go after a guy like that," I reply.

She grabs her drink off the table and tips it at me. "And that, my friend, is exactly why you have his attention."

I risk another glance in his direction, but he's not looking at me this time. His attention is tuned to Mullet Man who appears to be telling him a story while wildly gesticulating with his hands. There are, however, a new pair of eyes pointed my direction. The beautiful blonde beside Xavier shoots daggers at me with her stare from across the room and if looks could kill, I'd already be in a body bag.

Not wanting any trouble, I quickly look away and do my best to immerse myself in conversation with my cousin. Before I know it we are laughing and making plans for how much fun we are going to have this summer. Quinn goes on and on about how great her job at the bar is and how she promises I'm going to love it— especially the tips.

"Your boss does know I don't have a drop of experience as a server?" I ask as I start on my third drink of the night.

Quinn waves me off. "Hotness outweighs what a résumé says any day, Anna. Trust me on that."

"I'm just really nervous. It's my first job. Father is going to kill me when he finds out I'm choosing to serve drinks in a bar rather than using the degree he shelled out so much money for."

"We all have to start somewhere. Plus, it's not like there's hospitality management positions just lying around for recent college grads. Besides, most of us have to start from the ground up," she assures me.

"What are we talking about ladies?" My attention snaps to a tall, dark-haired man standing in front of our table with a couple of drinks. "I'm Brad, and this is my friend, Jared. Mind if we join you?"

My eyes flit to blond guy, Jared. He's wearing a hopeful smile that makes his brown eyes twinkle. Both guys are pretty cute. Nowhere near as attractive as Xavier, but cute nonetheless.

I glance over at Quinn, and she shrugs, pulls out a flirty grin, and turns her attention back to the two guys in front of me. "I'm Quinn, and this is my cousin, Anna."

Brad takes that as an invitation and takes a seat next to Quinn, sliding one of the beers he brought with him in her direction. "What brings you girls out tonight?"

Quinn explains we're just out having a drink to unwind, and I take a second to glance over in Xavier's direction as Jared slides a chair from the table beside us directly in front of me. Despite the obstacle I can still clearly see Xavier glaring at Jared's back, watching every move he makes.

"I'm Jared." I smile at him politely as he extends a hand toward me.

"Nice to meet you," I say after shaking his hand.

I know getting to know new people is high on Quinn's list of fun activities for us this summer, but I still can't help feeling awkward. My flirting skills need some work.

"So, umm, are you from around here?"

I can't tell if Jared's actually interested in me, or if he's just taking one for the team so his buddy can talk to Quinn. I shake my head and finish off my drink, feeling my toes start to tingle. I giggle as I wonder if this is what it feels like to have a buzz. "Nope. I'm actually from Portland."

"Wow. Are you just visiting or what?"

"I'm a transplant—moved here today, actually. Quinn is my new roomie."

I flick my tongue around in my mouth, amazed by how foreign it feels in my mouth as I speak, and giggle again. I lift the glass to my lips, but grow disappointed when I remember that it's empty.

"I really like these things. They taste so fruity. You can't even taste the alcohol."

Jared grins and taps my empty glass. "Let me get you another drink."

I rest my chin in my hand and smile, thinking of how nice Jared seems. "That would be great."

When he gets up, I glance around, noticing there are a lot more people in here than an hour or so ago when we first arrived. Just then a voice pipes up over the low music that was playing, and a DJ announces that he's taking over before an up-tempo song blasts through the speakers.

"Oh!" Quinn squeals in my ear. "I love this song! Let's dance, Anna."

She nudges me out of the booth before turning around and shouting at Brad to watch our seats. Typically I'm not a "dance in public" kind of girl, but with the way the liquor has me loosened up, and the heavy thump of bass pounding through me, all I feel like doing is letting go.

She stops at the edge of the floor. "Let's give them a little show, cuz."

I laugh as she grabs my hands and starts rocking her hips to the music, forcing me to follow her lead. "Where'd you learn to dance like this?"

"I should ask you the same question, girl. You've got some moves."

I grin. "My undergrad degree is in dance. I've always been fascinated. There was a girl in one of my classes who taught me a few freestyle moves and introduced me to the beauty of top forty pop."

"Oh, if Uncle Simon ever found out, you would've been toast." She laughs and tosses her dark hair around. "Whip your hair around. It drives guys crazy!"

I mimic her actions just as I feel a hand slip up on my hip and see Brad push up behind Quinn.

"You look great out here. Very sexy!" Jared says in my ear as he hands me a drink.

"Thanks!" I shout so he can hear me over the music as I lift the drink to my lips.

My arm stops in mid-air, and I stare down at the fingers wrapped around my wrist. My vision follows the thick fingers, to the wrist, up the tattooed arm, broad chest, finally resting on a light-blue pooled iris. Xavier's jaw flexes as he stares over my head at Jared, who has completely stilled behind me. "Don't *ever* take a drink from a random guy. That's lesson one in this cruel reality, beautiful. Not all guys are nice."

He grabs the drink from my hand and slams the plastic cup down on the floor, splattering its pink liquid all over a group of guys standing a little too close watching the action unfold. With a sharp tug he pulls me behind him, effectively putting a wall of muscle between Jared and me.

Xavier stares down at Jared, his fingers flexing into fists at his sides. It's like he's ready to rip into my would-be dance partner. "You think I didn't see what you put in her drink back there, motherfucker? There's no way in hell I'm going to allow a little pecker-stain like you to attempt to drug this girl and get away with it."

297

MICHELLE A. VALENTINE

All the blood drains from Jared's face, leaving his skin pale, and his mouth hanging open in shock. But more frighteningly, he doesn't deny the accusations. Xavier shakes his head in disgust. "You just gave me the green light to end your fucking world."

Jared raises his hands in surrender and takes a step back. "Hey, man. I don't know what you think you saw, but I don't want any trouble."

Xavier rolls his shoulders. "You should've thought about that a few minutes ago because trouble is my middle name, and my foot has been twitching all night to kick your fucking ass."

"I'm sorry, okay." Jared's voice shakes as his eyes flit to Brad, who seems content on staying the hell away. "We'll just go."

Some friend you've got there, Jared, leaving you to hang out to dry.

Xavier shakes his head and laughs darkly. "Go? You think I'll let you just leave after that shit? You must be out of your fucking mind."

Jared turns to leave but Xavier grabs him by the bicep, turning him back around before drawing back his fist to crush every bone in Jared's skull. The instant I realize what's going on I gasp.

I can't let this happen. He can't get into trouble over me.

I wrap both of my hands around his elbow, clinging on for dear life as I scream, "No!"

Xavier jerks his gaze to me, his thick eyebrows knitted in confusion. "You don't want me to pound this punk?"

I shake my head vigorously. "I don't want you to get into any trouble. He's not worth it."

"He's not, but *you are.*"

The intense connection that always pulls me to him assaults me full force and I can tell he feels it too.

I stare into his eyes as I cling to him, my fingers woven together so tightly that they're numb, while he waits for me to give the word to destroy Jared. I have to remain calm and try to defuse the situation before things get ugly, and Xavier gets arrested for murdering a man while defending me.

"Let him go and we'll leave."

His hard eyes soften a bit. "Together?"

I nod. "Anywhere you want to go."

A wicked smile cracks his face, and a weird tingle erupts in my belly. Maybe I shouldn't have promised that—who knows what's on that naughty mind of his. But if that means walking out of here without Xavier in handcuffs, I'm game.

Xavier directs his attention back to Jared. "Looks like it's your lucky day, fucker. You should kiss the ground this angel walks on because she just saved your fucking life."

He releases Jared's arm. "Don't let me catch you in here again. Beat it, you fucking pussy."

Jared and Brad push past Quinn, wasting no time getting as far away from us as possible. For a second I feel a little guilty for ruining my cousin's fun—Brad seemed nice enough—but the old saying that goes "a man is known for the company he keeps" rolls through my brain, so Brad's probably a date rapist too. In a way I guess I kind of saved her, well, Xavier saved her—us.

Quinn smirks as her eyes drift down to where I'm still tightly clutching my sexy savior and I quickly detach myself from him, only to be instantly reconnected with him when he grabs my hand and tugs me toward the exit. I turn and wave at my cousin as I'm pulled away.

He stops at the bar, where the blonde and Mullet Man sit chatting, a couple of empty beer glasses in front of them. The blonde's nostrils flare as she rakes her eyes over me from head to toe. Clearly she's not one bit impressed by me or my clothing. Her eyes zero in on my hand, held tightly inside Xavier's thick fingers, while he gives Mullet Man some instructions. "Make sure Anna's cousin gets home safe, Jimmy."

"No problem, boss."

Xavier takes a step but doesn't make it far because Blondie hops into his path. "You're not leaving with her." She glares at him with icy blue eyes.

He scoffs at her order. "Watch me, Deena."

Mid-pivot, Deena grabs his arm, but he jerks away like he's been stung by a bee. "I told you to never touch me again."

She narrows her eyes. "If you walk out that door with her, I'll quit—right here, right now."

"Promise?" he asks with a sarcastic tone to his voice as he pushes past her and tugs me along behind him, not giving her a second glance.

I, however, can't fight my stupid curiosity and turn around to catch her reaction. The look on Deena's face makes me believe she's growling and given the chance, she would pound me into oblivion.

I don't know who she is, or what kind of relationship she and Xavier have, but one thing is perfectly clear— Deena is pissed and believes I'm messing with something of hers. Alarm bells ring immediately as I return my gaze to take in the beautiful, strong profile of the man leading me out of the bar. He warned me that he wasn't a good guy, and by the looks of things, he leads a complicated life—stardom and women—that I'm sure I don't want to get mixed up in.

But for the life of me I can't fight the crazy attraction I feel toward this man. And after the way he just came to my rescue back there, I'm not sure I want to anymore.

About the Author

New York Times and USA Today Best Selling author Michelle A. Valentine is a Central Ohio nurse turned author of erotic and New Adult romance of novels. Her love of hard-rock music, tattoos and sexy musicians inspires her sexy novels.

Find her:

Facebook

Twitter:
@M_A_Valentine

Blog:
http://michelleavalentine.blogspot.com/

Website:
http://www.michelleavalentine.com

Acknowledgements

First off, I want to thank you, my dear readers, for embracing this series. Words cannot express how much it means to me that you've stuck with this series over the last couple of years. Thank you for loving my guys as much as I do. Love you all!

Now on to my thank yous:

Emily Snow, and Kristen Proby (aka, The Wicked Mafia) this past couple of years with you all have been amazing. Thank you for your love and support. Love you guys hard!

Holly Malgieri you freaking rock my world. Thank you for EVERYTHING you do for me. I couldn't make it on a daily basis without you. Your encouragement and undying support means so much to me. Thank you. Thank you. Thank you.

Jennifer Wolfel thank you for always being in my corner! You are the one person I depend on to give it to me straight. Thank you for your honesty and keeping me on task. Love ya!

Jennifer Foor thank you for being you and always making me laugh. You are a rock star.

Kelsie Leverich thank you for always lending your ear when I'm struggling. You don't know how much that means to me. Your one of the few people I can count on to run things by that totally gets where I'm coming from. Here's to hoping we have many more years to procrastinate together.

Claire Contreras you inspire me. Thank you for being such a good friend and an amazing soul.

Kelli Maine your friendship is invaluable and I look forward to many more years to come wading through this crazy book world together.

Ryn Hughes you kick so much ass, woman! Thank you for working with me through my crazy schedule. I always look forward to your red marks!

Jenny Sims thank you for your eagle eye on this book! You saved me a boatload of time.

My beautiful ladies in Valentine's Vixen's Group, you all are the best. You guys always brighten my day and push me to be a better writer. Thank you!

To the romance blogging community. Thank you for always supporting me and my books. I can't tell you how much every share, tweet, post and comment means to me. I read them all and every time I feel giddy. THANK YOU for everything you do. Blogging is not an easy job and I can't tell you how much I appreciate what you do for indie authors like me. You totally make our world go round.

Last, but always first in my life, my husband and son. Thank you for putting up with me. I love you both more than words can express.

Printed in Great Britain
by Amazon